Bal Harbour

W. E Smith

Also by W. E. Smith

Novels

Be True to Your Tribe
Tanaki on the Shore
Ver Sacrum: or, Heaven Help Us All
I've Got a Right to Sing the Blues

Story Collections

I Wanna Hear It Again
He on Honeydew Hath Fed

Bal Harbour

The Place

THE THINGS I'M ABOUT TO TELL happened a few years back, before they tore down the Sheraton and put up that buff-colored condo that sits across from the Shops these days. The Sheraton Bal Harbour may not have been South Florida's most glamorous beach resort, but there was something about the place that always made me feel like a piece of paradise—even more paradise than the rest of America's priciest zip code—had been plunked down on the beach beside Collins Avenue.

Whenever you went in the hotel lobby, people would be lounging on the sleek upholstered furniture, dressed in that casual rich way that says you don't have a care in the world—because you can afford anything, no problem. Light would stream in from windows behind the bar, where guys watched tennis or horse racing, sipping their beers and cocktails. Maybe there'd be some gal in a strapless dress nursing a daiquiri . . .

But it was when you slipped past the bar to the beachside grounds that the place got really stunning. They had these terraformed waterfalls, and the most gorgeous tangle of tropical vegetation I've ever seen (and I've seen plenty of it around here, believe me). A couple of jacuzzis occupied their own little grottos, and underneath the highest waterfall a school of big, fat koi fish, all mottled in different colors, milled about in a shallow pond.

Across that pond swung a hanging bridge like they'd have in those old jungle movies I watched on TV as a kid. It led to a lookout where you could see the ocean, way out beyond the beach gate. In between, the swimming pool snaked all over to hell and back. Whitewashed tortoises perched over the pool's edges, and its narrow places were arched over by sculpted concrete bridges. They had a band on one of those bridges every afternoon, playing their fannies off to keep the guests in a happy mood.

On the south side of the pool, near the poolside bar, a terrace offered yellow-striped rental cabanas. It was along that flank of the beachside grounds—veiled behind palm trees and thick bougainvillea—that sat the resort's best digs. Garden villas, they called them, with their own two-story wing. They were like condos, with balconies overlooking all that artificial Eden. What's more, every one of them had a terrific view of the ocean.

From there, a short stroll took you past the poolside bar to where two concrete pillars supported an iron grillwork gate. That was the beach entrance. Outside was a spigot to wash the sand off your feet. Just beyond that, a jogging path ran up and down the shore. Once you crossed that path you'd be on the beach, and as you walked toward the ocean, the rumble of the surf would slowly obliterate the hubbub from the pool. A man at a canvas booth there rented chaise lounges and umbrellas. Then it was just sand and water, and this famous Florida sun melting everything into one big haze . . .

Chapter 1

DRIVING ACROSS THE 123RD STREET CAUSEWAY I had a goofy feeling in the pit of my stomach. It wasn't just that I was on my way to a stiff scene. I've been a cop long enough to get the idea that people do some pretty rotten things to each other. It was an intoxicating day—Biscayne Bay glittered like a jewel, with a light breeze ruffling the surface—but that didn't explain my quivering guts, either. Since I quit Baltimore narcotics thirteen years ago to join Miami homicide, I've also figured out that this whole place is basically one big opiate.

The call from the Sheraton came in at 9:37. One of the maids found the body when she went in to clean the room. I was at the dentist's while my eldest, Sara—the one who thinks she's a singer—got her wisdom teeth yanked. Lori was over in Naples doing a catering job. I couldn't leave my baby half-looped on sodium pentothal, so I called Sanchez and asked her to start without me. When Dr. Lyndquist finished with my girl, I dropped her at the house. I asked old Mrs. Pruitt next door if she'd stop in on her from time to time and headed for the beach.

When I got to the Sheraton it was a circus. Word had shot through the hotel and spilled out onto the street. An ambulance was parked in the drive, and bystanders gawked from the sidewalk. A couple of our officers tried to keep a lid on the crowd of worried guests who paced around the entrance. There were two satellite vans in the parking lot, three or four camera crews around the drive.

Collins Avenue's royal palms waved in the breeze, and the red and white petunias that crowded the hotel's beds strained toward the clear morning light of a South Florida February.

I know what you're thinking. Another day in paradise, right?

Making for the front entrance, I recognized one of the reporters, one I knew was a real bulldog. She looked like she wanted to corner me, so I ducked in through the service doorway to the right of the drive. Grimy back corridors took me to the lobby. From there I glided past the bar and out to the beachside grounds. Once over the hanging bridge, I wound past the jacuzzis and the cabanas. They had already cordoned off the villa section with yellow tape. I said good morning to the officer guarding the gate and moved toward the second-floor unit with all the people going in and out from the balcony.

Sanchez came over when I got to the sliding glass doors. The corpse lay across the floor on the other side of the coffee table. Corinne, the medical examiner, crouched over it. A couple of forensics people moved around the room taking evidence.

"How's the kid?" Sanchez asked.

"A little spacey from the anesthetic, that's all. What's going on?"

"Corinne's working on the corpse. The rest of Forensics is in the other rooms."

"Let's take a look."

We stepped over to where Corinne was working on the body. She looked up at us.

"What's it look like?" I said.

"Blunt trauma."

She knelt by the man, cradling his head, and pulled his hair apart so that I could see the wound better. He was a decent looking guy, early fifties, I figured, blond hair in a stylish cut. He wore a fine, sandy-colored, summer-weight suit. On the floor beside him lay a statue, about a foot high, of that Greek goddess with the arm missing. *Venus de Milo*, Corinne informed me. A statuette, I guess you'd call it. It looked like it was made of marble. There was a blood smear along one side of it.

"Weapon?"

"Looks that way."

I turned to Sanchez. "What do we know about him?"

"His name's Robin Markson. He was some kind of composer. Classical, opera, that kind of thing. He lived out West, near Seattle. Checked in here four nights ago. The poor guy was supposed to conduct his latest opera down at the Arsht Center tonight."

"I suppose they've canceled the performance."

"Don't know."

"Any leads?"

"Not yet. We're looking for prints. We also checked the phone log on his mobile. Simmons is running it through our reverse number service. I'm betting on plain old robbery."

"Is his wallet missing?"

"No—"

I raised my eyebrows.

"I know it seems odd," Sanchez said. "But I figure whoever did it got surprised. Either they didn't know he was here, or he came in on them. They probably freaked out after they offed him, ran out. Maybe Markson yelled. Made some noise."

"Have we talked to the other guests?"

"I've got Willis on it."

"Did anyone look at the in-room safe?"

"Unlocked, and empty."

"Any sign of forced entry?"

"No, but . . ."

"I know. A lot of guests probably leave their balcony doors unlocked. They like to wander back and forth, feel the sea breeze. They figure they're safe. Hey, Corinne, what's your guestimate for time of death?"

"Around midnight, one o'clock."

"Where's the wallet?"

"Right here." She picked it up from where it lay beside her, waited while I donned latex and handed it over. "It was in his left back trousers pocket."

"Did you talk to the girl who found the body?" I asked Sanchez.

"I thought you'd want first crack at her."

"Where is she?"

"I'm not sure. She was pretty upset. The manager was with her when she left the room. I asked her not to leave the premises."

"Ask one of our officers to find her. Have them meet me in the lobby in half an hour."

Sanchez left the room and I took some measurements. Then I went out the sliding doors. I wanted to clear my head, step away from the whole awful scene. There was the body, legs hiked up the way he fell across the coffee table, blond hair falling over his forehead. Corinne was still finishing her work. Behind me I could hear kids roughhousing in the pool, strains of a reggae band and, in the distance, the surf.

Another cadaver, I thought, another day. But something told me this one wasn't going to be that simple, like this case would change my life in some fashion I could never have expected. Sure, it was just a feeling. But through my years as a detective,

I've come to believe in those kinds of hunches more than anything.

I opened the wallet. The plastic insert presented a typical assortment of items. There was a Washington State drivers license, credit cards, and a few photos of near and dear (an elderly couple, the victim with a teenaged girl, two boys standing in front of a brick rambler, circa 1960). In the bill compartment was a couple hundred dollars in cash, a dry cleaning ticket and the baggage receipt from his flight out.

Behind the credit card insert was an inner compartment. I dug my finger in there: that's where I always keep my most important stuff. I extracted a tightly folded piece of paper, an account card for Charles Schwab brokerage, an ornate business card from a Mexican hotel, and a dog-eared photo of a young woman in a floor-length gown. She was holding a bouquet of roses.

I unfolded the paper; it was a receipt. Fourteen thousand dollars for an emerald necklace. The address on the receipt was the Bal Harbour Shops, right across from the resort. It appeared that Markson had purchased the item two days earlier.

"Any sign of a fancy necklace?" I called through the door to all and sundry.

Sanchez came over. "We didn't turn up anything like that."

"You sure?"

"Yes, unless it's hiding someplace."

I handed her the receipt and she looked it over. "Ay caramba!" she erupted, "—a three karat emerald set with diamonds. Fourteen G's! Pretty classy."

"Pretty expensive, that's for sure."

"I wonder what he was doing with it. He doesn't look like the cross-dresser type."

"Good question. But here's an even better one. Where is it?"

"Stolen, most likely."

"You're probably right," I said. "But still, if this was a robbery, why wouldn't they take the wallet? That's what bugging me. Even if the perp was in a hurry, it was such easy pickings."

"If I got a hold of this necklace, I'd be a pretty happy camper," she said.

"Yeah, but the perp, or perps, probably doesn't share your taste in jewelry."

"You never know."

"Let me know if it turns up."

"Right."

I returned the receipt to the wallet and turned and looked out over the ocean. Past the breaker line, the water was a medium green, with frothy whitecaps kicked up by a light wind. Bolstered by a lungful of fresh air, I went back into the room and took a closer look.

Aside from the coffee table being askew, there was no sign of struggle in the living room. Nor was there anything unusual with the doors or windows. There was the statuette lying on the floor and, not far off, some scattered papers. I bent over to examine them.

It turned out to be some kind of music score. There were bloody fingerprints along the edges, like the victim—or somebody—handled it after he was injured. A title at the top of one of the pages said, *Biscayne Bay: An Opera in Three Acts.* I don't know much about music, so the rest didn't mean much to me. It was just a bunch of indecipherable markings. Hieroglyphics. There were a few words in what looked like Italian. *Forte, Allegro,* that kind of thing.

I got down on my knees and scanned the pages more carefully, and eventually I came to some words in English. It looked like a song, though I could only see bits and snatches.

The pages lay all atop one another, and I didn't want to mess with them. They'd have to go to the lab and get checked for prints with nihydrin. *The summer breeze off Biscayne Bay . . . your searching eyes . . . that old bandit time.* It was damned nostalgic. About some lost love, no doubt.

I left it for the forensics team.

Sanchez and I went through the other rooms, a bedroom and a bath. Everything looked like you'd expect. I put her in charge of the scene, left the suite through the door to the interior hallway and walked toward the hotel lobby. When I got there one of our officers was waiting. Beside him was a nicely dressed, forty-something lady. Sitting in one of the easy chairs was an Hispanic girl, about eighteen or nineteen. She wore one of the hotel's housekeeping uniforms.

Her face was stained with tears.

When I approached, the nicely dressed one stepped up and held out her hand.

"I'm Helen Merrett, hotel manager."

I introduced myself.

"Lucía is extremely upset. This has been such a shock."

I assured her that I understood. "Is there somewhere we can talk?"

She took us to an office off the lobby and I asked her to leave me alone with Lucía. Merrett looked stricken, but after reassuring Lucía that all would be well—and shooting me this wicked mother hen look—she backed out of the room. Out the office window I saw the ambulance with its lights flashing. Guests milled around. Palm fronds waved. Sun streamed into the room through the Venetian blinds.

I got the girl's name: Lucía Rodriguez.

"How long you been working here, Lucía?"

She was still sniffling. "Three years."

"I know you're upset. But I'm going to have to ask you some questions, so we can figure out who did this. Are you okay?"

"Yes," she sniffled.

"I need you to tell me what you saw when you went into Mr. Markson's room this morning."

She started to speak, but before she got past the word *He* she broke into hysterics. I let her cry for a minute, until she got what sounded like the hiccups. She sat there hiccuping awhile, and I handed her a kleenex. When she finally calmed down she slowly started to speak. From what she described, it didn't sound like anything had changed from the time she found the body until our personnel arrived at the scene. Other than the dead man on the floor, the statuette and papers, she hadn't noticed anything amiss in the room.

"What did you do when you saw Mr. Markson on the floor?"

"What do you think?" she said. "I screamed and ran out of there—about as fast as my little legs would carry me!"

"What did you do after that?"

"Jorge—he's one of the housemen—he must have heard me. He came running down the hallway, and I told him what happened."

"Did Jorge go into the room?"

"Yes, he went right in."

"Did he stay in there long?"

"No, he came running right back out. Dios, Dios! he kept saying. Then he went into another room and called security."

"Did anyone else go into Mr. Markson's suite?"

"No, not until security came. And Mrs. Merrett. They went in. I was so upset. Thank God Jorge was there. After that the lady detective came. She said I couldn't leave the hotel, and Mrs. Merrett took me to her office so that I could relax a little."

"Listen," I said, "I believe that Mr. Markson was carrying a very expensive piece of jewelry. A necklace, to be exact. Did you happen to see anything like that when you went into the room this morning?"

She cast her gaze downward. "No."

"Are you sure? Because it's missing now, and it's a very important piece of evidence."

She had a suspicious look about her, like she she feared that I was leading her into some kind of trap.

"Look," I went on, "if somebody picked up that necklace, there wouldn't be any problem if they wanted to return it. What I mean is, they wouldn't be in any kind of trouble. Do you understand what I'm saying?"

"I didn't take it. That's what you're saying, isn't it?"

"No, I'm not saying you took it. Anyone might have."

"Well, I didn't take it, and I don't know anybody that did."

"I understand."

She seemed piqued and stared into her lap for a moment. Then she looked toward the window. "But I did see it," she offered suddenly, quietly, a Venetian zebra striping her youth-fresh face.

"Wait, I thought you just said that you didn't see it."

"I said that I didn't see it this morning. That's what you asked, isn't it? It was yesterday, when I was cleaning the room. The guest—Mr. Markson—was there, but he told me to clean anyway. He said he wanted the suite to look nice, because he might have some company."

"Did he say who?"

"No."

"Where did you see that necklace?"

"It was on the desk where he was working. I told him it was beautiful, and he looked up and smiled. He had a very kind face."

"Did you see it again after that? The necklace, I mean."

"No."

"Can you describe it to me?"

"Yes. It had one big green gemstone—an emerald, I think—with diamonds clustered around it. There were other, smaller jewels, further up on this lacy chain."

"Did Mr. Markson say anything to you that would suggest that he was in danger, or that he felt threatened in any way?"

"No. He just asked if I knew a good restaurant."

"What did you tell him?"

"I don't know about restaurants." She almost laughed. "But I told him that a lot of guests go to Carpaccio, over in the Shops. I think it's real fancy."

"Did he say that he would go there?"

"Yes, he did. He called the concierge and asked him to make a reservation."

"Do you remember what time he made the reservation for?"

"Nine o'clock, I think."

"Do you remember anything else he said? Did he mention anywhere else he planned to go last evening, or who he was meeting? Anything?"

"No, that's all he said. I just cleaned the room and left. He was still working at his desk."

I thanked Lucía Rodriguez and led her out of the office. As we entered the lobby they were bringing the gurney through. Corinne walked beside it while a couple of uniforms cleared the path. Lucía broke down again. Mrs. Merrett, who was standing nearby, came over and took her under her mother-hen wing.

It was then that Ralph Owens came up to me. I don't know why I stopped to speak with him, since I had wanted to discuss a few things with Corinne before she left. I can only think of one thing to explain it: He bore an uncanny resemblance to the victim, only half his age. There was the same waved hair and high forehead, the same stylish summer suit. The kid's eyes were clear and intelligent. He was the type who looked like he didn't get his hands dirty much, but was nevertheless a decent guy, if you know what I mean. It was like I was looking at the stiff standing before me, twenty-some years earlier. But alive, of course, with all those twenty-some years still ahead of him. That sensation must be what transfixed me, kept me standing there listening to some music reporter in the critical first hour of a murder investigation.

"Excuse me, Lieutenant Nelson?" He held out his hand, but I didn't take it.

"I'm Ralph Owens, arts writer for the *Gazette*. I know how busy you are, but I wonder if I could ask you a couple of questions."

"Sorry, I don't have much time right now."

"Do you have any leads?"

"Nothing at the moment." I turned to leave.

The kid's voice sputtered behind my back. "Does he seem to have . . . suffered greatly?"

I pivoted toward him. For some reason his face was screwed into a pained whorl. It set me back, and I took a moment to respond. "I couldn't tell you," I said. "Now, if you'll excuse me."

I started toward the front entrance. It might still be possible, I was thinking, to catch Corinne before the ambulance pulled away . . .

"You realize," Owens blurted behind my back, "Robin Markson was one of the unheralded geniuses of our time."

I stopped. The kid spoke with such conviction. I approached him. "How much do you know about Mr. Markson, anyway?"

He looked me unflinchingly in the eyes. "I'd say I've followed his career as closely as anybody."

This guy might be useful, I thought. "You got a card? I might like to speak with you when I get a minute."

"I'd greatly appreciate that."

While he dug into the breast pocket of his sports coat I turned to see the ambulance pull away. I had missed Corinne. What's worse, that reporter I'd recognized earlier, the bulldog, had just walked through the entrance. She was striding toward Owens and me with a take-no-prisoners look on her face.

I hiked my head in her direction. "Look," I said to Owens, "you want to do me a favor? Get her off my tail."

He looked past me and nodded while I hurried toward the doors to the beachside grounds. As I looked over my shoulder, I saw him collide with my bulldog, just enough to knock her off her stride. The usual apologies, mutual introductions . . .

That Owens kid was all right with me.

Back at the crime scene Forensics was still working the room. They'd tagged the statuette and music papers and other miscellanea.

"Learn anything from the maid?" Sanchez asked when I came in.

I told her about the dinner reservation at Carpaccio. "And," I added, "Markson told the girl he was expecting company."

"Did she say who?"

"No, but I figure it was whoever he was supposed to have dinner with. We'll have to see if we can't track them down."

After I took some photos with my digital I asked Sanchez to walk with me. We went out through the suite's balcony, down the steps, and combed the surrounding area. An exhaustive search of the lush vegetation in which the villas were nested didn't turn up a thing. We went along the pool walkways and over to the beach gate. Nada. Not that I expected anything. The pool crew had done their usual thorough cleaning at the break of dawn. I asked Sanchez to see if she could collect the trash bags before they went to the landfill.

"How many ways are there for the perp to flee?" We were standing by the resort's beach gate, looking toward the villa wing.

She replied that the killer could have gone out the suite's sliding doors and down the balcony steps, then through the pool area and out the beach gate. If he wanted to avoid the lighted pool area, she went on, he could have skirted the front of the villas, using the plantings as cover, slipped past the tennis courts and gotten to the beach by hopping the fence. "Or," she said, "he could have used the suite's door to the interior hall-way. From there, he could have left the building through any one of the resort's regular exits."

"There must be a dozen of them."

"The easiest would be the one at the end of the villa hallway. That would put him near the beach, with just a short hop over that fence."

"Anybody spoken to security?"

"Willis did. They're trying to contact the night shift, but they haven't been able to reach them."

"What about cameras?"

"I'm not sure. We'll have to ask Willis."

I thanked her and asked her to let me know as soon as any-thing turned up with the phone records or hotel security. She planned to check with Willis and see how he was doing with the other guests. I went out the beach gate and walked south on the jogging path that runs along the shore there. I wasn't looking for evidence. I glanced around, sure, in case anything should jump out at me. But I was really just meandering, so I could think a little. We had a dead man, apparently whacked over the head with a statuette of a Greek goddess. There were some scattered music papers, a missing fourteen thousand dollar emerald necklace, and a dinner reservation at Carpaccio.

Not much to go on.

I'd have to locate the next of kin. Notify them. Sanchez was probably already on that. That's one thing I always liked about Sanchez. She thought of little chores I had to do before they even occurred to me.

I turned around and headed back toward the resort. There was a tall bank of sea grape massed along the path there. Vigorous, fertile and strong, it looked like you couldn't stop it growing if you wanted to.

When I got to the Sheraton's gate, and went into the pool area, it seemed that the usual spirit of fun was lacking. The sun worshippers were subdued, muted.

Or was it just me?

Things had returned to normal in the lobby, in any event, now that the body had been taken out and the ambulance gone. I went over to the concierge desk and introduced myself. I asked the concierge, a Mr. Bryant, if he remembered making a reservation for the victim at Carpaccio.

"Yes, I do," he said. "I'm a huge opera fan, so I was thrilled to help Mr. Markson. I can't believe what's happened. It's so sad. What's wrong with people?"

"You figure that one out, my friend," I said, "you can have my job. Do you remember how many the reservation was for?"

"Yes, two."

"Did he mention who he was dining with, by any chance?"

"No, I'm afraid he didn't. Our conversation was quite brief. It sounded like he was terribly busy. You know, the premiere of his latest work is tonight."

"Do you mean to say they're going to put on the show? In spite of what's happened?"

"That's what I understand. I had tickets, so I went to the website this morning to see what they had decided. Apparently José Diaz, the music director, is going to conduct."

I thanked him and left the hotel through the front doors. Before I got around the drive the bulldog was standing there, blocking my path.

"Okay, Frank," she said, "don't you think you've been avoiding me long enough?"

"I appreciate the fourth estate, Fiona"—Fiona, that was her name—"but I've really got to keep moving. This is a fresh investigation."

"Not so fresh you couldn't speak with Ralph Owens about it."

"A couple of words . . ."

"How about a couple of words for me, then? Like, what do you know so far?"

"Very little. There's a couple of words for you."

"Now, Frank." I stepped around her and headed for the crosswalk, but she tagged along beside me. "Can't you give me anything?"

"Okay, if you promise to get off my back."

"Fine."

"An emerald necklace is missing."

I often drop these tidbits to the press, so Fiona's pestering turned out to be convenient. Perps and their accomplices can be pushed into nervous errors when they know you're after something concrete. I guess that's what they call turning lemons into lemonade.

"Are you saying it was robbery?"

"That's all for now, Fiona. I've got to go."

We were at the crosswalk and the light had changed. Fiona looked exasperated, but she turned around and started to dial her cell phone. I crossed over to the Shops.

The Shops at Bal Harbour sits across Collins Avenue from where the Sheraton beach resort used to be. You would think they were put there together: as a set, so to speak. The Shops, you see, has all the swanky stuff the rich people who used to stay at the resort liked to buy. It's a two-story affair, with a Neiman Marcus at one end and Saks Fifth Avenue at the other. In between is a reproduction of Rodeo Drive, with all the fancy designer shops you can think of. Cartier's, Bulgari, Armani, Gucci, Versace, Dior. You get the idea. On the second level is an art gallery hawking paintings for more than my house is worth, by famous artists I've never heard of. Sometimes Lori and I dine at one of the restaurants and wander around. The mall is open to the sky, with koi ponds and palm trees, and Lori oohs and aahs over all the fancy duds and jewelry. Fortunately, she never expects me to buy that kind of stuff for her. She tells me that she just appreciates the artistry that goes into it. She's happy on a detective's salary, she says, and with what she pulls in from her part-time catering work.

I'm lucky that way.

The parking area in front of the Shops is ringed with Indian laurel trees. They're about twenty feet tall, all butt up against one another, and they trim them flat on the tops and sides like some crazy, gigantic hedgerow. In the evenings the big boat-tailed grackles gather in those trees in massive, thousands-strong flocks and set up a tremendous racket. If the sky's also cloud-streaked and mysterious at those times, you'd swear something strange was about to happen.

Armageddon, maybe.

When I got across Collins, I walked under the laurels and over to Carpaccio, at ground level on the street side of the Shops. They had a pretty good crowd at their sidewalk tables. I went over to the hostess station and asked about Mr. Markson's reservation for the evening before.

"Nine o'clock, you said? Yes, I have him here. Party of two."

"So, he showed up?"

"Well, he's crossed off the list," the hostess said, "but that doesn't necessarily mean he showed. After an hour or so we cross off the no-shows. Or, of course, if they cancel."

"Were you working last night?"

"No, that would have been Vanessa."

"Is she around?"

"Not yet. She doesn't come in until four."

"Is there any way to find out for sure whether Mr. Markson dined here last night?"

"You could check the charge receipts, assuming he paid by credit. The manager would have to help you with that, though."

I accepted her offer and stood by while the manager went through an evening's worth of charge slips at one of South Florida's most popular restaurants. You can imagine how thrilled he must have been, but he didn't complain. Unfortunately, there was nothing on Markson. Then I had him—a little grudgingly this time, it seemed to me—go through a second time. If Markson had dined at Carpaccio, he told me, he either paid in cash, or his mysterious dinner companion picked up the tab.

"Look," I said, "I'd really like to know for certain whether Mr. Markson was here last night. The gal out front told me that Vanessa worked the hostess station."

"That's right."

"She'll be in at four?"

"Supposed to be."

I told him that I'd return and left the restaurant. Wending my way back into the Shops, I found Cartier's. The manager introduced me to the sales girl who sold Markson the necklace.

"Did he say why he was buying it? Was there some special occasion, for example?"

"No, not that he mentioned," she said. "He just said he wanted something extraordinary."

"Do you happen to have another one here? Could you show me what it looks like?"

"It was a one of a kind, I'm afraid."

"Could you describe it to me?"

"It had three emerald pendants. The one in the center was larger than the other two. The smaller ones were a few inches higher on the chain. They were all rimmed with diamonds, and the chain was fourteen-carat white gold."

I thanked her and took the escalator to the second floor. There's a Cuban lunch place up there—Guantanamera Café—where I planned to order one of those sandwiches with the pork and pickles. They've become a particular favorite of mine over the years. While I waited at the counter, I rang up Lori and told her that we had a fresh case. She knew what that meant: I'd be pretty scarce for a few days. I also called home. Mrs. Pruitt answered, and I asked her to put Sara on. The kid was feeling miserable, but our nice old neighbor was applying cold compresses to her jaw. That seemed to help.

After the sandwich I crossed Collins back to the Sheraton. I ducked through the service entrance, in case Fiona was still lurking about, and made my way back to the villas. Forensics was finishing up, getting ready to pack out, so I asked Sanchez to pull our team together. That would be just her and Willis for the moment, since Simmons—who'd recently joined our team from the ranks—was at the station working on the phone records. I put Sanchez on the necklace and asked Willis if he'd learned anything from the other guests on the villa wing.

"I haven't been able to track them all down," he said. "The

people in the next room, for instance."

"Stay on it, will you?"

"Will do."

"What about security? Have you been able to contact the night shift?"

"Not yet."

"How about cameras? You should take a look at the tapes around the time of the murder."

"Anything else?" He gave me one of those funny looks he sometimes gets. I didn't need to ask what it meant.

I turned to Sanchez. "Did you learn anything about the next of kin?"

"I made some inquiries back in Washington State," she said. "He taught at a college out there. It looks like his only immediate family is a daughter. She's scheduled to check in at the hotel later today. She was coming in to see the opera."

"Wife?"

"It seems Markson and the girl's mother split about nine years ago."

"I hope the kid hasn't heard it on the news," I said. "That would be terrible."

"Her flight's scheduled to get in at two."

"Hmm, that's an hour from now. Where?"

"Lauderdale."

"I'd better hustle over there and wait at the gate."

"Shouldn't I come along?" she asked.

The force had recently instituted a policy for detectives to break this kind of bad news in teams.

"That's all right," I said. "I'll call the station and have the chaplain meet me. I need you to stay on things here."

I went back out through the service entrance, got my car and headed for the airport. Sanchez had given me the girl's name:

Morgan, Morgan Markson. I wondered if she was the pretty teen in the photograph in the victim's wallet. There was some resemblance, although the girl's long, wavy hair was dark, not blond like the victim's.

I called the station but the chaplain wasn't available. There had already been one other homicide that morning, and he was talking to *their* next of kin.

I made a quick calculation. It was too late to turn around for Sanchez. I couldn't allow Markson's daughter to get off that plane with no one there to meet her. They've got televisions tuned to news channels all over the airport, and there wouldn't be anything worse than letting the poor kid learn of her father's fate like that. The department's policy would have to wait for a more convenient moment.

The airline agreed to set aside a room where I could meet with Morgan Markson, and I went to the gate to wait for her. They got word to the flight crew to ask her to come to the counter when she deplaned.

I recognized her as soon as she cleared the gangway. It was the girl in the photograph, no question. She came to the counter and addressed herself to the attendant.

"This gentleman is here for you," the gate clerk said.

Ms. Markson looked at me quizzically. "Are you from the opera? The hotel?"

"Not exactly," I said.

"I thought my father was coming."

I introduced myself and showed her my badge. "May I ask you to come this way, where we can talk."

"Talk about what? I need to get to my hotel. I'm attending an extremely important function this evening."

"Yes, I know. I just need to talk with you a moment. It's about your father." We were walking now, and I asked if I could help with her bag.

"No, I'm fine. What about my father? Why isn't he here?"

"That's what I've come to talk with you about. If you'll just come this way . . ."

"Is something wrong? Is he ill?"

I didn't answer. I didn't want her to freak out in the middle of the concourse. It wouldn't be dignified, for one thing, and she might cause a ruckus. Fortunately we were near the elite lounge the airline had made available for me. They'd been decent enough to close it off to other customers until I finished what I had to do. An airline employee waited there to let us in.

"You're making me nervous," Ms. Markson said as soon as we walked into the lounge. "You're a policeman. That means something has happened to my father. Something bad." Her voice was shaky, and I tried to steer her toward a chair while I responded.

"I'm afraid something has happened to him."

She stood frozen, her eyes riveted on mine. I looked away.

"It's very painful to tell you," I said, "but your father has been murdered. His body was found this morning in his hotel room."

"Oh, my God! What are you saying?"

Her face ratcheted through all the phases of shock, terror and disbelief, until her mind finally began painfully to wrap itself around the unimaginable. For a moment she looked like she would implode; then she just fell apart. I reached out and helped her into a low leather chair. She sat there sobbing awhile, unmindful of my presence.

"What happened? Where is he?" she finally blurted.

"We've taken the body to the morgue. If you feel you could, it would be helpful if you would come downtown and make a positive identification."

She broke into a deeper round of pain and weeping, and now it was I who stood frozen. I wanted to reach out, comfort her in some way but, after all, I was a stranger. A stranger with a badge. I was vaguely aware of gleaming jetliners taking off through the lounge's high windows. Other than Morgan Markson's sobbing, the room was stone quiet.

"If you don't feel up to it," I said, "I mean going to the morgue, I could take you straight to the Sheraton."

She choked back her tears. "No, I want to see him. But I need to call my mother first." She dug around in her handbag. "Could you leave me alone for a moment?"

I told her that I would wait outside the lounge door.

After ten minutes I peeked through the door's glass panel. Morgan Markson had finished her call and now slumped in the black leather chair looking stunned. I hated to barge in, but I had an investigation in progress, and I had to keep moving. I walked over to where she sat. She reached a hand out to me. "Please help me up," she said.

It was a relief to be able do anything for the lady. She also let me take her bag, and I drove her to the medical examiner's building. Along the way she asked the usual questions. How did it happen? Who could have done it? I gave her the standard assurances: that we would do everything possible to find and prosecute the guilty party.

She turned her face toward the window. "Why now?" she asked, speaking more to herself than to me, "—when so much seemed to be coming to fruition for him?"

I broke in on her thoughts. "What do you mean?"

"All of the musical ideas he's spent his career developing," she said as she gazed at the passing scenery, "it was all coming together. And people—some of them, anyway—had really begun to appreciate what he was doing."

"I'm not much of an expert on the arts," I confessed.

She kept her eyes fixed out the window, daubing them at intervals with a tissue.

"Did your father have any enemies that you know of? Is there any reason why anyone would want to harm him?"

"No." She blew her nose. "He was the kindest, sweetest . . ." She broke down again.

After she identified the body I drove her to the Sheraton. I was concerned about her being alone, but she told me that she had called a family friend. When we pulled up at the hotel, a middle-aged lady stepped over to the car. Morgan hugged her long and hard before they walked into the lobby together.

The news crews were gone when I walked back to the villa wing. The crime scene cordon had been removed and everyone from our team had left the room. Kids shrieked in the pool, while adults lay splayed on chaises like fat, lazy lizards. It was back to normal for them.

It was back to normal for me, too, I said to myself. Hunting down killers *was* my normal.

I went back to the station to do some paperwork and check in with my team. Willis had talked to the guests next to Markson's room. They had heard some noises around 10:30, a couple of thumps and some groaning. Unfortunately, they figured their neighbors were just enjoying themselves and turned up the TV a little louder.

As for phone records, Markson had made and received several calls the day before. Simmons had a list of names, phone numbers, addresses and occupations. We would have to check them out. It looked like a surprised burglar, like Sanchez said, but it was way too early to jump to any conclusions. We didn't know the victim, I reminded the team. Who could say what kind of darkness he might have been involved with?

Sanchez was going to put in a late night so she could run down the usual suspects, hoodlums who never get out of bed until three in the afternoon. She was planning to beat the bushes in some choice locales. I put Simmons on it with her. A fourteen thousand dollar necklace doesn't disappear into thin air. If we could locate it, we would at least have something to go on.

I went into my office with the phone records to make some calls. Here's the list:

1) José Diaz, Artistic Director, Miami Opera Company
2) Ralph Owens, Arts Reporter, South Florida Gazette
3) Robinson's Dry Cleaners
4) Morgan Markson, daughter of Robin Markson
5) Olivia Taylor, voice coach
6) Several calls to the music department at the victim's college in Washington State
7) Various calls to the front desk

Ralph Owens was the arts reporter I met at the hotel. I figured he and Markson had done some kind of interview, probably not much of a personal nature. I'd meet with him later. I'd already spoken with Morgan Markson, and her father had likely called the college regarding his teaching duties. I'd have Simmons check in with them. That left Diaz, the opera director, and Taylor, the voice coach.

I decided to start with Diaz. The person who answered the phone said that he was in rehearsals and couldn't be disturbed, so I left a message. Next I dialed Taylor, Olivia. She answered. I introduced myself and asked if she was acquainted with Robin Markson.

"Yes, I knew him," she said.

I asked if she'd heard the news.

"Yes, I heard."

She spoke so softly that I could barely hear her.

Had she known him for long?

"We were acquainted . . . many years ago."

I remarked that he had called her two days before. Could I ask why he had called?

"He just wanted to say hello."

"I understand you're a voice coach."

"Yes."

"Is that like a teacher?"

"Yes."

"Were you involved with the production of Mr. Markson's current show? The opera?"

"No, I wasn't."

"Did he say anything that would indicate that he was in trouble, or that he was in any kind of danger?"

"No."

I sensed that she was softly crying, but I couldn't be sure.

"Did he mention what he planned to do last evening?"

"No." Her voice had grown shaky. "I don't recall anything."

"Ms. Taylor, please try to remember. It appears that he made a dinner reservation for two. Are you sure he didn't mention who he was dining with?"

She was distinctly crying now. "I'm sure. I told you, I don't know anything about it." There was a loud sniffle. "Please just let me go."

With that she hung up.

I considered ringing back but soon thought better of it. Maybe I had pushed too hard. I couldn't help wonder why she would be so broken up about someone she had known ages ago, as she herself said, but from what I hear those artistic types can be pretty emotional. For most people, I reminded myself, murder isn't an everyday affair. I decided to give it a rest. I could always check back with her later.

I took a look at my to-do list for the other nine cases our team was working. They would have to wait a couple of days while we chased down everything we could on this one while it was fresh. When I finished at my desk it was nearly seven, and I still hadn't heard back from José Diaz, the opera guy. I decided to drive over to the opera house and look him up in person.

Chapter 2

I GOT OFF THE CAUSEWAY at Biscayne Boulevard and parked out front. Terrazzo paving led past palm trees to a high glass entranceway. When an usher greeted me I told him why I was there. He asked me to wait while he went off to find someone else. A lady in a smart suit came over, and I explained the same business to her.

"I can appreciate your requirements, Mr. Nelson," she said, "but Mr. Diaz is conducting a performance in an hour. They're only just now finishing up rehearsals."

"It'll only take a few minutes."

She asked me to wait and disappeared into the hall. I figured she had to talk to another suit. After a minute she came back and asked me to follow her. We went through a side door to the backstage area. Black-clad stagehands hustled to and fro as we stood in the wings and watched Diaz finish his rehearsal. He had a group of singers off to one side, and he was making them sing the same bit over and over again:

> and the vastness of the ocean,
> and the endless pouring out of time,
> and the sun that drenched these beaches . . .

"That's better," he said when they stopped. "Just remember

what Robin said the other day. Think Greek chorus. Stately. A timeless voice of ancient ones. Do you understand?"

The singers, four gals and two men, said they did. Diaz dismissed them and turned to the orchestra.

"Let's do it up for Robin," he said. There were tears in his eyes. "Have a good show."

He turned to a man and woman who stood nearby. They were elegantly dressed, her in a long gown, he in coat and tails. They spoke quietly and then hugged and kissed each other on the cheeks—the men, too—before walking off the stage together.

"Okay," the suit who brought me back said, "he may have a moment now."

She took me down a hallway where there was a series of dressing rooms and a couple of sitting lounges. Orchestra members and singers, more suits and nicely dressed ladies milled around or moved on their way. My suit stopped at the door of one of the sitting rooms. She asked me to wait while she went in to speak with Diaz, who sat on a sofa speaking to a young man with a clipboard. After the suit spoke with him, Diaz looked at me, stood up and came over. The suit left us.

"Won't you come with me?" he said. "We'll go to my office."

"I appreciate your taking the time. I know how busy you are."

"Anything for Robin."

"Were you friends?"

"I've known Robin almost thirty years," he said. "He was the best friend I've ever had. Except my wife, Lily, of course."

"This must be rough for you. Having to work, I mean, what with it being so . . . soon."

"To tell the truth," Diaz said, "we almost called off the performance. But we had a meeting, a pretty emotional one. And we decided that if we canceled, we'd just be giving whoever

murdered my friend one more victory. This is the biggest moment in Robin's career, the premiere of his finest work to date.
It's up to us to make sure that whoever took his life didn't take
this away as well. So we're going to keep up our spirits and
put on this show. Just the way Robin would have wanted it, if
possible."

Those musicians have more guts than I thought.

"And you know what," he continued, "now that we've decided to do it, I'm feeling somewhat better. I think all of us are.
We're doing something for Robin, instead of just letting the
grief defeat us—along with Robin's soaring artistic accomplish-
ment. It lets us feel like, in some way, he's still with us. Do you
know what I mean?"

I told him that I did.

We got to his office and sat around a coffee table. I asked
him how much time he had, and he said he could spare ten
minutes.

"Let me get right down to it, then," I said. "When's the last
time you saw Mr. Markson?"

"I saw him yesterday, when he was over here rehearsing.
He was supposed to conduct for the premiere, you know. I had
been working with the company myself for weeks, of course.
But since he got in, on Thursday I think it was, he's been coming over to manage the sessions."

"I see."

"Afterward I drove him back to the Sheraton. We played a
couple of sets of tennis and then had a drink together."

"You said you'd been friends a long time."

"Yes." Diaz let out a long sigh, looked toward the hallway,
and then turned back to me. "We started our careers together
years ago. Right here in Miami, in fact. Robin was getting fill-in
work as an assistant conductor, and I was a struggling young

baritone. We were both trying to negotiate this crazy business. There were Lily and Olivia, our practice pianist Arturo, so many other friends. It's all so painful to remember." He looked away again. "This was supposed to be a joyous homecoming for Robin. So many of us knew him. The soprano, Lisa Malfi, our tenor. We were looking forward to a festive party tonight. Funny how quickly things change. We're going to have the party anyway, to celebrate Robin's life, and this great work. But it won't be so festive, I'm afraid. At least I feel good that, before he died, he was able to incorporate so many of his artistic ideas into this wonderful opera. Nobody can ever take that away from him."

"You mentioned an Olivia. That wouldn't be Olivia Taylor, by any chance?"

"Yes, it is. They were quite close back then. We were all great friends, of course. So young and hopeful. So full of life and music . . ."

"Can you think of anyone who would want to hurt Mr. Markson? For any reason?"

Diaz thought for a moment, furled his eyebrows. "No, I can't. He was one of the nicest men I've ever known. Always courteous. Decent and thoughtful . . ."

"I hate to ask you this, but forgive me, I have to rule some things out."

"Go ahead," he said, "do your job."

"Was Mr. Markson involved in anything illegal that you know of? Narcotics? Anything?"

"God, no," he replied. "An occasional glass of wine or two, a beer . . ."

"What about women? He didn't have any habits in that area that, you know, might have gotten him mixed up with the wrong kind of people?"

He looked at me like he couldn't quite process what I was saying. "You mean like . . . prostitution? S&M? Lieutenant Nelson, Robin was a decent, regular guy. He was devoted to his daughter, to his students, and especially to his art. Sure, he's done some dating since his divorce. But he wasn't involved with anything, you know . . . illicit, I guess you'd say."

"That's what I figured. Sorry, I had to ask."

"That's all right." Diaz rested his elbows on his knees, then he burrowed his hands into his hair and shook his head, as if he were trying to dislodge the whole painful idea of Robin Markson's murder from his mind. "Any idea who did this?" he asked. "Or why?"

"It was probably a burglary," I said. "He purchased an expensive piece of jewelry day before yesterday. An emerald necklace. Now it's nowhere to be found. Did he mention anything to you about that?"

He looked suddenly inquisitive. "No, he didn't."

"One other thing. He made a dinner reservation at Carpaccio, across from the resort, but it looks like he never showed. The reservation was for two. Did he say anything about dinner plans for last evening?"

Diaz's expression grew thoughtful. "Actually," he said, "I asked him up to our place. I'd organized an impromptu dinner party, just some old friends and a few principals from the cast. But Robin said that he had a prior engagement."

"Did he say what that was?"

"No, he didn't. And when I asked about it, he said he had better not tell me just yet, because he didn't want to *jinx* it."

"Any idea what that was supposed to mean?"

"I couldn't tell you. It could have been an interview with one of the big newspapers, *Time* or *Newsweek*. Maybe he'd secured a deal with a record company, who knows? Then again, he may have simply gotten himself a date. There are quite a few attractive women in the show."

I glanced at the clock on the wall and saw that our ten minutes was up.

"I'd better let you go," I said. "Thanks for your time. I may need to contact you again as the investigation continues."

"I'll do anything I can to help."

We both stood up. I assured him that the department would do everything in our power to find his friend's killer.

Without warning, he put his arms around me and hugged me heartily. He even pressed his face into the shoulder of my sports coat. I was half afraid he was about to plant a wet one on me, to tell you the truth. You never know with these artistic types . . .

"Listen," he said after he released me, "I don't know if you'd be interested, but you're welcome to stay for the show. I can put you in a box. We always reserve a few seats for last-minute VIPs."

I hadn't thought about staying, but it didn't seem right to say no. Not only would it be disrespectful to the memory of Mr. Markson, I had a hunch that seeing the opera might help me with the case. Diaz accompanied me into the hallway. He hailed the kid with the clipboard and asked him to take me out front and set me up with a seat.

I'd never been in the hall before. The kid put me near the stage in one of the boxes, little balconies that jut out from the sides of the theater. The whole place was done up in rich gold tones, and several stories high. There was a balcony all across the back, at least four stories up. Those are the cheap seats, and still too pricey for a cop's blood.

It was already past seven-thirty, and people were coming into the hall. The show wasn't supposed to start until eight;

I made a few calls while I waited. First I checked in at home. Sara was doing better. Mrs. Pruitt had brought her some home-made chicken soup, and thanks to the pain meds, she wasn't feeling too uncomfortable. I told Lori I'd be late. Then I contacted my team.

No news.

About ten of eight Morgan Markson—the victim's daughter—came into the box, dressed to the nines. She was with the same middle-aged lady who met her at the hotel that afternoon. She too was decked out in a fancy evening gown. Ms. Markson said a somber hello and introduced her friend.

At eight sharp, after flickering a few times, the lights went down. A spotlight dug into the pit and picked up Diaz walking across the front of the orchestra. Everybody in the place started to applaud, so I joined in. When the clapping finally stopped, Diaz raised his baton and the orchestra began to play.

I must say, I was impressed.

The few times I had heard opera, to be honest, I found it a little hard to stomach. My father had a couple of old records he'd play now and then, all scratchy, with this guy croaking out stuff you could make neither heads nor tales of. Later, there were occasions—on a Saturday afternoon, I think—when I would come across it on the radio. The music seemed a little overdone, if you know what I mean. The singers, it's more like they were shouting half the time than singing. What's worse, to stretch things out between all the bellowing, they would just tra la la along, sort of half-singing, half-speaking. That might have been all right, if you had any idea what they were talking about. But the problem was, it was always in some foreign tongue. Every now and then, I have to admit, there'd be a really gorgeous bit. Some gal singing like an angel, just reeking with emotion, or some fellow belting his heart out. But it seemed like you had to sit through a fair amount of filler to get to the good stuff.

When Diaz started to wave his baton, I got the sense that this was going to be different. At first the music was velvety and sleek, and sort of modern (don't get me wrong, it was pretty serious stuff, but with a hint of, say, a tango—and I know a thing or two about the Latin dances, because I took some lessons to humor Lori.) In the next part it was like a Parisian café, all airy and light. Eventually the melodies grew more somber, but still it didn't have that bombastic quality I've sometimes heard. It was more like the breakers crashing in when no one else is around: a little lonesome, and even a little terrifying. There was somehow something heartbreaking about it, and the drama hadn't even begun. Finally everything got real peaceful, like we were drifting into dreamland or something. That could have been a problem had it gone on too long.

Us homicide cops never get enough sleep.

With the music quivering in that eerie state, a pool of soft lighting pointed up a raised area at the back of the stage. A middle-aged man is sitting at a desk in a beautifully appointed room. He's wearing the same type of summer-weight suit Robin Markson wore the evening he was murdered. The man stands up, goes to a piano and begins to tinker, like he's trying to figure something out. There's a well-weathered Panama hat sitting there. He takes it in his hands and ponders it for a moment. Then he looks off, as if he's trying to remember something . . .

At that moment a spotlight hits the front of the stage. The guys and gals I had watched Diaz rehearsing were standing there. They were singing that same bit from the rehearsal, over and over again in a drony, hypnotic manner:

> . . . and the vastness of the ocean
> and the endless pouring out of time

and the sun that drenched these beaches . . .

The man at the piano appears to be transfixed by the singers, and the stage went dark. Then—within seconds—the lights came up again, but not on the man at the back of the stage. He now sits in the shadows, looking on as the opera begins to unfold before his eyes . . .

Two young lovers step from the wings and come strolling along a backdrop of Biscayne Bay chatting, in song, about their lives. The gal, Caroline, confides to Tom, her boyfriend, about the rigors of her life as an aspiring prima donna. Though her luxuries are few, she sings, and she seldom knows where next month's rent is coming from, the opportunity to make beautiful music makes it all worthwhile. Taking up the same theme, Tom sings that he's happy to be scraping by on pick-up work with the local opera company, so long as he can nurture his dream to one day compose operas that will last through the ages.

I note immediately that the Tom character wears the same style Panama hat the older man had toyed with at the piano. I'm no expert, but that made it plain to me that Tom was a younger version of the piano guy. What's more, judging from the fine summer-weight suit, the piano and the opera gig, I concluded that both of them represented Robin Markson at different stages of his life. It looked like staying for the show had been a decent decision. It would give me an opportunity to learn something about the victim, straight from the horse's mouth, so to speak.

In the next scene several young people are gathered on the stage of a theater. They're all great friends, and they sing to us, as a group, about how they are, each and every one of them, fired-up crazy to craft music to nourish the souls of their fellow human beings. One of them, Antonio (who reminded me an awful lot of the opera director, Diaz) steps forward. He sings that he's Tom's best pal, and that they're all waiting for Tom and Caroline to arrive so they can begin their rehearsal. As it happens, they don't have to wait long, because no sooner has Antonio finished his number than Tom and Caroline come back on stage, professing their love for one another in soaring melodies. After some humorous greetings, these two join their friends in the joyous work of making an opera production.

All is well in their world.

But as the rehearsal winds down, Nick Portfino, a rich, older man who helps pay the company's freight, comes into the theater; he's going to be a sort of dark cloud over the story. We quickly learn that his business connections are none too savory, but what's worse, he's a lecherous bastard. He's after all the young women in the company, and he's especially gunning for Tom's gal, Caroline. Backstage after the rehearsal, he tries to get her in the sack by promising her a plum role in the next production. He even suggests that he can help Tom's career along if she gives him her body. In short, he's just the sort of scumbag that can sometimes make me wish my Sara was born a boy.

One bit that really got me, when the scenes changed, was how that soft lighting would come up on the older man at the piano. Sitting there alone, he would silently watch the group in the spotlight drone those same lines from the rehearsal:

> . . . and the vastness of the ocean,
> and the endless pouring out of time,
> and the sun that drenched these beaches . . .

. . . or sometimes adding others, like . . .

> . . . the corridors of desire,
> my restless, fleeting soul,
> your eyes that never leave me . . .

Anyway, thanks to the magic of opera, we're soon at the

beach ourselves (at least there's a super backdrop, with a perfect blue sky, puffy white clouds, and even a few sailboats). Tom kneels in the sand—real sand, mind you!—and asks Caroline to marry him (in song, of course). But since he's so poor, he sings, he suggests they keep their engagement unofficial until he can bag a more regular gig (bad idea). With that, the two lovebirds burst right into a duet about the trials and hardships of struggling young artists, living on a wing and a prayer in their low-rent dives. Then, while they're still warbling like parakeets, the rest of the gang shows up. Raising their hearty voices together, they remind one another that, in spite of their poverty, they will always have their incomparable dreams and one another's priceless friendship.

Sparkling, youthful dreams: how beautiful they always are! Unfortunately, those of Tom and Caroline are about to get a devastating kick right in the seat of the pants.

The lecher character—Portfino—has shifted his sexual harassment of the company's young women into high gear. We watch, shocked and disgusted, as he pops into the dressing areas unannounced, making inappropriate comments and getting grabby with the singers. One afternoon he as much as brings Caroline to tears with his unwanted and ungentlemanly advances.

That evening Caroline shares her distress with Tom, though softening the rough edges, and this is where the young Markson character makes his fatal mistake. Upset about Portfino's treatment of the company's females, and especially his own gal, he decides to play a little prank on the old rascal. We watch it all happen one afternoon while Tom is rehearsing the company in the opera hall. Portfino comes in to observe, as is his custom, and after Casanova gets himself seated, Tom gives the company a signal (because, you see, they've planned everything in advance). Suddenly dropping what they've been working on, the troupe commences to act out a classic opera scene where a dirty old man makes a fool of himself chasing after the story's young female characters. At the climactic moment, the old lecher turns around to reveal a sign reading "Portfino" on his back. The whole company cracks up, and Portfino, red in the face, goes storming out of the theater. But sadly, Markson's (I mean Tom's) satisfaction is short-lived, because from that point forward, without warning or explanation, the Miami opera ceases to call him for work.

In the next scene Antonio hears through closed doors that Portfino had arranged to have his friend edged out, just as we had imagined. After angrily confronting the man, Antonio severs his own connections with the Miami company. He and his gal, Delores, move out West, where they both have friends and opera connections.

For his part, the Markson character now confronts a bleak situation, having lost both his job and his best friend. But the worst part of the whole business is that Portfino now has Caroline right where he wants her. Dangling the prospect of restoring Tom's position in front of her eyes, he tightens the screws, pouring on the pressure to get her in the sack. It gets so intense that Caroline appears to break down under the stress. She experiences the occasional dizzy spell, and sometimes feels so fatigued she can hardly get out of bed. Her joints begin to ache. She visits several doctors, but none of them can arrive at a diagnosis. In the final scene of the first half, Caroline is rehearsing with the opera company, singing one of those old-fashioned belters, and she drops right out on the floor.

The lights came up for intermission, and I wandered out to the lobby with everybody else. The clothes on the spectators were almost as dazzling as the performers' duds, or the Arsht

Center's gilt, velvet and chandeliers. That is to say, silky gowns and sleek tuxedos. They all milled around sipping champagne and eating hors d'oeuvres, bathed in some special kind of light. It wasn't only that wonderful dressed-up look, but a deeper warmth, as if all that rich opera music had done something marvelous to their souls. Some kind of mood elevator. I went to the snack bar and got myself a diet coke.

While I stood there sipping my soda, Morgan Markson's friend—Donna Sullivan was her name—came along.

"Lieutenant Nelson, isn't it?"

I fessed up.

"I want to thank you for being so supportive with Morgan this afternoon," she said.

"Thank you, but I was just doing my job."

"Morgan told me what a gentleman you were, though. That's all too rare these days. I consider it above and beyond, and it meant a lot to her."

"I'm glad I could be helpful," I said. "I just hate to meet people under these circumstances. I hope we can get her some kind of closure on the whole thing."

"I'm sure you will, Lieutenant."

"I wish I could be as confident as you," I replied, "but we'll definitely give it our best shot."

Before we knew it the lights in the lobby began to blink and everybody, including me and Ms. Sullivan, started to move back to our seats. Along the way we came across Morgan Markson. She was chatting with two older couples who handled her with a sort of exaggerated care. It gave me a real lift to see that kind of human decency on display.

We all got settled in the box, the house lights went down, and the stage lights came up again.

Young Tom is in his World War Two vintage apartment now,

with musical instruments and papers scattered everywhere. He looks toward the audience and starts up this slow, mournful song, like one of those tangos they used to play at the dance classes. Without the work he was getting at the opera, he sings, he's poor as a church mouse. What's worse, Caroline—who's health has continued to deteriorate—requires all kinds of expensive specialists. Tom can't imagine, if they are to marry, how he'll ever come up with the scratch to properly care for her. He goes to the window, opens it and gazes down on the traffic, looking so woebegone you're afraid he's about to jump. I guess it was the cop in me, but at that moment I actually twisted in my chair, like I ought to dash onto the stage and restrain him. But just then the phone rings. Markson's—I mean Tom's—pal Antonio has called from California. It seems that Diaz (I mean Antonio, of course) has gotten wind of an opening for a conductor out west. What's more, he sings that Tom is a shoe-in for the position, if he wants it. Tom, holding the receiver out to his side, proceeds to musically agonize over the decision in a gut-wrenching number that nearly blew the roof off the concert hall. I guess Antonio didn't mind holding the line, because after concluding that he has no better options, Tom takes up the receiver again and agrees to join his old friend in Los Angeles.

After a spate of wild clapping for Tom's song, the stage went dark. The older Tom watches the droners again from his perch near the piano, and then we find the young Tom and Caroline together. This is the difficult moment when Tom must tell Caroline about his plans to move to California. After breaking the bad news, we watch him croon, in soaring tones, that he will send for her as soon as he gets settled in Los Angeles. But listen up, because this part was really great. Caroline looks toward the audience, like she's speaking to us and Tom can't hear, and in the show's most wrenching number sings that she knows

Tom will never send for her, but that she will always love him, anyway. Holding him in her arms, she gives him her blessing, and the stage went dark again.

It felt like the entire audience had sucked in their breath, that singing lady unleashed so much emotional power on us. Someone shouted brava!, and the place burst into a thunderous applause that kept up for five, maybe ten minutes. When everybody finally settled down, the curtain opened for what turned out to be the final scene.

Tom is in Los Angeles now, where he has just wrapped up a rehearsal with his new opera company. He turns to the audience, like he's just noticed we're there, and sings how the company is a start-up outfit that can barely keep the lights on. Paychecks, meager as they are, come in fits and starts. He croons how he misses Caroline terribly, but sings that he's in no position to support her. He writes less and less because there's jack for good news to report. Their correspondence, he concludes sadly, has dwindled to a trickle.

At that moment, while Tom is collecting his things, Antonio bursts in: and he has terrible news! It seems that Caroline—Antonio bellows in his deep baritone—has married the old lech, Portfino. Young Tom literally reels from the shock. He sings that he can't imagine how he'll go on, with his fondest dreams for the future shattered. But his stalwart friend, with that low, booming voice of his, convinces him that he must stay the course. Finally, with Diaz bracing him up, Markson resolves to throw himself into his work, singing that he will strive to one day create something beautiful enough to make Caroline proud that she once loved him.

Those guys' rousing duet had about the same effect on the audience as Caroline's farewell number.

It brought the house down.

When everybody finally finished with the bravos and the clapping, the main lighting went down and the lighting at the back of the stage came up. This was the part the program called "Coda." The older Tom is at the piano again. He's gone back to his tinkering, but now he's begun to get some real music going. Before you know it, in fact, he's playing that peaceful melody from the overture. He then begins to sing, telling how painful life's lessons can be, how youth is wasted on the young, and how he once had the whole world in his hands but was too clueless to realize it! The lights came up again now at the front of the stage. The young people are there dancing, singing and having a grand, carefree time. Their young music grows louder and louder, and they're all singing, until at last the older Markson—I mean Tom, of course—comes downstage and joins them. When the music finally fades, they all walk offstage together and everything goes dark. I was about to start clapping—I mean, my hands had almost touched—until the spotlight captured that chorus group, standing at the lip of the stage, for one last go:

> *... and the vastness of the ocean,*
> *and the endless pouring out of time,*
> *and the sun that drenched these beaches ...*

The little group sang their chant for several more rounds, growing more and more quiet, until their spot finally faded. After a long, pregnant pause, someone who must have been in the know began to clap their hands. A few others joined in, and then the whole place exploded. The cast started to come out and take bows, and pretty soon the entire audience was on its feet. People shouted *bravo!* and *brava!* and *bravi!* while various members of the cast came on in different combinations. Someone tossed a bouquet of roses up to Caroline who, incidentally, was back on her feet and in fine health. I've attended rock concerts where the clapping went on for quite a stretch, trying to squeeze a few more numbers out of the band, but I'd never seen anything to match this. They clapped and clapped and hooted and hollered. Finally, probably because everybody's hands were rubbed raw, the applause died down. The curtain closed for the last time and people began to leave the hall.

I turned to Morgan Markson and complimented her on her father's show. There were tears in her eyes, but she was gently smiling. I told her that I would keep her informed about the investigation.

After leaving the box I found my way to the backstage area. Aside from wanting to thank Diaz for letting me stay, I had some questions for him. Chiefly, I was wondering if Markson's opera, as I suspected, was about Markson's real life. There was a big crowd in the hallways, orchestra players and cast members still in their costumes or half out of them. They all looked happily flushed—I mean, the show had been a huge success— but somehow still sad on account of Markson's death.

About halfway down the hallway I spotted Diaz. He stood among a small group, resting one hand on the handle of a wheelchair. A striking looking, fiftyish lady sat perched in it with her legs crossed one over the other. I walked over to the group and stood by while they finished something they were talking about. Then I stepped in and held out my hand.

"I just wanted to thank you for the show. I really enjoyed it."

"I'm glad you could stay," Diaz said.

The lady in the wheelchair glanced in my direction but quickly averted her eyes. She had a finely chiseled face, golden brown hair swept back on both sides and a look of tremendous courage about her. It's not that she wasn't feminine, or beautiful. She was both.

She looked as though she had been crying.

I turned to leave. This didn't seem to be the time to probe

Diaz about the opera, with all those people around. But he grabbed me by the arm.

"Lieutenant," he said, "let me introduce you to Olivia Taylor. Livy, this is Lieutenant Nelson. He's working on Robin's case."

Hearing Diaz's voice suddenly drop into somber tones, I felt like a black hole, bearing death wherever I went.

I looked down at Taylor and she held out her hand.

"Pleased to meet you, Lieutenant," she said gravely.

"Likewise," I replied. "We spoke on the phone this afternoon."

"That's right. I hope you're successful in your investigations."

I told her that we'd do everything we could, and then I thanked Diaz again and made my way out of the opera house. I was dead tired but wanted to catch the Carpaccio hostess while her memory was fresh. Also on my agenda was one last visit to the hotel before the day was out; I hadn't yet seen the crime scene at night. Biscayne Boulevard was a breeze, and the 96th Street Causeway got me to the shore in minutes. After pulling into the Shops parking lot I went over to Carpaccio's hostess station. They were winding down for the evening, and Vanessa wasn't busy. I had the playbill from the opera with me. She took a close look at the photo of Markson, which was positioned over top a brief blurb about his career.

"Yes, I do remember him," she said. "He was so courteous."

"So he did dine here last night."

"Actually, no, he didn't. He apologized, but he said that his friend wasn't feeling well, and that they couldn't stay."

"Could you describe the friend to me?"

"I'm afraid not. I never saw his companion."

"Are you sure that no one was with him?"

"Lieutenant, things get awfully chaotic at that time of the

evening, with everyone trying to get seated. I don't always notice everything. But I'm pretty sure he was by himself."

That wasn't much, but it was something. I could place Markson alive, around nine o'clock, at Carpaccio's hostess station. I could only hope that his mystery dinner companion would come forward. They could help us fill in some important details.

Then again, I thought, maybe they didn't want to come forward. They could be a person of interest . . .

I went out through the parking lot, crossed Collins to the Sheraton and walked back to the beachside area. On the far end of the villa wing I noted the exit near the beach, and also an alleyway that ran behind the tall chain-link fence that separated the Sheraton from the condo building next door.

The front side of the villas described an oblique angle to both the pool and the ocean. The vegetation there, tall and lush, was filled with shadows. Someone leaving the villas on that side of the structure could easily have gone unnoticed. The pool area was deserted as I snaked my way through its winding walkways to the beach gate.

Out on the damp sand, the volleyball net stood empty of sport. A toy truck, half-buried, lay abandoned. Further on a beach towel languished, twisted and dirty, in the sand. I went down by the surf. A huge orange moon rose out of the ocean. The salty wind poured in from offshore and pressed against me hard. As the moon crept up from the horizon it gradually changed color until a giant, yellow, Lemonhead candy hung out over the sea.

I thought over the day's events. A man was dead, violently killed not two stone's throws from where I stood. That may sound obvious, but when I start a case, I find it useful to step back and remind myself of the fundamentals. A dead person, his life violently snuffed out by another human being: that's what this whole exercise was about. With all the forensics, the interviewing, all the minutiae of the investigation, I couldn't let myself lose sight of one essential fact. Robin Markson, dead. It was for him that we were going through all of this. It was also for his family, his friends and, sure, for all of us who want to experience the natural span of our years without somebody cutting the party short on us. For all of us who want to live out our days in peace, Robin Markson was the latest poster child.

I got to thinking about Professor Swanson. He was this old coot I dealt with on a case I had worked two years earlier. We had a Haitian victim who was into voodoo, and Swanson was a specialist in religions and cults. I'll never forget how he explained the man and the snake. He was telling me why people put their faith in superstitions and the supernatural—in any kind of religion, for that matter. "Consider a man walking down a path," Swanson said to me one day, peering at me through his thick glasses, "and let's say, for argument's sake, that that man gets bitten by a poisonous snake and dies. Well," he went on, "our amazing modern science can tell us exactly how the venom traveled through the man's bloodstream, how it interacted with his body chemistry and, then, how that chemical reaction stopped the beating of the man's heart, thereby putting an end to his life. But all our glorious modern science," Swanson concluded, his eyebrows knitted up like he couldn't quite grasp it himself, "cannot answer the million dollar question: *why were the man and the snake on the same path at the same time?*"

When I work a case, I like to probe into the victim's life, reconstruct as much about it as I can. I'm looking for that chain of necessity, the things that add up, one by one, until the victim ends up on the same path as the snake. Call it crazy, but you can ask my colleagues, I didn't rack up the highest conviction rate in the division by bungling cases. Frankly, I'm not sure myself how it works. It could be that, in the process of digging into the victim's life, I happen to stumble onto clues that lead to the solution to the case. Maybe it's something more mysterious. Who knows? It works, so I don't question it. Of course we do all the customary procedural stuff, good solid police work.

I had my team on that.

As for Robin Markson, what did we know after one day of investigation? He came into town five days earlier to prepare for the premiere of his latest show. After his arrival, he went to the opera house several times to work with the orchestra and cast. He played tennis with his old friend José Diaz and called another old acquaintance, Olivia Taylor. His daughter, Morgan Markson, arrived in the afternoon to attend the performance. A dinner reservation was made for two at Carpaccio. Markson canceled it, explaining that his friend wasn't feeling well. The day before his death, he bought a ridiculously expensive necklace from Cartier's. It was nowhere in sight. I had Sanchez on that. If anybody could find a hot necklace in South Florida, it was Sanchez.

Then there was the opera. The main character seemed to represent Markson himself as a young man, an aspiring composer and opera conductor. It was the last show he did, and it opened the day after he was killed. I couldn't help think that there was something significant in the opera's story. Mental note: visit Diaz again, find out how much of Markson's opera was based on the real facts of Robin Markson's life.

I pivoted away from the offshore wind and looked toward the hotel. From the towers that rose into an indigo sky random windows shone with a yellow glow. The banks of sea grape that draped the dunes along the jogging path formed thick, nameless shadows. Up and down the coast, the gleaming lights of one elegant high-rise after another bespoke luxury, ease and the fullness of life. Yet here, on this night, I knew there was a stain. A stain of evil. There was treachery, malfeasance, and spilled blood.

I glanced up at the coconut palms that lined the shore there. Their fronds drooped with shame. I felt that surge of helplessness I always experience when I start a murder investigation. The world is vast, life indescribably complex, and I'm supposed to figure out how—and why!—a person's life ended. I looked around. The abandoned child's toy, the chaise man's silent tent, the dark and fertile sea grape clusters were of no help. I turned again toward the surf. In its endless cycle of rushing and collapsing, gurgling and slapping, fizzling and sloshing, it seemed to bear some message. But it was not one that I could decipher. The moon rose higher and grew whiter and rounder. If it had any answers, it wasn't giving them up, either.

Tomorrow was another day. I longed to get home and find myself in Lori's warm arms. She couldn't solve my case, but in her own, magical way she could keep my worries at bay until morning. If it weren't for her keeping the home fires burning, I told myself, I couldn't do this.

As for the toll it might be taking on her, and the kids, that was another story. But they're not the kind who would complain.

As I said, I'm lucky that way.

Chapter 3 (Ralph Owens)

ROBIN MARKSON'S DEATH IS A SHOCK, to say the least. He was, for me, the brightest light on the horizon of contemporary American music.

His wasn't a household name, to be sure. But then, he didn't follow the ready route to musical fame: the three-minute pop ditty, love and longing on the run. I don't mean to sound the snob. I've spent untold hours myself wafting on the waves of our popular songsmiths. I even fancied becoming one of them, back in my rock band days. But college drew me to more expansive pursuits, serious literature and classical art forms, and I've found a home these days as the arts reporter for a medium-market newspaper. It's not a bad gig, and I can only hope that exposure to the Robin Marksons of this world might sharpen my own creative visions, visions I struggle to make concrete in the novel that owns my spare hours . . .

No, Markson was not a household name. In fact, the vast majority of my fellow citizens have never, I am quite sure, heard of him. But among a growing circle of cognoscenti, he had come to be considered a modern American classic, an unsung genius quietly sowing the seeds of transformative artworks. Markson was well—and unsentimentally—aware of his obscurity. I spoke to him about it only days before his death.

"All I can really do," he said, "is produce my work. The life of an artist—I'm sure you know—is not what many people suppose. We don't spend all day having fun. I mean, I love my work, and in that sense, it's quite rewarding. But let's make no bones about it. Making art is damned hard business. Especially the big, comprehensive sort I try to create."

"Opera . . ."

"Exactly. And since I not only score my shows, but generally write the book as well, I've really got my hands full. That's on top, mind you, of the teaching and arranging I do to keep the bills paid. And if you're to be honest—that is, if you consider art to consist of an uncompromising effort to get at truth, if not *the* truth—you have a grueling process of self-discovery on your hands. That task is, of course, never-ending.

"So, with all of that to deal with," he continued, "who has time for self-promotion? To worry about whether anyone wants to experience the art you're creating? I mean, it's only natural to care. If you're a normal human being, and I believe I fit roughly into that category, you feel part of your community, and you want to make a contribution. But you're also driven by inner, well . . . demons, if you will . . . to create art that says things you feel need to be said, and in the manner you feel you need to say them."

I asked whether he thought that anyone working in his medium—modern opera—could realistically expect to gain a wide audience.

"Good question," he said with an amiable laugh. "Modern opera, along with modern symphonic and chamber music, has had a hard time achieving an audience. Audiences seem to like music that they can hum, and in dispensing with things like melody, tonality, and regular rhythms, modern composers of what we call serious music—of the ilk of say, Schoenberg—have often left their audiences confused, bewildered and, Im afraid, disengaged. Don't get me wrong. I don't think that all music has to be hummable. I just don't think it all has to be not hummable. You might say that I'm for a mix of the hummable and the not hummable."

We touched on the difficulty of getting modern works, even more accessible ones, on opera companies' programs.

"Yes," he said with a resigned but still congenial air, "the typical company does take refuge in the old warhorses, and that leaves precious little space in their schedules for anything new. Believe me, I adore the great masters. I cut my teeth on them, and they are still my touchstone. But how can we keep a tradition alive with nothing in our repertory but operas that are a hundred, two hundred years old? Certainly they should be performed, and performed regularly. They're priceless treasures of our civilization. But so much has happened since Verde, Puccini, and Wagner. There has been so much history, and so many new departures in music (too many new departures, some might argue, and not all of them worth pursuing). But if we are to maintain a vital, living culture, we have no choice but to try, do we not? Must we not forge on, and attempt to make sense of our modern world in our own, modern terms? What I'd like to see is a greater spirit of adventure on the part of audiences and those who program operas, and a stronger desire to meet the audiences halfway on the part of composers."

"Don't the substantial costs of mounting an opera," I suggested, "inhibit risk-taking on the part of programmers?"

"Putting on an opera is indeed enormously expensive," Markson agreed. "And that does engender a play-it-safe attitude among those who program companies' schedules. With tickets starting at one hundred dollars for obstructed views in major cities, our audience is pretty much limited to the well-off. That means it's normally an older crowd, not the kind of folks most likely to try something new. I'm excited, though, about the growing interest in chamber opera, productions with smaller ensembles and less spectacle, but more affordable ticket prices. That puts a little more pressure on us composers to keep the *music* interesting. But that's what we're here for, isn't it?"

To my mind, Robin Markson had managed, through dint of a struggle the intensity of which I can only guess at, to create structures that satisfy the highest demands of artistic rigor yet still pulse with the living breath of his culture and times. The first time I heard his work (a concert performance of his early opera, *Rosemont Street*) I sensed a kindred spirit, a man striving to meld the prodigious formal achievements of western music to a modern age where so much is transitory and topical. I have avidly followed his career ever since, often traveling significant distances to see rare performances of his works, as none of his operas has yet been recorded. And I have never been disappointed. Instead I have noted a growing mastery and, indeed, had come to believe that Markson *would* one day be a household name, so seamlessly was he weaving the most vital elements of our lives into his musical dramas. The orphic heights reached in his latest work, premiered here just last night, were nothing short of miraculous.

But all of that is now at an end, finished by a hard blow to the skull with a blunt object: a statuette of the *Venus de Milo*, it has been reported. It is some small consolation that tomorrow morning I will write a review of *Biscayne Bay*, in which I will have an opportunity to laud this great American artist.

More than anything, though, I am anxious to speak with Daphne. Like a child running to his mother, I admit, it is she I yearn to see when things go badly. When I suffer.

Right now I am suffering.

I wasn't able to see her this evening; I had to attend Markson's premiere. She would have loved to go, she said, but she hasn't had her restaurant gig at Saudade for long, and she was afraid to risk asking the night off.

"A regular gig, for real money," she said when I chided her about missing what promised to be the most important premiere of our lifetimes. "Do you know how many singers are lined up to take my place? Naturally, I'd love to go, especially since Livy used to work with him."

Oh yes, I forgot to mention. Daphne's voice coach, Olivia Taylor, was once acquainted with Markson. Taylor was a rising diva when she was struck by some debilitating condition. *Myasthenia gravis*, I believe it is called. Now she works as a voice coach, and my Daphne is just crazy about her. I can personally attest that the lady's an incredible artist, because I've seen the occasional recital. She's a beautiful human being, too, from all reports. These are mostly from Daphne, but then, her word is golden to me.

Chapter 4

THE ALARM RANG way too early, but I had an eight o'clock with my team. Sara was moaning with pain, so Lori took her some ibuprofen while I got Andrew moving. As he groped for his clothes, he asked if I could come to his baseball game that afternoon. He was a freshman and had made starting shortstop on the junior varsity squad; it was their first game of the season. I told him we'd have to wait and see and got in the shower.

The team was waiting when I reached the station. Sanchez and Simmons had spent the night beating the bushes in Liberty City, Opa-locka and Hialeah, looking for that emerald necklace. They hadn't been home, and you could tell from the looks—and the scent—of them.

"We checked in with the pawn shops, talked to the usual bad actors. Put heat on the known fences. Didn't turn up a thing."

I asked Willis if he'd been able to speak with the hotel's night security detail.

"Yeah, I caught up with them."

"Did they notice anything unusual?"

"Nothing. Not that I expected much."

"Security cameras?"

"Problems. First of all, their system's limited. It's the usual thing. They feel they've got to respect their guests' privacy. So no cameras in the guest hallways."

"Yeah," Sanchez said, "a lot of these guys traveling on business don't want a record of who's coming into their rooms. I wonder why?"

"Sanchez," Willis said, "just because your ex was a jerk, don't go painting every dude with the same brush."

"In my experience," she replied, "one brush is about all it takes."

"In any case," I interrupted, "it doesn't help us any, does it? Willis, what have they got?"

"That's the other problem. They've got cameras at pinch points—entrances and exits—but the recording system was on the fritz yesterday. They're getting their outside computer company in to look into it. They recently upgraded to this new digital system, and it's been acting a little wiggy."

"Technology's great, isn't it?" Simmons said resignedly, "—when it works, that is."

"The important question for us," I said, "is why their surveillance system happened to be out the night our victim was wasted. Willis, I want background checks on the entire security team. Have a talk with anybody that works with the surveillance system. Bring them in if you have to. Check their alibis. I mean, it's probably just a coincidence, but we need to check it out."

"Will do."

"We haven't got much to go on," I went on, "but let's not lose our focus. So far the missing bling is the one tangible object that might solve this thing."

"And it's history," Willis said.

"Not necessarily," Sanchez stated confidently.

"Granted," Willis conceded. "But Miami's a big place for a

little old necklace to be hiding."

Sanchez dismissed Willis's remark with a wave of her hand. "I've been thinking, Chief," she said, "shouldn't we have a case on the Shops? Suppose there's a theft ring stalking the jewelry places. Waiting for some mark to buy something, so they can jump him?"

"You know," Simmons piped up, pretty excited, "that would explain why Markson's wallet wasn't taken. Whoever busted him seemed to know exactly what they were after—that necklace!"

I loved Simmons' zeal. It reminded me of when I was new to homicide. I commended Sanchez on her idea. "Fact is," I said, "I thought of that last night myself, while I was lying awake at three in the morning. Then I promptly forgot about it. There are just too many damned details to manage. I'm glad you brought it up."

I put Willis on it. I told Sanchez and Simmons to go home and get a few winks and check back with me in the afternoon.

The meeting broke up. I went to my office and dug in my wallet for the business card I had gotten from José Diaz, the opera director. The previous night's performance had made a distinct impression on me. More and more, I was seeing the main character, who sat at the back of the stage reminiscing about things that had happened when he was a young man, as Robin Markson. Robin Markson, whose life—if I can put it that way—was now in my hands. All I'd known of the man was the sight of his semi-rigid corpse canted across the floor of a garden villa at the Sheraton beach resort. That is, until the opera. Now I'd seen another piece of the puzzle. I'd seen the *living* Robin Markson. Even if it was just a singer pretending to be our victim, for me it was as real as it was going to get. I'd gone to bed with Markson's music running through my head, woke up with those same melodies floating around in there, picturing scenes from the show. Maybe this was the thread that would lead me to whatever I needed to know to wrap up my part in this whole, sad affair. I didn't know how and I didn't know why. But I wanted to talk to Diaz, who seemed to have been as close to the murdered man as anyone. If anybody could tell me how much of the opera was taken from real life, it would be him.

He was cordial on the phone. "It's fortunate you called this early," he said. "We've got rehearsals starting at one, and I won't be home for long. You're welcome to come over before that if you wish. I'm happy to help in any way I can."

I got in the car and hustled over to the beach, where Diaz and his wife lived in a condo tower on the Intracoastal. Diaz greeted me at the door of their seventh-floor unit and led me through the living room to the balcony. There was a magnificent view of the ocean all up and down that stretch of coastline. Directly below, a couple of cabin cruisers chugged along the Intracoastal canal. The placid waterway split just south of there to make its way around a small island. On that island sat a beautiful estate ringed with palm and bougainvillea. As long as I've lived in South Florida, I never get over some of these spectacles; even if, on a cop's salary, I just hover around the fringes of paradise, never allowed permanent entrance. I savored the view as I took the seat that Diaz offered. The fringe is better than nothing.

"So, what can I do for you?" he asked.

"I just wanted to ask a few follow-up questions. Incidentally," I added, "that was quite a show you put on last night. I enjoyed it more than I thought I would."

"I'm glad it surpassed your expectations," he said with a sort of wry smile.

"I've never been a big opera fan," I confessed. "I've always found it difficult to get into, to tell you the truth. I don't suppose you could understand that."

"No, I absolutely do," he protested, "in which case your reaction to last night's performance is all the finer a compliment, both to the company and to Robin. Opera is a difficult taste for most of our contemporaries. We in opera are probably as much to blame as anyone. After all, in the days of Bellini and Donizetti, the opera was a cherished entertainment of the Italian masses. The great singers of the day were the equivalent of today's rock stars. So there's no reason that a sung drama, with serious music, can't entertain the common man. It was one of Robin's greatest gifts to see how that might happen again, but in today's cultural context."

"About Mr. Markson," I said, "I can't help wonder how much of his opera is taken from real life. I mean, specifically, from Mr. Markson's life."

"That's a difficult question to answer."

"I know it's pretty personal. But it would help me tremendously if I could get a better idea of the big picture."

"I understand," he said. "But it's not so much that it's personal. It has more to do with the process of artistic creation."

"What do you mean by that?"

"Well, if I say that Robin set out to build an opera about his life, we must be aware that such a story would merely be *his* view of the events that shaped his experience. Now, I probably don't need to tell you, Lieutenant, that we ourselves are typically not the most faithful observers of our own lives. Beyond that, the story that Robin constructed would only be one manner, among endless options, of portraying the myriad events that make up any person's existence."

"I see."

"In any case," he went on, "when authors use real life as a

basis for the stories they tell, they always take a certain number of liberties . . . for purposes of dramatic effect."

"Okay," I said, "but granting all of that, could we say that the opera was roughly autobiographical?"

Diaz looked toward the ocean, thought long and hard. "Lieutenant, if I discuss this with you, do I have your word that the things I tell you won't appear in the press?"

I assured him that I would use any information he gave me for the sole purpose of furthering my investigation, and that nothing would be put in the public record unless it had a direct bearing on the prosecution of Robin Markson's murderer.

"Well, then," he said, "I will start by saying that the opera was indeed based on the life of my old friend. I myself am portrayed in the show, as well as my wife."

"I thought so. That guy Antonio definitely reminded me of you."

"Yes."

"And the gal in the opera—the one you, or rather, Antonio, went out West with—that's your wife? You really ended up getting hitched up?"

"Yes, and we're still quite happy."

"Things didn't seem to go so well for Mr. Markson."

"No, I'm afraid not. But they didn't go so badly, either. It's true that he struggled in his personal life. He was married for the better part of a decade to quite a nice woman, a fellow musician. They had a wonderful daughter, Morgan. A lovely, intelligent girl. But they were really just roommates, Robin and his ex. They never became soul mates, if you know what I mean. I don't suppose that's something you can become, though, is it? It's more something you have to start with."

He looked off into the sea haze.

"Sort of like the main couple in the opera," I offered, "—the composer and the singer . . ."

"Yes," he replied, turning to me again, "exactly like that. In any case, in spite of his personal difficulties, or perhaps because of them—who knows?—Robin achieved a degree of focus in his art that was extraordinary. More than anyone I've ever known, he was attuned to the pulse of human life. And he spent his career mastering how to put down those soundings on sheets of music score, music woven around dramas that bring us together in our shared humanity. Particularly with this last work, he's pointed the way forward for anyone serious about keeping opera a thriving art form into the future."

"If we can get back to the details of the story," I said, "I'd like to ask about the woman called Caroline in the opera. Is she still around, by any chance?"

"Yes, she is. You met her last night, backstage."

"You mean Olivia Taylor?"

"Yes."

"Ah, the wheelchair! I see. Is that because of the illness she suffered as a young woman?"

"That's right," he said. "It was really sad, because Olivia had such promise. That voice of hers! So crystal clear, like the most limpid stream. And always such feeling in it! It's because she has such an open heart, of course. That's where it all comes from, you know. As much as we work on our vocal apparatus and technique, and that's all necessary, of course, but without this"—he tapped lightly on his chest—"you have nothing."

"They never made it clear what she suffered from," I said. "It seemed like fibromyalgia, or maybe multiple sclerosis."

"Actually, she was eventually diagnosed with a condition known as *myasthenia gravis*. It was really tough on her, being a singer. Because, you see, this work we singers do takes a lot of effort. We may be smiling up there, and believe me, it's a kick. But we're also working our little—or in my case, not so little—butts off. That's not to mention the constant training, practice, and rehearsals. The main thing about this condition, myasthenia gravis, is fatigue. Depending on the severity of her symptoms at any given time (because the disease can fluctuate wildly) a person who suffers from the syndrome has to dole out her activity in manageable periods. Then they need to rest. Often the voice is affected, and sometimes it can be difficult to breathe. You can imagine the problems for a singer. They say it's some kind of auto-immune disease, where the body's own defenses prevent nerve signals from reaching the muscles."

"It sounds like a damn tough hand to draw."

"It is, awfully tough. But Olivia is such a beautiful person, and she's borne it well. At the initial onset she tried to ignore it. Of course she went to all the doctors, the specialists. But she continued to work with the company, although it was getting harder all the time. One day she just collapsed, right in the middle of rehearsal, as was portrayed in the opera. I think that's when she realized that she couldn't force her way through this thing, no matter how much she wanted to share this beautiful gift of her voice . . . and her spirit."

"What about Mr. Markson? What was he doing at this time?"

"I'm afraid Robin had his own troubles. He had been getting regular work with the opera company, as you saw in the show. In fact, we all thought they were grooming him to step into the assistant conductor's role. Everything seemed to be going his way, and no one deserved it more. But one day, with little explanation, they up and stopped calling him. Just like that!"

"In his opera he makes it look like there was some trouble with another man, that older individual who was interested in

Caroline. Or rather, Olivia."

"It wasn't only Olivia he was interested in, believe me. He's largely the reason Lily and I moved out West. And listen, I really need to ask your discretion here, and I'll tell you why. This man we're talking about, he's still influential. He's rich as sin, and one of the opera's biggest backers. If he were to think I had crossed him, he could definitely make life difficult for me."

"Look," I said, "everything I'm asking you is solely for internal purposes, to help me get my bearings with this investigation. I won't be broadcasting it around town."

"Okay, then," he said, taking a long glance out over the ocean before he continued. "The man's name is Donald Kessel. He owns real estate all over South Florida. Big, commercial buildings. That's how he supposedly made his pile."

"Supposedly . . . wait, what do you mean *supposedly*?"

"There were always rumors floating around about the guy, that he was involved with criminals. Drugs, I think. Or maybe it was money laundering, something like that. In any case, he was already well-off in the old days, and it was never clear how he got his grubstake. He just came out of nowhere and started to contribute heavily to the opera. He was eventually appointed to the board. We used to say that he bought his way into the company, bought his way into art. It was like he thought he could . . . own us. He was forever dropping in on rehearsals. He'd come back to the dressing rooms and chat with the singers. Especially the young women singers."

"In the opera he comes on pretty heavily to Ms. Taylor."

"He was coming on to many of the younger women in the company. But Olivia was, I guess you could say, his primary target. At first she made light of it. Actually, we all considered it something of a joke. In the beginning, that is."

"A joke? How's that?"

"Ah, yes, I guess that wouldn't be obvious to a non-opera fan." He smiled congenially. "But it was exactly like a number of the classic operas, where you have an older, wealthy lecher trying to get in the way of true, youthful love."

"I see."

"The scary thing is," he went on, "Kessel began to play his part too well. I mean, the thing got way too serious. He just wouldn't leave Olivia alone, although everybody knew that she was Robin's girl. It became very uncomfortable for her."

"Did he tell her that he would boost Mr. Markson's career if she slept with him, like they showed in the opera?"

"It might not have been that blunt, and perhaps Robin took some artistic license. But in the main I believe it. He certainly said some pretty insulting things to Lily."

"Wasn't there anything you young people could have done? Couldn't you have gone to the opera management?"

"It's hard to say. Sexual harassment was swept under the rug in those days. It still is, in many cases. We were all so green, so young. And the career of a singer—of any young artist, for that matter—rides on such a slender thread. You're taught to look at the managers of the opera world as your benefactors. You just want to make beautiful art—and let them know that you can do it. The last thing you want to do is cause problems, make waves. Robin thought he could shame Kessel with that stunt he borrowed from *Hamlet*. In retrospect, that obviously wasn't the most effective course."

"It didn't appear to work out so well."

"No, Robin didn't figure—none of us did—on how despicable the guy could be. I'm convinced that, somehow, he had Robin pushed aside. Imagine the pressure on Olivia, seeing Robin's chances ruined because she wouldn't sleep with Kessel."

"The opera made it seem like all that stress may have

brought on Ms. Taylor's illness."

"Who can say?" Diaz said with a sigh. "Myasthenia gravis's causes are still a mystery. But it's well-documented that emotional stress can worsen symptoms. Perhaps Livy was already developing the condition, on a sub-clinical level, and the anguish that Kessel put her through pushed her into crisis stage."

He looked out at the ocean. Sunlight washed over the condo towers along the beachfront. Beyond them, an indistinct glare poured off the silvered surface of the sea.

"So," I said, "it seems Mr. Markson came out West to join you. But Olivia didn't come with him?"

"You have to understand," Diaz said, "that this was a wrenching time for Robin. He was so poor, and Olivia needed all these expensive specialists. None of us had any health insurance. Olivia's parents were paying for the doctors. I found out about that opening in L.A., like you saw in the opera. It wasn't anything too secure, just a shot with a start-up company. But it seemed the career lifeline that Robin needed. Thanks to our buddy Kessel, as I've said, he was at the end of the line with the Miami troupe."

"But that meant leaving Olivia behind."

"Yes, it did. But to be honest, Lieutenant, I feel that the strain of worrying about Olivia had gotten to be too much for Robin. I hate to say it, but he wasn't the strongest soul in those days. I'm sure he thought he would send for her, but it's not easy keeping aloft in that damned city of angels, let me tell you. And Olivia just kept getting sicker. The pressure on Robin was considerable.

"Also"—and here Diaz hesitated—"I don't want you to think I wasn't being forthright with you yesterday, when you asked about Robin being involved with anything illegal. Because this is all long past, decades ago. I mean, what I'm about to say."

"Go ahead. I won't take it wrong."

"Okay then," he said. "The L.A. start-up company went the way of most of these endeavors. That is to say, they couldn't pay anybody half the time, and the company didn't last a year. But just as the start-up was winding down, Robin met someone in the television business. They were impressed with his talent, and he agreed to do some arranging work. It wasn't what he wanted, by a long shot, but he badly needed the money."

"What do you mean, wasn't what he wanted?"

"You may find this hard to comprehend, but it nearly destroyed Robin to sell his talent as a hired gun. That's the way it is when any true artist burns with . . . inner visions. To stand in the way of that is like telling a woman in labor to try and prevent her child from being born . . ."

He stared off. He seemed to be thinking, and his expression turned a little sad. "Robin was still in touch with Olivia," he went on after a moment, "but her news wasn't getting any better. You know how these things are, Lieutenant. At first everybody tries to stay optimistic, put up a brave front. They tell the patient she'll beat it, that they'll pray for her. If there's a one-in-a-million chance of recovery, they figure their friend is the one who's going to get it. At first even Olivia—as I mentioned—said she would never give up her career."

"I can understand that."

"But then," Diaz continued, "reality sets in. And the patient, and her friends and family, realize they're going to have to settle into a hard struggle, and some abandoned dreams. Frankly, all of that was just too much for the kind of guy Robin was back then. He was a sweet, decent guy, mind you. But like I said, a weak reed, I guess you'd call it."

"So he stayed out in L.A.?"

"Yes. He was getting more calls for the television work and, little by little, he was getting sucked into that whole L.A. scene. They were throwing major money at him, no question about it. The problem was, he knew that he was denying his truest impulses. In fact, the prospect of making a comfortable living in the television business placed him in an excruciating dilemma."

"A dilemma? How's that?"

"Ah, yes," he said, "I'm afraid I've left you behind again, haven't I? My apologies, but again it has to do with that imperiousness of the artistic calling. If Robin had been content to make a career with television, where there was plenty of loot to go around, marrying Olivia, even with her medical issues, wouldn't have been so daunting. But it would have come at the expense of his own artistic visions. You see, he was already mapping out incredibly powerful strategies for creating opera. But what he needed was time, and the freedom to create in his own way. I've always thought it was the strain of that Hobson's choice—to stay true to his art, or to accept financial security not only for himself, but for Olivia as well—that pushed him, almost irresistibly, into his cocaine addiction."

"Ah, cocaine. That's the illegal part you referred to?"

"I'm sure you can imagine," Diaz picked up again, "what that Hollywood crowd was like. Especially in those days. There were a lot of temptations, I mean, the stuff was everywhere! In short, Robin fell in with some serious partiers. It started with the occasional line at a studio, or some gathering he attended with his television acquaintances. But before long he was self-medicating on a nearly continual basis. If you ask me, he was trying to crank up his system enough to push through a problem even as smart a guy as Robin Markson couldn't sort out."

"Were you still in touch with him?"

"Yes, and I tried to talk to him. I felt responsible, at least in part, since I was the one who had encouraged him to come out west. Nonetheless, there was only so much I could do. We saw him less and less, the more he got sucked into that cocaine lifestyle. But then one night, at two in the morning, he showed up at our apartment door."

"Yeah?"

"He had gotten some devastating news. Olivia had married Kessel."

"So that was for real? She married the lech? Boy, that must have been rough on him."

"Catastrophic. He even asked if he could stay at our place for a while. He said he didn't think he could deal with being alone. On the positive side, though, he finally admitted that he needed help with his addiction. He wanted to get away from that party scene he'd been involved with."

"I see."

"So, with a little TLC, and the help of some good people, he began to get his act together. Looking back now, it's clear that it was the shock of Olivia's marriage that put him on the right track again. It made him realize just how far he'd wandered from his true path. And after he got sober, he went back to concentrating on his own art. Slowly. Steadily. Unhurried. And you know what, the universe started to help him out. Have you ever heard that line from Aeschylus: *when the spirit is willing, the gods join in*? Well, it was like that. It was at this time that he got his teaching post up in Seattle. It wasn't anything big or important, just enough to pay the bills. But it was steady, and it gave him stability. More importantly, it gave him the quiet time he needed to create. He lived, and he learned. And by golly, he figured out how to make an opera as beautiful as what you saw at the Arsht Center last night."

He seemed to choke up, and his eyes teared over. He took a long swallow.

"What about Ms. Taylor?" I asked after he'd braced himself up. "I can't believe she married this Kessel character."

"I was shocked, too, believe me. We all were."

As he spoke I became aware of a rustle of clothing. A nice-looking lady, fiftyish like Diaz, stepped onto the balcony.

"You've got to think of the woman's point of view," she said as she breezed over to us. "Olivia was at sea. She was losing her ability to work, and needing more medical attention all the time! She wasn't the kind to go crawling back to her parents' home to live as a spinster in the attic. It was all so new for her, everything she was dealing with. And terribly frightening. From her point of view, Robin had abandoned her. What was she supposed to think?"

I stood up. The lady turned to me and smiled. "Excuse me for butting in, Lieutenant. I'm Lily Diaz. I couldn't help but overhear your conversation from the kitchen. Welcome to our home. Has José offered you coffee? Anything?"

I protested that she wasn't interfering and said that I would be happy to accept some java. She went back inside and moments later returned with a steaming cup. After she handed me the coffee, she stood beside José's chair and put a hand on his shoulder. He laid his hand on hers.

"But why Kessel?" he said. "That's what I could never get. With his track record!"

Lily Diaz drew back her hand. "Track record? You mean that he was after women? And how did that distinguish him from any other man, except for a few monks? We've gone over this all before, darling."

"Yes, I know, but I still don't get it. Maybe I just don't want to get it. From what Lily has told me, Lieutenant, Olivia didn't know anything about Kessel's less-than-scrupulous business dealings."

"No, she didn't," Lily said. "She found out about that later, not long after they were married."

"But the other women," Diaz said, still perplexed. "Why did he marry her, if he didn't really want her?"

"Men like Donald Kessel like to possess things, love. And Livy gave him that connection with the arts. Can't you see? It gave him a kind of legitimacy he craved, a sort of status he couldn't achieve by just owning buildings. Let's not forget the fact, incidentally, that she was quite the looker. She still is, in fact. He figured Olivia wouldn't mind him running around, since he was doing her such a favor by marrying her. You know, taking on the hardship case. But he didn't count on Olivia's sense of dignity. She's a sensitive woman, but her pride is non-negotiable, I can tell you that."

"It sounds like their marriage didn't work out so great."

"No," Lily said. "Breaking it off wasn't easy for Olivia, because she was still learning to deal with her condition. But there's a tough woman underneath that vulnerable-looking shell. After she and Donald divorced, she took some help from her parents and set herself up on her own. Fortunately, with time, her condition leveled out. It became more predictable. She learned when she could be active, and when she needed to lay low. Eventually the doctors were able to calibrate her medications more effectively, to the point where she could often function with few symptoms. There have even been several periods of remission, when the syndrome has barely affected her. She found work coaching with the opera company and giving private lessons. She's also had some postings at area colleges. Over time she's figured out how to get along. Quite nicely, in fact. As a voice coach, there's no one who's in greater demand."

"And this Kessel," I said, "he's still around, you say, and still a supporter of the opera?"

"Oh, yes," Diaz said.

"Do you know if he came to the premiere last night?"

"I didn't see him there."

"Neither did I," Lily said, "but I'm not surprised. The subject matter of the opera was no secret, after all. Though the connections to real life weren't spelled out, Donald was aware of the basic story line, and he could have imagined how he would fit in. I don't suppose he would have expected it to be an especially flattering portrait."

"I'm sure he's not happy about the production," Diaz weighed in. "General audience members wouldn't know, but those who've been around the company awhile, older board members and such, would know exactly who was who."

"I'm surprised he didn't use his pull with the board to nix the production," I said.

"What could he say," Lily said with a little laugh, "the lecherous creep in the story is me? From what I've heard, he just made himself scarce for a while."

"Point granted." I looked out toward the sea while I collected my thoughts. When I turned around, I took both of the Diazes into my gaze. "This may sound crazy," I pronounced slowly, carefully, "but if he couldn't use his influence with the board, might Mr. Kessel have done something more drastic to stop the opera from going forward?"

Both of their faces registered a sudden shock.

"You mean . . . like . . . kill Robin?"

"We have to consider everything."

They looked searchingly at one another, and then Lily turned to me.

"I don't think he has the guts."

"God," Diaz put in, "the thought never occurred to me. We were all intimidated by him in the old days, but he's on the far side of seventy now. Since his marriage to Olivia, he's been nothing but the picture of respectability."

Our attention was drawn to waves of laughter and good cheer rising to the balcony from a sleek yacht chugging past the Diazes' building on the Intracoastal. We were aware again of the clear morning light, shadows playing across the surrounding high-rises, and an astringent breeze that washed over us from the sea. I got up, walked to the balcony rail and looked down on the passing craft and its passengers. They seemed so far from the world of sad mayhem that I—and now the Diazes with me—were caught up in.

I turned and realized that Lily had been left standing, her husband and I occupying the only two chairs on the balcony. She agreed to take my seat. While she got situated, I leaned against the rail and collected my thoughts.

"There's one other thing you've got me curious about," I said to Diaz.

"What's that?"

"It seems you and Kessel didn't have the friendliest of partings in Miami. If the opera was true to life, in fact, you told him off in some pretty pointed terms. And you say that Kessel is still influential with the opera. So, how is it you came to be the company's artistic director?"

A quizzical smile creased Diaz's face. "I'm not sure we understand that ourselves."

"I think it was Olivia's doing," Lily remarked.

"How's that?"

"We'd been out West a couple of years." she explained, "and Olivia and Donald had gotten married. Then one day, completely out of the blue, José gets a call from Miami's artistic director at the time. He wants him for Iago in Verdi's *Otello*."

"What a role!" José exclaimed.

"I suppose you took the offer."

"How could he refuse?" Lily said. "It turned out to be his breakout! He sang beautifully, of course, and the reviews were incredible. After that, the offers just came pouring in."

"Yes, it was quite a run." Diaz reached over to take his wife's hand. "It seems like I was constantly on the road. Lily had her own productions, too, so we met for dates between our different shows. It was an amazing time for both of us."

"Extremely romantic," Lily said.

"And did you ever work in Miami again?" I asked.

"Yes," Diaz said. "That's the crazy thing! They called me back for something almost every season."

"Did you have any dealings with Kessel during that time?"

"Frankly, I rarely saw him."

"I think he was pulling strings behind the scenes, though, the way he does," Lily said. "If you ask me, he was trying to make up for his earlier egregious behavior. Living with Olivia no doubt had a civilizing effect on him . . ."

"Here's something else intriguing," José Diaz said. "Around that same time—the time of my first call from Miami—Robin also got a call from the company, offering him conducting work. By then, unfortunately, he didn't want anything more to do with the Miami opera."

"I'm sure Kessel was behind that, too," Lily said. "Trying to salve his guilty conscience."

"Anyway," Diaz picked up again, "for whatever reason, I seem to have become some kind of favorite with the company here."

"Lieutenant," Lily said, "don't believe that *for whatever reason* for a minute. José earned every bit of his success with tremendous talent and hard work. Even if Kessel instigated it, the other board members—not to mention audiences and critics—loved him."

"Thank you, babe." Diaz squeezed his wife's hand and then turned to me. "Anyway, a few years back—to answer your original question—Miami's artistic director post opened up. Lily and I were getting weary of living on the road, and I was starting to have some difficulties with my voice. Recurring nodules on the larynx, to be exact. I'd been pushing my instrument too hard, unfortunately, and I wasn't getting any younger. I decided to take a flyer, and I wrote the board a letter offering my services."

"We figured this would be the real test," Lily said. "If Donald wanted to stand in José's way, here was his big chance."

"But obviously he didn't, and you got the job."

"That's right," Diaz said.

"How have things been with Kessel since then?"

"The fact is, I only see him at board meetings, and he rarely has much to say. His pull with the opera is significant, due to the financial support he offers. But he has very little involvement with the day-to-day running of the company."

I thanked them for their time, promised to keep them informed of the investigation, and rose to go. As we were walking through the living room, José Diaz stopped me short.

"Wait a minute, Lieutenant. There's something I'd like to share with you."

He walked to a set of shelves stuffed with CDs and DVDs. After scanning the spines of the shiny plastic boxes for a minute, he pulled one out.

"Here," he said, "please take this. It might help you understand our world a little better. Our world as opera singers, that is. Who knows, it might even help you with the case."

He held out the box. The words *La Bohème* were floridly penned across the top in a deep blue script. I butchered the pronunciation, but Diaz corrected me nicely.

"Bo-emm," he said. "French pronunciation, never straightforward. Have you ever seen one of the opera classics?"

I confessed that I hadn't.

"I think you might enjoy this one. Many consider it the best of the old warhorses."

I told him that a homicide cop's free time was pretty limited, but that I would try and take a look. I thanked them both again and went out the front door.

A walkway ran across the front of the Diazes' building, the side that faced away from the ocean. From up there on the seventh floor, you could see way out to the west—over Hollywood's commercial strip, over its rooftops and palms and bougainvillea—toward the neighborhoods, far from the beach, where working stiffs like myself live. The sky was a beautiful blue, with towering white clouds piled on the horizon, the air fresh and sweet. It was my favorite time of year in South Florida: early spring, before the horrible heat and humidity get up; when every day is like a fragrant bouquet or a splash in a fountain. Looking out over everything it hit me, like it sometimes does, how beautiful the world is, or at least can be, and the familiar aching came on me. I had like a catch in my throat trying to swallow how anybody, in all this beauty, could do anything so ugly as snuff out the life of a fellow human being.

But there was no time to think about it, there never was. I had to keep moving while we still had a chance of finding fresh evidence. I made my way along the balcony to the elevator bay and caught the lift down to the parking lot.

Chapter 5 (Ralph Owens)

IT IS TWO DAYS AFTER Robin Markson's death, and it is only now sinking in. I am not ashamed to admit that this morning, as I sat at my desk to start my review, I found myself shedding tears for the loss of a man I had met only twice—at performances of his works—and interviewed once on the telephone. I say I did not know him, but why is it that he seems more familiar to me than many people with whom I live in close association day by day?

After I allayed my grief, the words came pouring out. And I felt that something of the spirit and energy of *Biscayne Bay* found its way into my review:

> *. . . and the vastness of the ocean,*
> *and the endless pouring out of time,*
> *and the sun that drenched these beaches . . .*

> *With the hypnotic chant that opens and ends this splendid opera, and is woven throughout, Markson puts us on notice that he has chosen the arena of his latest work to grapple with timeless questions: What in this world is truly of value? Is happiness possible? To what should we turn our greatest energies?*

****

Between these opening and closing chants, delivered by a chorus reminiscent of Greek drama (but draped not in chitons, but in beach towels!) Markson presents a tour of the musical choices facing an American composer at the turn of the 21st Century. Against a foundation that is essentially elegiac, and loosely tonal, this most highly inventive of composers nods to everything from ragtime to minimalism. But we are always returned to the simple chant of the opening, as if to a temple where peace can be regained, insight and clarity restored . . .

****

. . . The opera is based around a story that is simple enough, and not particularly original. But aren't all fundamental myths timeless and spare? Two young people meet and are drawn to one another. They experience the joys of youthful love as well as its struggles. A challenge arises to their budding relationship, and the young man—the opera's hero—fails the test . . .

****

. . . From the work's opening strains we perceive a startling fact, which the remainder of the opera only confirms: we are in the presence of a composer who has managed what his contemporaries have thought impossible. Refusing to take sides in the ongoing battles between tonal and atonal, modern and ancient, serious and popular, Western and non-Western, Markson

has incorporated the competing strains of our culture's diverse musical lexicons into his palette and, through some awakened alchemy, transcended them all! He finds invaluable treasure in every mode in which humankind has attempted to convey the stirrings of its soul through sound, and in the process delivers to his audience a motherlode of energy such as this reviewer has never before witnessed. We continually feel ourselves quivering on the edge of some profound journey, to be plunged, at critical points in Markson's drama, into depths impossible to describe with words (for that, one would need Markson's masterful deployment of his large orchestra, and the fulsome gifts of Miami's extraordinary singers) . . .

****

. . . His respect for Ives is evident in his eclecticism (I think of Ives' remark that it would be as senseless to avoid tonality as to avoid atonality), his intimacy with the great warhorses manifest in the snatches of famous arias which punctuate the struggles of the aspiring singers who populate his story. Though he makes ready and fluent use of popular forms—tango and blues, recitative which suggests Bill Evans's soulful improvisations—he thoroughly integrates these into the work's larger structure, much as the romantic masters wove towering works out of folk melodies gleaned from Europe's peasant classes . . .

****

> *. . . With this opera Markson has shown him-*
> *self to be the musical hero we have waited for:*
> *one who has forged a path out of the dilemma*
> *of modern music, indeed of modern art in gen-*
> *eral. That is all the more reason to mourn the*
> *passing of this great American artist. He will*
> *be sorely missed. But he leaves us with a musi-*
> *cal drama by which, paradoxically, we are both*
> *humbled and exalted, a fitting testament to a*
> *life well lived.*

After getting the review off to my editor I fell back on the living room sofa, exhausted with the strain of the events of the previous twenty-four hours. When I awoke, around noon, Daphne was on my mind. We had made a loose lunch date the day before, when I had called her with the news of Markson's death.

Her voice was sunny when she answered the phone. I pictured her sitting on the second-floor terrace outside the apartment she rents in a grand old house in Del Rey, surrounded by tropical vegetation and singing birds.

"Review all finished?" she asked.

"All done."

"Good, then you're mine for the rest of the day."

"All yours. Until evening, anyway."

"Where do you want to go for lunch?"

I hadn't thought about it, and I reflexively suggested the Shops at Bal Harbour.

"So close to my job?"

"If you don't want to . . ."

"No, I don't mind. As long as it's not Saudade."

"I hadn't thought of going that elaborate, anyway," I said. "Why don't we go to that little Cuban place upstairs? We can have a light lunch, and then spend the afternoon on the beach."

"That would be great. I'm in the mood for a good empanada."

We agreed to meet at one and signed off.

Returning my phone to its holster, I wondered why I had suggested the Bal Harbour Shops so automatically, so unthinkingly. But it didn't take long to figure it out. Like a trauma victim reliving a soul-shaking experience, I wanted to be near the site of Markson's murder. I was clearly grieving, and I could only hope that I wouldn't be a downer for Daphne.

She looked lovely coming across the ceramic tile floor on the second level of the Shops (in a dress of bold, bright colors, her long, dark hair falling across her shoulders) towards the table I had taken near the railing that overlooks the lower level of the mall.

"I thought this would be better than the counter inside," I said after we embraced.

"Perfect." She glanced around approvingly.

We held hands across the table. "So how are you?" she asked.

"Could be better, I suppose."

"I know. But are you handling this okay?"

"Sure, I'm handling it. But it's eating at me. Such a huge loss . . ."

"Give it time. It only happened two days ago."

One of the café's black-vest- and white-shirt-clad waiters came over and took our order: Cuban sandwiches and empanadas, a café con leche for me and lemonade for Daphne. He called the order back to the kitchen through the headset he wore, one of the touches I love about the place, and then rushed off to another table. Daphne and I sat in silence, caressing one anothers' hands. I gazed at her seriously composed face, which peered off into the far reaches of the mall.

"I can't imagine how Livy must be taking this horrible

crime," she said, more to herself, it seemed, than to me.

Livy is how Daphne refers to Olivia Taylor, her voice coach. "Do you think this is difficult for her?" I asked.

She seemed startled by my question, as though I had broken unexpectedly in on her private thoughts. And when she finally responded it was with hesitancy, as if she were groping through some inner fog for the right words. "I always knew that Livy and Markson used to work together," she said. "It was many years ago, right here in Miami, as I have told you. But I never had a very clear idea how close their relationship had been. Until recently, I always assumed that they were just friends and colleagues . . ."

She fell silent.

"I see, and . . ."

She moved her spoon slowly around her coffee cup; again there was the hesitancy, the groping. "But then, last fall," she went on after a moment, "when I was working on one of Markson's arias—remember, that one you put me on to?—she treated the score as if it were her first born child or something! I had never seen her bore into an aria like that. It seemed that she was looking for something beyond the music, something of deep, personal significance . . ."

"Interesting!"

"And when I said something complimentary about the piece, she brushed right by it, acting as if it were all the same. I don't know, call it woman's intuition, but I couldn't help feel that she was, or at least once had been, in love with the man."

I told her about Markson's opera, about the young composer in love with a diva who is struck by a mysterious illness. "I don't have any idea to what extent the work is autobiographical," I quickly added. "Markson may have created the plot from whole cloth, for all I know. Or, more likely, he started with assorted elements from real life, and then reassembled them into a story he felt would be of interest to his audience. Who knows, maybe *he* was in love with *Olivia* back then. He could have put that element into the opera's plot, along with the fantasy that they had actually *been* lovers. Sort of how Hemingway dealt with the Catherine character in *Farewell to Arms*. Writers of stories can be pretty darned devious in that way."

"You ought to know." She smiled coyly as she gently brushed the top of my hand with her fingertips.

A black-vested, headset-wearing waitress brought our lunch.

"It's all so mysterious." I cut into a steaming empanada. "There may ultimately be no way of knowing how much of the opera's plot is from real life. I mean, you could ask Olivia . . ."

"No," Daphne said decisively. "She's so private. And this is such a delicate matter."

I agreed, in spite of my curiosity, both personal and professional. Our conversation moved on to other things while we ate our sandwiches and empanadas, and when we finished the lunch we paid the cuenta and got up. As we wended our way through the tables, Daphne drew my attention to a lone man, tall and darkly handsome, who sat at a table near the rail sipping coffee and jotting notes in a notebook.

"Look at that guy." She drew herself close to me and whispered. "I'll bet he's a spy."

"Funny."

"No, I mean it. He's got that look about him. Kind of furtive."

"He just looks lonesome to me."

"Yeah, he does. He needs a honey, I'll bet."

"Why don't you go over and plant a wet one on him? See how he likes it?"

"Oh, stop it!"

"Well, you seem pretty interested in him." I knew my jealous insecurities were bleeding through, but I couldn't help myself.

"I'm just interested in you," she purred, nuzzling her face into my neck as we turned into the stairway and walked down to the street level.

Once out in the parking lot we got our beach things from the cars. We had both worn swimsuits under our street clothes; we pulled off our shoes and left them in my Miata. Donning beach sandals, we applied generous doses of sunscreen.

"Which way now?" she asked.

I looked across Collins Avenue toward the Sheraton. "The closest way to the beach is through the resort."

"Are you sure it won't be too . . . yucky?"

I have always loved the way Daphne can perfectly sum up a situation with what, on the surface, seems a childishly ridiculous choice of words.

"We're just walking through," I said, though I knew there was more to it than that: a magnetic pull towards the scene of an artistic hero's demise.

She looked deep into my eyes. "Okay," she conceded, "if you're sure it won't freak you out."

"I think I'll be all right."

I took her hand as we walked under the crisply manicured trees that ring the Shops parking lot. We crossed Collins Avenue, made our way around the hotel's flower-adorned drive, and entered the lobby. A guard at the far end of the hanging bridge wanted to see our guest keys, but I was able to make up something with my press pass and got us through.

It was a gloriously sunny day, the resort's pool alive with splashing spray and people having fun. But my gaze was drawn involuntarily to the garden villas, where I sought out the balcony on which uniformed police officers and detectives in dull suits had gathered two days earlier. Daphne followed my eyes. She snugged an arm around my waste and said, "Come on, now, it's not good for you." I looked at her and kissed her, for who else in the world cares half so much about me? We walked around the twists and turns of the snaking pool, past the bar, and then out through the ironwork gate to the beach.

We spent the afternoon lounging on the sand, listening to music on Daphne's boom box, and taking occasional dips in an Atlantic surf that had lost its winter chill. Towards day's end we took a leisurely stroll along the beach. When we reached the inlet, where Atlantic waters surge through seawalls to Biscayne Bay, we walked over to Collins and made our way back toward the Shops. I had one hand around Daphne's rib cage and she had an arm around my waist; the air was redolent with jasmine and oleander and life seemed good. But Robin Markson had been unceremoniously bludgeoned to death just blocks away for reasons unknown, and it was as though the structure of my happiness had had a hole kicked out of it, and I could not conceive of how I might repair it.

Daphne sensed my unease. She didn't say anything but put her head against me and said that everything was going to be all right. We parted at the Shops. She had to get ready for her restaurant gig, and I had to attend an art opening.

"When's your next lesson with Livy?" I asked.

"Tomorrow, why?"

"I don't know."

"Are you thinking, since she once knew Robin Markson, she might say something that will make it all make sense?"

"Could be, who knows?"

"I don't know if anything can ever make this brutal crime make sense," she said, wise girl that she is. "You just need a little time to process it all."

"I guess you're right." I looked across Collins toward the Sheraton. The late afternoon sun limned an abrupt shadow midway up the looming, whitewashed structure, and the plantings that adorn the front entrance looked especially lush in the blue and shady light. The big grackles that roost in the trees surrounding the Shops parking lot were setting up such a din that I nearly had to shout to make myself heard.

"It just seems so wrong."

Daphne put her face close to mine and spoke in my ear. "Of course it is, sweetheart. Try not to worry about it. Call me tomorrow."

We embraced one last time. She got in her car and made her way out of the lot onto Collins. I headed home to dress for my evening assignment.

Chapter 6

AFTER I LEFT the Diazes' place I went to the station. Sanchez sat at her desk with a cup of coffee, poring over her computer screen.

"I thought you were going to get some sleep," I said.

"Are you kidding? On the second day of a homicide case? I went home and freshened up a little, got the kids off to school, made a few beds, and cleaned up the kitchen. I'm completely good to go."

Sanchez was a full-time mom until her thirty-fifth birthday. About that time she got her criminology degree and came to work for the force. What's the point of raising up her kids good and strong, she once told me, if they're just going to get mowed down by some freakcase with a gun.

Hell of a cop.

Since she was there, I said, how about doing some research on Kessel? Then Simmons came straggling in, great new guy enthusiasm . . .

"Get any sleep?" Sanchez asked.

"Couple of hours. Where's the coffee?"

He stumbled off toward the caffeine while I went down the hallway to update the chief. When I got back, Sanchez was standing by the printer pulling pages off.

"This guy looks like big business," she said. "Owns stuff all over Miami. He doesn't smell too sweet, either."

"Got a record?"

"No, but he was indicted in '96 for tax fraud. He beat the case when the prosecution's star witness disappeared. Under highly questionable circumstances, I should add. Who is he, anyway?"

"Maybe nobody. He used to know Markson, way back when."

"What's the connection? Is he a suspect?"

"I don't know yet. There was some bad blood between him and Markson over a woman. Olivia Taylor, ex-diva. In Markson's opera, he portrayed the guy in a decidedly less than flattering light."

"Wait, Chief," she said. "The opera didn't open until the day *after* Markson was murdered."

"I know. But this Kessel character is involved with the opera company. He's on the board, in fact. He was in a position to know about the show in advance."

"Are you saying that he killed Markson over an opera?"

"People have killed for less."

"Word."

"Besides," I said, "if Kessel's involved in business dealings that aren't on the up and up, Markson's opera could blow his cover. Bring unwanted attention. There goes the facade of legitimacy some of these guys like to keep up. Drill into the tax fraud case, will you? That is, after you've exhausted your search for the necklace."

"What are you going to be up to, if I might ask?"

"I think I'll pay our Mr. Kessel a friendly visit."

Sanchez walked off and I went to my desk and called over to Kessel Enterprises, Kessel's real estate development company. The gal who answered the phone said he'd already left for the day.

"He doesn't keep regular hours here any more," she said when I asked when they expected him back. "You might say he's semi-retired. He left shortly after noon."

I looked at my watch as I crossed the station's parking lot: three o'clock. Andrew's ballgame had just started. I calculated that I could swing by before heading over to Kessel's home off Millionaire's Row in Lauderdale. I could only stay a few minutes, but I figured that was better than nothing.

When I got to the school I parked and made my way toward where a couple dozen spectators stood near the ballfield fence. I approached from behind the bleachers and tried to blend in. I knew that if Andrew saw me, it would just make it harder to get away. I felt stupid hiding from my own kid. But we had a fresh murder on our hands, and what's the use, like Sanchez says, of raising up your kid good and strong, if there's nothing to grow into but a free-fire zone?

I was able to stay long enough to see him handle one at-bat. He struck out, but in the next inning he fielded a nice grounder, and he topped it off with a terrific throw to first.

Kessel's home was what I expected. That is, a palace. Hidden behind high stone walls overflowing with bougainvillea, it was shaded by hundred-year-old banyans and malaleucas. Its spacious grounds ended at a private pier near where the New River empties into the widest portion of the Intracoastal. A maid answered and asked me to wait. In a few minutes a man in his late sixties or early seventies, tall and erect of bearing, came into the foyer. He was immaculately dressed, his graying hair neatly cut and combed. He introduced himself as Donald Kessel.

I told him I was investigating Markson's murder and asked if we could talk.

"I'd be happy to." He led me through a formal sitting room

to a lanai at the back of the house. Sumptuous opera music played throughout the ground floor, a swelling orchestra and the high, sweet tones of a soprano. Kessel picked up a remote from a side table. "Let me turn this music down," he said. "Can I get you coffee, tea? A cold beverage?"

I declined.

"So, what can I do for you? Shame about Robin."

"Sure is."

"Do you have any leads?"

I was about to answer when we were interrupted by a fortyish blonde in tennis clothes. She breezed into the room, but she came up short when she noticed me sitting there.

I stood up.

"Hello, darling," Kessel said. "This is Lieutenant Nelson, Miami-Dade police. He's investigating Robin Markson's death."

"How sad," she said." But why are you here?"

"We're just talking to people who knew him, people involved with the opera. It's standard procedure."

"Well, we hardly . . ." she began.

"It's all routine police business, sweetheart," Kessel said. "Nothing to concern yourself with. Off to your lesson?"

"Yes."

They said their goodbyes and Kessel sat down again.

"So?" he said after we were settled.

"To answer your question," I said, "we don't have much in the way of leads. That's why we're talking to people who were acquainted with the victim. I understand you knew Mr. Markson."

"It's been a number years since we had much to do with each other. I believe he's lived out west since, oh, the late seventies, I think."

"So I understand. Have you seen his new opera?"

"No, I haven't."

"Isn't it odd that you'd miss the premiere, what with you being on the opera's board?"

"To be honest, Lieutenant, I wasn't particularly interested. I'm a fan of traditional opera. These modern composers leave me cold, to tell you the truth."

"Weren't you once married to Olivia Taylor?"

"Ancient history." With a look of distaste, Kessel glanced out at the Intracoastal, where magnificent yachts from up and down the East Coast strutted their stuff. "What would my marriage to Olivia have to do with any of this?"

"I don't know. I'm just trying to get the picture straight. Are you aware of what goes on in the opera?"

"I heard something about it. I didn't pay much attention."

"Let me refresh your memory," I said. "There's this young couple, and they're in love. He's an opera composer, struggling to keep his head above water. She's a singer. There's also this older man—one of the company's backers—who's after the girl. This guy's money isn't all that clean, if you know what I mean. But what's worse, he comes on to the singer in a way that most people wouldn't consider very gentlemanly. He even goes so far as to ruin her beau's career with the company, all because she won't sleep with him."

A smile formed on Kessel's lips. "It sounds like your typical opera plot to me," he said. "You've got the young couple in love, a dirty old man after the girl. What of it?"

I spoke deliberately, choosing my words carefully. "In the opera, the girl ends up with a debilitating illness. The young composer goes out west. Now, I've been told that Robin Markson and Olivia Taylor were intimately connected when he was with the Miami company. Olivia Taylor, I've learned, was struck with a debilitating illness. Markson, as you said, moved out west . . ."

"And I married Olivia," he said wearily. "So what does it all add up to? I'm not sure I know what you're driving at."

"It's just that I've talked to some people," I said. "And it's been suggested that you might not be extravagantly happy about seeing this opera produced."

"Oh really? I'd be curious to know who you've been talking to that's supposed to know what might or might not make me happy." He stood up and took a few jagged steps around the room. "Diaz? Is that who it was?" There was a tautness in his voice, a sort of simmering resentment. "What does he know about me? He's never liked me, in spite of everything I've done for his career. I know how he and his friends used to look at me—the barbarian, crashing the gates of the refined citadel of the arts! Why? Because I had *money*, unlike he and his broke friends. It never occurred to them that I got involved with the opera because I happen to enjoy the music." He let out an exasperated sigh, turned on himself, and then faced me and took up again. "Who do you think keeps an opera company going? Who supports the careers of all these singers? People with money, that's who! Operas don't run on oxygen, you know."

"Wait a minute, Mr. Kessel," I said. "There's no reason to get excited."

"Who's excited?" He came over and rested a hand on the back of the chair he had been sitting in. "But it sounds like you're treating me like a suspect. Do you have a single shred of evidence? I mean, beyond the wild talk of some overly emotional guy like Diaz?"

"No one said you're a suspect. I'm just trying to understand the big picture."

"Very well. I hope that clears it up. Is there anything else you need to know?"

"Mr. Kessel, you were indicted for tax fraud in 1996. There were implications of money laundering . . ."

"I don't see how that would be relevant to Robin's death. Besides, the case was dismissed. They expunged the record six years ago."

"Yes, I know. But it appears that a key witness in that case—someone who had been prepared to testify against you—went missing, and under highly questionable circumstances."

"They went through all that at the time, Nelson. I had nothing to do with it. He was one of the hoodlums who was trying to set me up. If you want my opinion, the thing was getting too hot for him to handle, and he somehow fled the country."

I didn't know if I believed Kessel's explanation, but until I got more information from Sanchez, I was in no position to challenge it.

"So, is that everything?"

"I guess that will do it for now." It didn't look like I would get any further with Kessel. Not that day, in any case.

"Then if you'll excuse me," he said, "I have some important calls to make."

"I'm sure you do. I appreciate your taking the time."

I got up from my chair, and we walked toward the front door.

"There is one last thing I have to ask you." We were moving through Kessel's formal sitting room.

"Shoot."

"Where were you Monday evening, about ten-thirty?"

The question was a wild swing—even wilder than a few I had witnessed at the junior varsity baseball game. A maid was dusting furniture. Through the windows I saw a whole team of landscapers grooming the grounds. A guy like Kessel would never kill anybody. He would buy somebody else to do it, just like he bought them to do all the other chores he'd rather not dirty his hands with.

"Right here in my bed," he said. "And I've got three people who can testify to it."

"I had to ask."

"I understand. Do let me know if there's anything else I can do. And Lieutenant," he added as I grasped the door handle, "let me ask you something."

"What's that?"

"Would you say that you're the same man you were twenty-five years ago?"

"I'd like to think I've learned a thing or two since my salad days."

"Exactly. So have I. People change. Maybe you can tell that to your friend Diaz for me."

I left Kessel's place and got on the road. Rush hour was at full tilt and traffic moved at a crawl. Instead of going to the station I decided to drop by the Bal Harbour Shops and check in with Willis.

I got out of the car under the big laurels. The boat-tailed grackles were screaming to high heaven. I know it sounds crazy, but to me their cries bore a message.

Murder unavenged.

I went in past Carpaccio. There was already a crowd dining outdoors. I went up the stairs to the second level and found Willis at one of the tables outside the Cuban lunch place. He was sipping coffee and writing in a notebook.

"Your novel?"

"Yeah, it's called *Five Dozen Ways to Mess Up Your Fellow Human Beings*. You should read it."

"That's all right. I've seen the movie, a few hundred times now."

"Actually, I'm making some notes." He pushed one of the

unoccupied chairs away from the table with his foot. "Seat?"

I sat down. Willis had chosen a table beside the railing. From there he had a vantage all along the lower level of the Shops. Cartier's, Bulgari, Tiffany's, Versaci: they were all lined up in a row, though the view was partly obscured by the coconut palms that grew out of big square planters on the ground level.

"This place is something else," he said. "Where do people come up with this kind of scratch?"

"They earn it. Most of them, anyway."

"They sell belts here that would bust me for the month."

"It's all a façade. It don't mean a thing."

"It does to some people."

"I guess you're right, or it wouldn't be here. Seen anything else of interest?"

"Other than expensive belts, I guess you mean?"

"Other than expensive belts."

"Several beautiful women. There was one over there at lunchtime who was a complete knockout. Sitting with some soft-looking character . . ."

"I keep telling you, Willis. You'll never understand a woman's real beauty until you unconditionally devote yourself to her."

"Jeesh, you married guys . . ."

"You ought to try it. You might like it."

"Chief, you keep talking like that, I'm apt to start having breathing trouble."

I shook my head.

"I'm not saying I'm against marriage. As a concept, anyway. I just need a little time. Five, ten, maybe twenty years . . ."

"Watch out about time. You take too much of it, and before you know it, there won't be any more of it left."

"I don't suppose you stopped by to check on my love life?"

"Why not?"

He ignored my remark. "I made the rounds of the stores, asked if anyone had seen anything unusual. I showed the salespeople Markson's photo. You know, the usual fishing."

"Anything?"

"The day he got killed, our victim bought a new shirt and a pair of gold cuff links. He also stopped in at the art gallery, up here on the second level. He put a painting on hold but, for obvious reasons, he never came back to pick it up."

"Do they still have the painting?"

"Yeah, the guy showed it to me. It cost a small fortune. They weren't sure what to do with it. They'd seen the news on Markson's murder, but they didn't know how to handle the deposit."

"We'll put them in touch with Markson's daughter. I don't suppose you've seen any sign of punks lying in wait for wealthy jewelry shoppers?"

"Chief, what do you expect? They're not going to come around two days after offing the guy, are they?"

"You never know. Sometimes they're that dumb. Besides, with everything still fresh, we need to be here. Incidentally, have you made any progress with the hotel security team?"

"I popped over there earlier and was able to run down a couple of them. One is the guy who generally handles the surveillance system. I also spoke with the security chief. They're running background checks on the whole lot at the station."

"Sounds good. Come on, let's walk."

We got up and made a circuit around the upper-level shops. It was dinner hour, and there wasn't much traffic up there. When we got to the art gallery, I asked Willis to introduce me to the owner.

The man showed me the painting Markson had put on hold the day he was killed. It was truly gorgeous. Biscayne Bay stretched across the canvas, bigger than life, bluer than blue. The Rickenbacker Causeway arched over it, fluffy white clouds dotted the sky, and the wakes of boats cut across the water. I have to admit, I was dazzled.

"He came in the other day," the owner said. "He walked around the shop a few times, but he kept going back to this one. It's a beautiful piece, and Marjorie Hopkins is certainly big these days. Mr. Markson stood in front of it for quite some time."

"Probably sticker shock . . ." Willis said out the side of his mouth.

"Could be. Our pieces aren't cheap. The gentleman did remark that the cost would be a stretch for him. But then, you get what you pay for."

"What was the price on it?" I asked.

"Let me see." The owner stepped over to a desk near the front of the gallery. "The price on this was twenty-eight thousand, five hundred. It's one of our more affordable pieces."

"Mr. Markson gave you a deposit?"

"That's correct. He really wanted the piece, but he said he didn't know if he had enough available credit. He said that if we could put it on hold for a few days he thought he could work it out. Then, of course, we never heard from him."

"How much was the deposit?"

"Five hundred dollars. I have the credit slip right here."

"This painting seems awfully expensive for a man of Mr. Markson's means," I said. "Did he say why he was buying it?"

"No, just that he liked it a great deal."

"Did he say anything that struck you? Did he discuss his plans for the day, or mention anyone he might be meeting later on?"

"Not that I recall. We simply discussed the painting and the terms of the sale."

We thanked the art dealer and left. After we finished our circuit of the upstairs shops we went down to the lower level. It was livelier down there, where several restaurants' seating spilled into the tiled corridors. At a Brazilian place called *Saudade*, this gal was singing beside a koi pond with floating lilies. She was an attractive girl, with long dark hair and a flower behind her ear, and she was singing one of those bossa nova songs that was a hit when you were a kid but now you just hear when you're grocery shopping. The singing sounded real nice, even if I couldn't understand the words, which were in Portuguese.

Willis spoke in my ear. "Chief, that's the babe I saw today at the Guantanamera Café! God, she's hot."

"What you need is one good woman," I said. "Some merciful angel to help you get over this romantic ADHD."

"I'll work on it," he said, but he made no effort to disguise the ridiculous smirk that spread over his face. We stood and listened until the maitre d' came over and asked if we wanted a table.

I suggested to Willis that he keep up his surveillance for another day or two, using what spare time he had to stay on the security team angle. When I got out to the parking lot it was seven-thirty, the last light draining from the day. The grackles were squawking louder than ever. Across Collins, the Sheraton resort, with its whitewashed exterior rising into the half-light, palm fronds waving below, looked peaceful as a chapel.

I missed Lori and wanted to see my kids, but that old bogeyman duty was nagging at me. Without really thinking about it I walked through the Shops parking lot and crossed Collins. I went to the Sheraton's desk, showed the manager my credentials and got a key to Markson's suite. We were nearing the end of our second day on the case and still hadn't gotten anywhere. I thought I'd spend a little more time at the crime scene, drill a little deeper. Maybe something would occur to me while standing there in the middle of it, something I'd missed on the first go-round . . .

The room was immaculate. You would have never guessed it was the scene of an ugly bludgeoning only two days earlier. I went in the living room and over to the sliding doors, pulled the curtain back and saw the full moon rising out of the ocean. I turned on all the lights in the suite and walked over every inch of it, examining everything closely. The only thing that caught my attention was a mark on one of the walls where the hallway opens into the living room. It was about three inches long, and two feet off the floor. If the rest of the suite hadn't been so pristine I would have never noticed it. It was just a mark, but it caught my attention: it could be evidence. I used my shoe to take a rough measurement and made a note to ask Forensics if they had done anything with it.

I turned out the lights and made my way out to the beachside grounds. After crossing the jungle bridge over the waterfalls and the koi pond, I wound my way past the jacuzzis and cabanas to the pool deck. There were still a few bathers, but the band had packed up and the bar was closing down. I climbed up on one of the whitewashed concrete bridges that spanned the pool at its narrow places and turned toward the hotel. I tried to take it all in, assess what it all meant—my murder case, that is. I thought of people still living who must go on with their grief and their pain. I pondered anew how such a heinous crime could occur in a place of such startling beauty. I shook it off and headed out to the beach.

There were often night fishers at the pier beside the inlet north of the hotel. I trudged through the five blocks of sand, watching hunting pelicans skim the water and gulls whirling overhead. I walked out onto the pier. There were a couple of guys fishing, but they hadn't been out the night of Markson's death. I asked them to call me if they heard any scuttlebutt from their fellow anglers, and then I walked along the inlet toward Collins Avenue.

As the last golden sunrays washed over the bridge where Collins crosses the inlet, the dark ocean sucked through the seawalls into Biscayne Bay. I climbed up there where I could be in the middle of it all. The sun was at my back; the moon hung over the vast ocean ahead of me. Below me, the wild waters of the inlet thrashed and galloped inland. None of it brought me any closer to knowing who had killed Robin Markson, or why. Watching the last light faded from the sky, I walked off the bridge and made my way along Collins to my car.

It was past eight o'clock when I left the Shops and headed home. There was paperwork to be done at the station, but I was feeling guilty about missing Andrew's game, my baby girl was still hurting from her tooth extraction, and I'd hardly seen Lori for two days. On my way in I thought through the case. It had been a decently productive day. My meeting with Diaz was instructive. It confirmed my suspicion that Markson's opera was based on real events. That opened up a number of leads: chiefly, for the moment, Kessel. I didn't have any evidence linking him to the crime, but given the way he was portrayed in the opera, he had motive. I was anxious to learn what else Sanchez might have dug up on him. I wasn't convinced that he was involved in Markson's murder, but I wasn't convinced that he wasn't.

Then there was Olivia Taylor. I didn't know what to make of her. She had had so little to say when I phoned her the day before. Maybe she was just stunned. But if she and Markson had been lovers, you'd think there would be more there. And her marriage to Kessel, what was that all about? I made a mental note to schedule a visit with her. She could probably tell me more about Kessel, if she wanted to. More to the point, she could fill me in on what went on between him and her and Markson in the old days.

Forensics had finished with the prints from the crime scene. They didn't give us anything. The bloodied marks on the music score all belonged to Markson. The others didn't return any matches. Any number of people with the opera might have handled the score during rehearsals. To be thorough, I figured, we should print every one of them, see if we could rule out some of the latents. There were a few usable prints on the vase, but they didn't turn up any matches, either. We'd have to print the hotel's room staff to see if we could eliminate them as well.

All we'd learned at the Shops was that Markson's purchase of the necklace was only part of a small spending spree. The painting was gorgeous, and I could see why Markson might want to own it, what with his opera being titled *Biscayne Bay*. But how could he afford it? It was our understanding that he was a professor at a college in Washington State. While those guys usually make more than say, a cop, it's not enough to finance too many fifty-thousand-dollar shopping orgies. I was going to have to talk to his daughter, Morgan Markson, about the deposit.

The DVD that Diaz loaned me lay on the passenger seat. La Bo-*emm*, not bo-*heem*. The plastic case depicted a young couple dressed in ratty clothes. They stood on a cobblestone street in front of a quaint old building. Diaz seemed like a decent guy, and he was easy to talk to. It surprised me, but I actually found myself looking forward to watching the opera. Maybe, I thought, I'd review it later that evening. That way I could relax a little and still feel like I was keeping my hand in with the case. Maybe, I thought, I could even get the family interested.

When I pulled into the drive I saw that Andrew had mowed the lawn and put the sprinklers on. Did I say that I had a couple of really good kids? Lori met me at the door with a nice kiss and hug. I smelled corned beef and cabbage coming from the kitchen.

My youngsters were watching TV in the family room. I went in and sat on the sofa beside Sara. Her cheeks were still puffy from the tooth extraction. I put my arm around her shoulders.

"How's my girl?"

"I'm okay," she mumbled.

"Does it hurt?"

"I've been better."

"Are you taking the pain meds?"

"Yeah," Andrew put in, "she's become a downright junkie! You might need to put the narc squad on her before long."

"Did anybody ask you?"

Sara reached behind me to swat at him.

"I'll be okay," she mumbled.

I stood up and complimented Andrew on his fielding play.

"What, you were at the game?"

"I stopped by for a while."

"Dude, why didn't you come and say hey? I never even saw you."

"I didn't want to get in the way."

"Get in the way? You're my dad, for chrissake."

"Besides, I didn't have much time. We're working a fresh case. Didn't Mom tell you?"

"Who got offed this time?" Sara mumbled.

"An opera composer. He was staying at the Sheraton Bal Harbour Beach Resort."

"That's pretty swanky, isn't it?"

"About as swanky as it gets."

"Opera?" Andrew said. "Isn't that where there's a crew of fat ladies decked in bizarre costumes, caterwauling in some unintelligible lingo?"

"They're not all fat. In fact, some of them ain't half-bad, from what I saw. Not as gorgeous as your mother or anything, but . . ."

"Excuu-use me," Andrew clowned, "I didn't know you were such a fan!"

"I went last night. It was part of working the case. And I've got to admit, it was pretty interesting. It's not all that fat-lady screeching anymore. Take this guy Markson—the one who was killed. It was his opera I saw. It had all kinds of different music in it. And it was in English."

"I wouldn't mind seeing one sometime," Sara mumbled.

My kids never cease to amaze me, just like everybody else. I knew Sara liked music. In fact, she thinks she's some kind of singer. But opera had never seemed like her style. Anyway, I saw my opportunity. "Then you're in luck," I said, "because I happen to have one right here. In fact, I thought we might put it on a little later."

I showed them the DVD.

"Whoa, dude," Andrew said. "I don't know if I'm ready for this."

"Open your mind," Sara mumbled. "How can you know you won't like it, if you don't give it a try?"

"I just have a feeling," he said. "A pretty strong one, in fact." He looked at the DVD cover. "La bo-heem? What's that?"

"La Bo-*emm*, dude," my girl mumbled in perfect French, just like Diaz had pronounced it. Did I mention that my kids were awfully bright?

"La *bo-emmm*." Andrew stretched his pronunciation to the breaking point, trying to sound funny in a French kind of way.

"Think about it," I said. "I'm told it's one of the greats. It might even help me with the case. That is, of course, if Mom doesn't mind. Meanwhile I need to get some food. I'm starved."

I went into the kitchen. Lori, true to form, had waited to eat with me. First she just let me eat in quiet for a while. She knows how I like to stuff my face, especially when I'm hungry. Then, once she saw that I was slowing down a bit, she asked me about the case. I sketched in what I knew, without going too far into the weeds. She told me about the catering job she had done in Naples, and then we talked about Sara's condition.

"I'm sorry I'm home so late," I said.

"You don't need to apologize. I know you can't always control your schedule." She rubbed my forearm in a nice, wifey way.

"I know," I said. "Still—"

I didn't finish my remark because, frankly, I couldn't conceive of what more could be said. Lori and I had a long-standing arrangement. She knew what my job involved and never complained. I focused on my work and let her take care of the rest. As to the family, I saw them when I saw them.

It was my fate to be a cop, I always figured, so what else could I do?

Lori went back to eating in that careful way she has, picking at each morsel like it's a precious jewel or something. Me, I started to think. Something was bugging me, some feeling I couldn't ignore. I even forgot about my food for the moment. Sure, I said to myself, Lori and I had an arrangement that had worked, more or less, over the years. But what was this new signal pinging its way through the mental noise? The message it bore sounded an awful lot like "life passing me by." It hit me, just like that, while I sat at the kitchen table watching Lori fork peas off her plate. I was getting on in my forties, I reflected.

Maybe it went with the territory. On the other hand, maybe Markson's opera was to blame. How, when he looked back over his life, he didn't like all the choices he had made . . .

I glanced at Lori's face. I had known her since we were fifteen, and I had never seen anything half so beautiful, or met a woman nearly as sweet. How much time did we have left? I wondered. Most people live into their seventies or eighties these days, but who could say? My father keeled over at the age of fifty-seven from a massive heart attack. How many evenings had I spent at the station hacking through paperwork or out chasing down leads, while my neighbors kicked back on their patios with their sweethearts, or took their families to the movies? I'm not saying that I regretted a thing I had done. It was a difficult job, but somebody had to chase down the ne'er-do-wells who are determined to make the rest of us as miserable as they must be inside. Still, I found myself thinking, the day may come when it's time to hand on the baton to some other schlepper, preferably while Lori and I still have time left to enjoy ourselves . . .

She snapped her fingers in front of me. "Hello in there. Anybody home?"

I apologized for daydreaming. "It's been a long day."

She told me not to worry about it. "I'll do a quick clean-up," she added, "then we can put on that opera you mentioned."

"Are you sure you don't mind?"

"I've never seen one. Like Sara said, don't knock it if you haven't tried it. It's got to be better than what they're watching now. Some vampire thing, I think."

I went back to our bedroom to wash up and change. When I returned to the family room everybody was arrayed on the sofa staring toward the tube. Lori had made some popcorn.

We put in the DVD and settled back.

As soon as they got past the overture and started singing, we realized that the entire opera was in French. But here's the beauty part: there were English subtitles, so you could follow the story perfectly. The whole thing kicks off in this crummy Paris walk-up on Christmas Eve. There are two seedy characters sitting among an odd assortment of broken down furniture. They're shivering with cold, because they can't even afford a few sticks of wood for their fire.

One is a poet, the other a painter.

"Note what happens with these artistic types," I couldn't help say, out the side of my mouth, to Sara (like I've mentioned, my daughter thinks she wants to be a singer, but I've advised her to plan for a more secure career). She shot me that ironic face she's been making since she was about five, and Lori said, "Why don't we just watch the opera."

We turned our attention to the screen again, just as two other blades are arriving at the crash pad. They all four live in the flat, it appears, crowded into one room like Cuban boat people or something. One of these new arrivals is a musician, the other some kind of freelance scholar. In other words, there's not a steady paycheck among the lot. When their landlord shows up to collect the rent, they resort to teasing him about his love life, shamelessly flattering the old buzzard to distract him from the fact that they're months in arrears on their payments. They finally manage to bustle the old koot out of the place, and since it's Christmas Eve, the gang decides to go and hang at the local watering hole. Only Rodolfo, the poet, stays behind, saying he has to finish an article he's writing and will join them later.

Rodolfo's decision turns out to be a fateful one, because no sooner have the others left than there's a knock at the door. Answering it, he finds a young lady standing there who says she lives upstairs. Her candle has gone out, she tells him, and she asks if he can give her a light, so to speak. Rodolfo, whose hormones are as active as the next guy's, invites her in.

The girl tells him that her name is Mimi and that she takes in seamstress work. All in song, of course. Just as you'd expect, Mimi and Rodolfo hit it off in about two minutes flat, and because it's opera, they croon to each other for about fifteen straight minutes. Now, I say *young* lady, but the actress who played Mimi looked about as old as my mother. I do have to admit, though, the music was pretty darned beautiful. What's more, the romantic angle seemed to keep Lori interested.

"This is lame," Andrew said.

It's too bad the gal who came for a light wasn't a little younger, I thought to myself, and a lot shapelier. "Just stick with it awhile," I said. "It might grow on you."

"What, like some kind of fungus?"

"Try not to be gross," Lori said, and she reached around and tousled his hair. Twisting and groaning under the pressure, he bumped into Sara, and she shoved him and said, "Dude, control yourself, will you?" and then stood up and adjusted the throw she had wrapped around her shoulders. My instructions to Andrew to settle down were greeted with a lopsided face and a devilish grin, but he did collect himself. He even put his arm around his sister's shoulders in a nice, brotherly way.

When we finally got back to the opera, Rodolfo and Mimi have joined the others at the local café. Here we meet a second female. Her name is Musetta, and she goes with Marcello, the painter. There's just one hitch. Musetta also accepts the attentions of a rich, older sugar daddy. "Make a note," I said to Sara. "He's *not* the artistic type. He's got enough scratch to keep his rent paid, buy some decent clothes . . ."

"It would be nice if we could just watch the show," Lori repeated calmly.

We settled back in. Andrew's interest had perked up considerably when the Musetta gal came along. She was quite a bit sleeker than old Mimi, the poet's girl. Lori seemed content, maybe because we were all together for a change, and Sara had stopped groaning and holding her jaw. She now peered intently at the screen, lost in a world of her own . . .

The youthful gang of artists really hoots it up at the café, with plenty of drinking, singing and general larking around. To top it off, the youngsters decamp on the sly, sticking Musetta's clueless old sugar daddy with the evening's tab.

I glanced down the sofa. The festivities on the screen must have been infectious, because everybody looked strangely happy. Unfortunately, the story was about to take a dark turn.

Months have passed since the joyous Christmas Eve shindig. The candle girl is standing in the snow outside a tavern where the painter Marcello now lives, pitiably unburdening herself to Rodolfo's old pal. She and Rodolfo have become an item, but as is often the case with young men, Rodolfo appears to be making a hash out of their love affair. He subjects the poor girl to constant jealous accusations, Mimi sings to Marcello, and he has now stormed out, leaving her to wander the frigid streets of Paris searching for him. Marcello notices her persistent cough, which looks suspiciously like tuberculous, and suggests that she forget about Rodolfo and go home.

"I've had enough," Andrew bleated. He acted like the show wasn't cool enough for him, but if you ask me, he couldn't handle the sorrow of it. Lori, who had been on the go all day, like usual, had begun to nod off against my shoulder. She roused herself and said that she would turn in, too.

"Do you mind if I stay up, Mum?" Sara mumbled. "I want to see how this ends."

Lori said she didn't mind and padded down the hallway. Andrew went into the kitchen, where I heard him guzzle about half a gallon of milk. Before heading off to bed, he stuck his head in to ask Sara if he could catch a ride to school with her and her friends in the morning. After a spate of the usual sibling banter, he headed off to bed.

Drawn by impassioned, male voices, Sara and I turned our attention again to the screen. Rodolfo has come out of the tavern, where he's been temporarily holed up with Marcello, and he is singing to his friend that his jealous outbursts with Mimi have really just been a cover. The true reason he's trying to break off with the poor girl, he bellows—with so much anguish you thought his throat would crack—is that he's afraid his girlfriend is dying. Convinced that living in his unheated hovel through the harsh Paris winter, with hardly a decent meal, is the reason for her illness, he is wracked with guilt and remorse. Mimi, who's been standing in the shadows listening to all of this, now emerges from hiding and approaches the men. Both she and Rodolfo are overcome with painful feelings, and after some serious musical emoting, they agree that it's best they split up. To round off the scene, Marcello also breaks up with Musetta, realizing she's one of those females who isn't interested in tying herself down to one man.

"She's probably just trying to provoke the guy to get a decent job," I remarked to Sara.

She moved over and laid her head against my shoulder. I could see that she was feeling distressed by the turn the story had taken. All that relationship dysfunction!

The opera's young male characters, for their part, don't appear to be feeling any pain. They go back to being goof-offs, like young men always do when they don't have young females around to keep them on mission. All that jackpotting comes to a screeching halt, however, when Musetta comes to their crash pad to announce that Mimi—the poor candle girl—is dying.

I've got to admit, when Mimi sang her swan song, I had a hard time keeping my eyes dry. For one thing, it's an incredibly beautiful number. For another, boy could that fat lady sing! On top of that, for some reason a dumb thought struck me. *What if that was my Sara?* She was holding my hand now, tears streaming down her face, and finally she mumbled, "Oh, Daddy, it's so sad." I was about to turn off the set, but before you knew it it was over and the audience set up a thunderous applause that lasted for the better part of ten minutes. Different players came out in different combinations to take their bows, and people threw flowers up to Mimi from the audience. Sara and I just sat slack-jawed, watching everybody applaud, because it helped to take away some of the sadness we felt from the story.

I told Sara that she ought to get to bed and reminded her about her antibiotic, and then I went to the kitchen to get a glass of water. As I stood there, looking out the back door, I realized that I had actually forgotten about my murder case for a couple of hours, caught up in the lives of some fictional Parisians from two centuries ago. I guess that's one of the great things about the arts. They give you a break from life.

As I thought back through the opera's story, it was plain why Diaz had loaned me the DVD. You had the young artistic types, struggling to get by; the older, wealthy man interested in their gals; and an illness that comes between a couple of soul mates. The main difference, in my murder case, was that the young woman didn't die.

But what was I supposed to learn from it all?

I would have thought that Markson had patterned his show after *La Bohème*, except I now knew that the plot of *Biscayne Bay* was patterned after Markson's own life.

Is that what they call life imitating art?

I got to thinking about Olivia Taylor. Watching the Mimi character in *La Bohème* did help me to understand the people of the opera world better, just like Diaz said it would. I couldn't help but wonder if Taylor ever had the kind of lungs that Mimi singer had. Whew could she belt it out! And if the Mimi character was at the center of *La Bohème*, I asked myself, could Olivia Taylor somehow be at the center of the Markson case?

I'd have to pay her a visit and find out.

I wandered down the hallway, heading for bed, but when I passed Sara's door I heard some faint singing in there. I stopped and listened. What first arrested me was that it wasn't the usual stuff she listens to (don't ask me the names of the groups, the ones with black-dyed hair plastered against their heads and body piercings). And there were no words, just a sort of high humming. But after listening for a minute, I recognized that it was that Mimi farewell number from the opera. Sara's voice was high and clear, though a little jagged from the pain in her gums. What really floored me, though, was this delicate beauty in it, a sort of subtlety I would never have expected from my kid. Her light was out. I figured she was lying in bed, remembering the opera.

Then again, maybe she was gazing out the window, dreaming some teenage dream . . .

Without warning I found myself having that father moment, the one every guy with a daughter has sooner or later. It's that moment when he realizes that his little girl isn't a *little* girl anymore. For me it came a bit late, on account of being caught up with homicide cases morning, noon and night. Since becoming team lead, I simply hadn't been around enough. But thinking about the way we sat watching *La Bohème* together, it was almost like we were on the same plane, feeling the same things. There was also that bedroom singing. So fine and mature. The realization struck me that there was a budding adult in there, one whom I hadn't done enough to get to know. What's more, she was one who might soon need her daddy's help to negotiate her entrance into the wonderful world of adulthood. In a few short years, I realized, she would be gone, and it would be too late.

I went to bed. Lori was asleep, but when she sensed my presence she helped arrange the covers and moved closer . . .

Chapter 7

I MET THE TEAM at the station. Sanchez and Simmons hadn't been out so late the night before; they had done everything they could on the necklace. I said I wanted them to keep an ear to the ground, but meanwhile asked them to work the Kessel angle. "Check his alibi, ask around. Dig into his finances and business dealings."

I mentioned that Willis would be spending another day at the Bal Harbour Shops.

"Rough assignment," Sanchez said. "The poor guy could sprain a wrist, lifting all those café con leches to his lips."

"Jealousy doesn't become you, dude," Willis said. "Besides, who else is going to do it? All those gorgeous women would be wasted on a married slug like Simmons here."

Simmons just smiled. He hadn't been on the team long, but I had already come to appreciate his cool under fire.

"Rough assignment or not," I said, "we need someone over there another day or two. You know how criminals are. They have a dumb way of repeating themselves. Sometimes I think they want to get caught. And with it being so close to the hotel, who knows what might turn up?"

"I guess I can struggle through another day among the rich

and beautiful." Willis clasped his hands behind his head and rested back in his chair.

"All right, Mr. Self-Satisfied," I said. "How about the hotel security team? Any further progress?"

"Yeah, I went over there yesterday after the Shops closed and caught up with the night shift. All their alibis sound good, but I'll check them out further when I get a chance."

"Good work."

I checked in with the team about a few of our older cases and reminded them that we would soon have to get back to them. If nothing new turned up, Markson's would join them: one more unsolved murder to rattle around in our files while we worked the same tired leads, hoping a breakthrough might fall out of the blue . . .

After the meeting broke I drove over to Olivia Taylor's home. I didn't call in advance. She had been so uncommunicative during our phone call, I was afraid she would blow me off.

The house was at the end of a quiet street on the outskirts of Coconut Grove. It was a two-story Spanish Colonial number canopied by mature trees. When you went in the front gate there was a garden off to one side. It was full of banana trees and flowers, and there was a birdbath and a small gurgling fountain. Two or three cats lounged on the flagstone patio.

As I approached the front door I heard a female voice singing in what sounded like Italian, with piano accompaniment. I figured Taylor was in the middle of one of her coaching sessions, or maybe rehearsing for something. I didn't want to interrupt, so I followed a walkway into the garden and took a seat at an ironwork bench near the fountain. A couple of cats came over to investigate. One of them rubbed against my legs, so I picked it up and stroked its fur. The morning air was still cool, Taylor's garden as peaceful a place as you could find in South

Florida.

There were French doors giving onto the garden on that side of the house, and in the darkened interior I made out someone standing beside a piano. Every now and then the piano would stop. There would be some talking, and then they would start up again with the singing.

I guess that was the coaching part.

Sometimes a voice would rise up over the singing. "Watch that *B*," the voice would call out. "You're sharp almost every time." Or, "Don't run that together. It's not that *legato*." Or, "I know that's your *passagio*, but sing through your *mask*. Try to maintain your *timbre* through here!"

I suppose every profession has its own lingo. But I was enjoying just being in the cool, shady garden with the cats. In fact, I didn't notice the music stop, or the French doors open, until a crystal clear voice cut through the quiet of the morning.

"Is there something I can do for you?"

Sitting in the doorway was Olivia Taylor in her wheelchair. What appeared to be a younger woman stood behind her in the shadows. Taylor wore a glossy blue dress with a silk scarf and a light sweater. When I stood up she seemed to recognize me.

"I'm Lieutenant Nelson," I said. "Miami-Dade police."

"Yes, of course. Good morning, Lieutenant." Taylor sounded breathless. "Why didn't you ring the bell?"

"I didn't want to interrupt."

"It would have been better than scaring us half to death. Daphne had her cell at the ready to dial 911."

"I'm sorry," I said. "I guess I didn't think I looked that frightening."

"You never know, looks can be deceiving. And with everything that's happened lately . . ."

"You're absolutely right," I said. "And you're smart not to

take chances. It was thoughtless of me, and I apologize."

"No harm done," she said. "We who work in opera, I realize, probably have overactive imaginations. After all, everyone in our world is either madly in love, desperate with grief, or seething with hatred. I see you've made friends with Giovanni."

"He's pretty affectionate."

"Oh yes, he's a great romancer. We can't keep him away from Carmen. Or Leonora, even though they've both been neutered. We didn't do him. I know it's bad, but we didn't have the heart. Perhaps in you he's found a kindred spirit?"

"Me," I said, "a romancer? Nah, just a happily married, hard-working cop."

"Daphne and I will be finished here in five or ten minutes, if you care to wait."

I peered into the darkness to see who Daphne was. I guess Taylor saw me squinting.

"Oh, excuse me," she said. "This is Daphne Courtwright. Daphne, this is Lieutenant Nelson."

Daphne stepped into the light. I knew I had seen her somewhere, but it took a minute to place it. Then it hit me.

"You sing over at Saudade, in the Bal Harbour Shops, don't you?"

"Yes, but I don't like to talk about that around Livy." She smiled. "I'm not sure that she approves."

"Now, Daph," Taylor came in, "I've always said that some of the modern—by modern, Lieutenant, I mean after 1920—ballads are very finely crafted. All that Cole Porter, Hoagy Carmichael, Duke Ellington. Even those Joni Mitchell songs you're so fond of are quite exquisite in their own, quirky way. As for the bossa nova tunes you do, you know those numbers hold a special place in my heart. They speak to me of . . . my younger years. Yes, Jobim was without doubt a genius of popular song.

But with your potential, my dear girl, if you really made a commitment to opera, what I could do with that voice! So clear and fine. And with such delicacy of feeling! And after all, where does one find music to test the frontiers of the human vocal apparatus as in the realm of opera?"

"You're too kind, my dear maestra," Daphne said.

"Not a bit," Taylor rejoined. "And don't think you're going to get me off your back that easily." She turned to me. "Lieutenant, I don't pester all of my students like this, but this one"— she reached over and took Daphne's hand—"this one is special to me. And not just because of her voice . . ."

Daphne squeezed Taylor's hand and smiled at her.

"Now, Lieutenant, if you'll excuse us . . . we won't be long. Please make yourself comfortable."

The ladies went back to their singing; meanwhile I deepened my acquaintance with the cats. Before long Daphne Courtwright emerged from the French doors and stepped across the garden to me.

"Livy asked me to tell you that she's ready to see you."

"Thank you."

"Aren't you investigating the Robin Markson murder?"

"That's right," I said.

"I hope you find whoever did it."

"I do too."

She walked across the flagstone walkway and out the front gate.

I went to the French doors and stuck my head in. Taylor was still in her wheelchair, close to the piano, and invited me to have a seat. It was a pleasant spot, comfortably furnished, with floor-to-ceiling glass looking out on the garden. She asked if I cared for coffee or tea.

I told her a cup of java would be great.

She wheeled over to the base of a stairway and called up the steps.

"Alice! Can you please come down and get Lieutenant Nelson some coffee?"

She wheeled back to the sitting room. "Alice is a godsend," she said as she canted in her chair, crossing one leg over the other and smoothing her dress. "I don't know what I'd do without her. Your coffee won't be a minute."

I didn't want to start right in on Markson. It seemed too brutal. Instead I found myself staring at Taylor's wheelchair. I didn't want her to think I was rude, but something was bugging me. Maybe because it was the old, manual type. It looked so, well, mechanical. You don't see people using them much anymore.

"I couldn't help notice that you use a manual wheelchair. It seems like most people have gone to the electrics these days."

"Yes, that's true. And it would probably be easier," she said. "But I prefer the old-fashioned kind. I guess I'm old-fashioned in a number of ways. I occasionally need some help, but I manage. This one keeps my upper body strong. I've always thought it better to challenge myself, rather than just give in to the inertia."

Alice, a sturdy-looking, middle-aged lady in jeans and a tee shirt, came into the room with my coffee. I thanked her and turned back to Taylor.

"Ms. Taylor," I said, "I was hoping I could ask you a few questions."

"I thought you took care of that the other night, on the phone."

"Well, yes. But you were probably suffering from shock when I called. After all, that was right after it happened. That's natural for anybody who knew the victim. The thing is, we're not getting anywhere with the case. I thought that maybe, now that a little time has passed, you might remember something further. Something that might aid in our investigation . . ."

"I really don't know what you'd be looking for."

"One thing that's nagging me is this dinner reservation. Mr. Markson reserved a table for two at Carpaccio—you know, across at the Bal Harbour Shops—and then canceled. He told the hostess his dinner companion wasn't feeling well."

"The reservation was before he was . . ."

"Yes, we think so. The medical examiner says he died shortly after midnight. He was injured around 10:30. Now, whoever was supposed to meet him for dinner, you'd think they would have come forward after hearing the news. But no one has. I'd feel a whole lot better if I knew who he was supposed to meet. It probably has no bearing on the case, but you never know."

"I certainly wish I could help."

"Let me ask you one more time to try and remember. He called you the day before, isn't that right?"

"Yes, I told you that."

"You're sure he didn't say anything about a dinner reservation?"

"Not that I recall." Her expression had grown blank. Maybe I was boring her.

"Did he mention anything about a necklace? It had emeralds and diamonds."

"A necklace?"

"Yes, a very nice one, and expensive," I said. "He had bought it that day, and now it's gone. Are you sure he didn't mention it?"

"It was probably stolen, don't you think?"

Taylor's face had now morphed into some kind of frozen china doll.

"Ms. Taylor," I said, "I hope this isn't too delicate a topic. But many years ago you and Mr. Markson were on somewhat intimate terms, weren't you?"

"Yes, but I don't see what that would have to do with any of this."

"The thing is, I've started to look into this dust-up between him and your ex-husband, Mr. Kessel."

"You mean we have to talk about *him*?" The blood suddenly returned to her cheeks.

"It would be helpful, if you don't mind."

"There was no love lost between Donald and Robin, that's for sure."

"You were at the opera the other night. Is Mr. Markson's story true to life? I mean, did the things he showed in the opera actually happen?"

"There's always some poetic license, Lieutenant."

"But did Kessel really bust up Mr. Markson's career with the opera because . . . well, over you?"

"Who can say? Robin believed that, but there was never any proof. In reality, the board may have made their decision for any number of reasons."

"How long were you married to Mr. Kessel?"

"Three long years."

"Can I ask why you divorced?"

She fussed with the hem of her sweater. "You're getting very personal, you know."

"Let me put it another way. Was Mr. Kessel involved in anything unscrupulous—anything that troubled you—during your marriage?"

"Other than running around, you mean?"

"I mean with his business dealings."

"I can't say. I don't understand these things. There were tax matters, I believe. That's not why I left him."

I sensed that I was losing her. Her expression had turned flat again. It was time to get to the million dollar question. "Mr. Kessel was portrayed in a very poor light in Mr. Markson's opera. It seems that he would be pretty unhappy about that."

"You'd think so. But the man can be terribly thick-skinned."

"Do you think he would be capable of doing something to stop the opera from going on?"

"You mean like murdering Robin? Is that what you're asking?"

"We can't rule anything out."

"I don't know," she said. "I've hardly seen Donald for some twenty years. Who knows what people are capable of?"

She set her face toward the garden with what looked like a mixture of fatigue and frustration. A tear had formed in her eye. I had that feeling, known to any married man, that I had tripped over some female sensitivity without knowing it.

"I'm feeling awfully tired, Lieutenant," she said. "My condition is acting up lately, and I really must get some rest before my next student."

It hadn't been much of an interview. I had gained little of value, and what was more troubling, the lady exhibited several indicia of lying that we detectives are trained to observe: repeating my questions, offering helpful suggestions, stalling, incongruous affect. I felt like she was trying to throw me off the scent, but I had no idea what the scent was. In any case, with nothing more concrete to go on, there was little choice but to break things off. I rose to go.

Taylor pushed down on one of the wheels of her chair to back away. She seemed distracted, and she ran up against the wall.

"Now look at that," she said, "I've gone and scuffed the wall.

Alice is going to have to clean it."

"I'm sorry if I've upset you."

She told me to think nothing of it, but as she repositioned her chair, smiling at me weakly, I couldn't help but wonder how often wheelchairs leave scuff marks on walls. And as I stood to go, I sidled around so that I could get a better look at the one Taylor's chair had made. It was about eighteen inches off the floor, and an awful lot like the one I had noticed in Markson's suite the night before.

I thanked her for her time and turned to leave. On the way to the door I noticed a stack of flyers on a table. They advertised a recital Taylor would be doing that weekend. Front and center was a nice publicity photo of the lady.

"Do you mind if I take one of these?"

"Are you an opera lover?"

"I'm getting to be one, more and more."

"I'd love for you to come."

I thanked her again and headed for the French doors.

"And Lieutenant."

"Yes." I turned.

"I believe I see Alice in the garden. Would you mind asking her to come in for a moment?"

"Not a bit."

Alice was watering a bed of day lilies at the edge of the garden when I approached her.

"Ms. Taylor asked me to let you know that she needs you."

"Thank you."

"Incidentally," I said as she messed with the hose nozzle, "were you here two nights ago?"

"That would be Monday?" She was still struggling with the nozzle. It seemed to be stuck.

"Yes, Monday."

"No, that's one of my evenings off. I had to help my sister with something. Here, will you hold this thing? I have to turn it off at the spigot."

I stood and watered the lilies while she closed the valve. When she returned, we watched the last of the water drain from the hose.

"Do you know if Ms. Taylor had plans that evening?"

"Not that I know of." She took the hose from me. "Thanks for the help."

"One other thing."

"What's that?"

"Does Ms. Taylor drive?"

"Oh no," she said. "She would need help with her chair."

"Her chair? Does she always use it?"

"She prefers to walk, and she usually can. But the way her condition works, she's never sure when the fatigue might come over her. She has her good days and her bad days. Other factors, like stress, or how well she's slept, can have a lot to do with it. To be on the safe side, unless it's a real short errand, she likes to have the chair handy. I guess it's one of her quirks. It's almost become like an accessory. She'll go shopping and ask one of the stores if they'll watch it for her while she bops around. It doesn't seem to bother her."

She shook the nozzle until it stopped dripping and began to unscrew it from the end of the hose. "You could say the chair is a sort of security blanket," she went on. "Ms. Taylor's the type of lady that would hate to get stranded somewhere, or have to rely on the kindness of strangers. She's real independent like that."

"How does she get around. I mean, since she doesn't drive?"

"When I'm here, I drive her."

"And when you're not?"

"She takes a cab."

"Any company in particular?"

"Same company every time, Ocean Cab. Why do you ask?"

"No reason. I'm just curious how a lady like that gets around."

"Well, that's how." She walked toward the hose caddy at the spigot and I walked toward the gate.

"Thanks again for the assistance," she called out.

I drove over to the Sheraton. I wanted to take a closer look at that scuff mark I had noticed on the wall of the villa suite. I planned to scrape some off, take an accurate measurement. I can't say that I seriously thought that Taylor had gone over to the Sheraton and wasted her one-time lover. But the scuff marks did look similar, and her behavior during the interview was awkward. Our investigation was in early stages, and I was just operating on automatic, following leads and trying to put two and two together.

When I got to the room, Lucía—the girl I had interviewed the day after the murder—happened to be on her way out. She was startled to see me standing in the hallway, about to swipe the key card they gave me at the front desk.

"I'm just finishing," she said. She looked flushed, and stray wisps of dark hair floated out from under the edges of her prim housekeeper's cap.

"I don't suppose there was much to do. I was in the suite just yesterday, and the place looked like it was back to normal."

"It was. We cleaned it real good. A special company even came out to fix the carpet. But the housekeeping manager's so picky. There was this little mark on the wall, so she made me come up and scrub it off."

I couldn't believe what I was hearing. "Is that what you just did?" I strode by her into the room. Sure enough, other than a wet blot, already melding into the clean, white wall where it was drying around the edges, the place where the scuff mark had been was now as pristine as the rest of the suite.

Lucía read the disappointment in my face. "Did I do something wrong?"

I assured that her she had not and stood wondering if Forensics could do anything with the soapy rinse water in Lucía's bucket. It didn't take long to realize that I was grasping at straws. If there had been any evidence in that mark, it was gone for good. I would still check with the forensics team, though. Maybe they had included it in their initial investigation. I measured the height of the mark from the floor and made a mental note to do some research on Taylor's wheelchair.

Next I went to my car and retrieved the flyer for Taylor's upcoming recital. They let me make some copies on the office's copy machine. I spoke to the doorman, but he hadn't been on duty Monday evening. Then I took one of the flyers around to security. The chief agreed to show it to his crew and ask if anyone had seen Taylor at the hotel. I knew it was a long shot, but it was what I had to work with at the moment.

I decided to cross Collins to the Shops and check in with Willis. I figured I could grab a sandwich at the same time. My interview with Taylor had made me hungrier than I should have been at that hour.

All Willis had to report was that he was getting friendly with a couple of the café's waitresses. I told him to stay at it another day. After that I was going to have him gather prints from folks at the opera and the hotel. I wanted to see if we could rule out some of the latents found on the statuette and the music score.

This case wasn't working with me. We had under-fastidious security systems and over-fastidious cleaning crews. But every case has its problems. What *did* we have? Kessel was a little unpleasant, and clearly hot over the opera, but we had nothing concrete on him. As for Taylor, even though the scuff mark was probably stretching things, her odd deportment during our interview stuck in my craw. It was like she was putting up a façade: a facade of steadiness. I had heard her quietly weeping on the phone, and there were tears backstage the night of the premiere. But when I questioned her about Markson's murder she seemed studied, too calm and in control. Until I brought up Kessel.

Why?

Meanwhile our team was coming up empty-handed on the necklace. It looked like the Markson case was quickly winding into that zone where unsolved murders go to die. We needed a fresh approach or a stroke of luck. Maybe, I thought, I needed to step back from it, give it some perspective. I decided to head to the station and catch up with paperwork on some older cases. As mindless as the red tape is, it sometimes helps to clear my head.

I stopped by Forensics first thing. No one on the team had worked the scuff mark. "Walls are full of scuff marks," the tech on duty told me. "Not that one," I said, making a mental note to ask for a review of departmental policy. I went back to my desk and reviewed our caseload, carefully documenting our progress on each and every one of them.

It was a relief not to think about the Markson puzzle for a couple of hours. I stopped for coffee around three, and while I stood in the canteen looking out over the parking lot, I remembered that arts reporter who had approached me at the hotel the day Markson's body was discovered. I don't know why he popped into my mind, probably because I wasn't having much luck with the obvious leads. The kid had said that he knew as much about Markson's career as any living person. There was also the way he reminded me of what Markson himself might have been like twenty years ago.

I knew that talking with a reporter about the case was questionable. In fact, a lot of my colleagues would have said I was crazy. But I felt like I had to shoot the moon a little. Besides, for some reason, I felt in my gut that I could trust this kid with my life. I dug through my wallet and found the guy's card: Ralph Owens, *South Florida Gazette*. When I got back to my desk I gave him a ring. He said that he had some work to finish at the paper, but he agreed to meet me at six for a drink.

Chapter 8 (Owens)

AN UNEXPECTED CALL came today at the paper: Frank Nelson from the Miami-Dade police. He wanted to meet for a drink, and I was more than willing to oblige him. He's working the Markson case, and I was eager for any news on the investigation.

"If it's all right with you," he said, "we can meet at the Sheraton beach resort. They've got a decent bar there. It's off to one side of the main lobby, before you go out to the pool area."

A few minutes before six I pulled into the lot at the Bal Harbour Shops, parked under one of the ficus trees and got out. The blackbirds had begun to roost. There was an unceasing rustle and twittering as they settled in, a prelude to the delirious cacophony I knew would follow as darkness overtook Bal Harbour. The late-day sun sliced through the royal palms along Collins and gleamed off the shining bodies of the expensive chariots that wheeled down the avenue.

I crossed over to the hotel and found Nelson waiting for me. There were a dozen people at the bar watching a golf tournament on a television mounted from the ceiling. Over in the main lobby flushed, weary-seeming travelers stood waiting to check in.

Nelson stood and greeted me.

"Thanks for coming," he said. "I wanted to talk to you about the Markson case."

I told him that I was happy to help.

He asked what I was drinking and called over the bartender. While we waited for our drinks, Nelson stared toward the front entrance. Having never known a homicide detective, I took the opportunity to take stock of him. My existing impressions derived chiefly from *Law and Order* and old episodes of that seventies classic, *Columbo*.

He was in his mid-forties, of medium height and build, with indifferently combed dark hair. He wore a cheap sports coat over a nondescript shirt and tie. As I watched him peer across the lobby, I detected a note of weariness in an expression that bespoke, if I might so venture, a philosophical nature.

The bartender put our drinks on the bar with a faint clink. Nelson turned to me, raised his glass and said, "Cheers," and then again fixed his gaze toward the entrance.

"I keep seeing them wheel that gurney through here the other day."

"In time," I said, "maybe we'll all forget about it."

Nelson glanced in my direction. "Don't count on it." He sat in silence a moment, staring into his drink, before going on. "I still remember every one of them," he said soberly, "going back almost fifteen years now. And, mind you, it's not just that cute little girl, raped and brutally killed my second year in homicide. Or the cop gunned down on a traffic stop, a guy I used to chat with over coffee in the canteen. Even thugs, iced over drug deals and stupid turf wars, I never forget any of them. When you see them lying there lifeless, and know they're never coming back, you see a child that a couple of parents—or at least one parent—put their lifeblood into raising up. You see a unique human being, with a unique potential. And there it is, gone in an instant. As much as I've seen it, it still seems impossible that such things can happen."

Apparently I hadn't misjudged Nelson's bent toward the philosophical. I was at a loss for words, and feeling distinctly out of my depths. What could I say about murder that hadn't occurred to Lieutenant Nelson at least a thousand times? "It must be shocking," was my lame attempt at a response.

Nelson turned on his seat and looked through the wall of glass that gives out onto the resort's beachside grounds. It seemed he was trying to clear his head—to absorb something of the fading daylight, and the lush tropical vegetation that surrounded a cascading waterfall—something to put into the balance against all the evils we do one another. When he finally turned back to the bar, a cloud had lifted from his expression.

"The other day you said that you were an expert on Mr. Markson."

I protested that I didn't know if *expert* were the right term, but said that there were few people in the world who had followed Markson's career as carefully as I had.

He wanted to know about my phone interview with Markson, whether he had told me anything about his plans. I told him that we had confined ourselves to a discussion of his music.

"You know," Nelson said, "I'm just getting my feet wet with opera. I've never really been into it, if you know what I mean."

"For most modern people," I remarked, "opera is definitely an acquired taste."

"It's funny you say that," he replied, "because I think I'm beginning to acquire it. I mean, I've seen a couple now, and it's not half bad when you understand what they're singing about. Those subtitles are great. And when you get all the sets and the drama, it's a heck of a lot more enjoyable than listening to people belt out unintelligible stuff on the radio."

I agreed with his analysis, and we fell silent again and sipped our drinks. I knew he hadn't invited me out to discuss opera.

"Are you making any progress on the case?" I finally asked.

"Not much," he said. "But that's not unusual. Investigations take time. Sometimes we stumble onto things. Sometimes things stumble onto us." He stared into his drink. "And some- times . . ."

He hesitated.

"Sometimes?" I asked.

"Sometimes we never figure out what the heck happened." He threw back a quick slug of his cocktail.

"Do you think this could be one of those cases?"

"I hope not. You never know. We're working several leads." He glanced up briefly at the golf tournament on the television, without appearing to take notice of the state of play, before abruptly turning my way. "Let me ask you something."

"All right."

"You were at the premiere of Markson's opera, weren't you?"

I said that I was.

"Did Mr. Markson mention anything about how he came up with the story? Does a guy usually make this stuff up, or does he take it from real life?"

I pleaded ignorance regarding the genesis of Markson's plot for *Biscayne Bay*. During our telephone interview he had been expertly evasive about the details of his upcoming premiere. "I can tell you," I said, "that Markson hasn't generally worked from autobiographical plots. One of his earlier operas dealt with the life of Lincoln, and another was built around a labor dispute in West Virginia's coal mining region at the turn of the last century. The one just prior to *Biscayne Bay* portrayed the Antarctic expedition of Douglas Mawson. But that's not to say that he would never generate a plot from his own life."

"Well, I've been told that's exactly what he did with this one."

"I'd be very interested to know about that."

"First of all," Nelson said, "I've got to ask, can we make this off the record?"

I readily agreed. I wasn't reporting on the case, I told him. My interest was more personal than professional.

"Okay, then," he said. "There's this guy, Antonio Diaz . . ."

I told him that I was familiar with the Miami company's director.

"Perhaps you're aware, then," he went on, "that he was a big chum of Markson's when they were younger."

I told him that I knew they were both affiliated with the Miami opera and added, "That was back in the seventies, I believe."

"Exactly. Their friendship goes back many years, to when they were first starting out. Anyway, I spoke to Mr. Diaz yesterday, and from what he tells me, the story of *Biscayne Bay* is very close to the story of Robin Markson's actual life."

"That's intriguing," I said. "The plot has so many elements you find in the famous opera warhorses. Innocent young lovers, a wealthy older man after the young women, betrayal, a frail heroine beset by an untimely illness. I assumed that Markson had simply mined opera history for his plot."

"Not according to Diaz. And he was right in the thick of it."

I asked if Diaz was the character named Antonio in *Biscayne Bay*.

"That's what he says."

"And his wife, Lily?"

"She was the Antonio character's lover."

"What about the lover of the young Markson character?

And his nemesis, that older businessman?"

"Here's where I really need your confidence," Nelson said. "Because with an ongoing investigation . . ."

"You can count on it." I looked forthrightly into his eyes; I wanted to leave no doubt that he could rely on me.

Nelson looked away for a moment, seemed to be weighing something in his mind. Then he fixed his eyes at the back of the bar and spoke deliberately.

"The older guy is patterned after a big real estate developer. Name of Kessel."

The name was familiar. I told him I had seen it on signs at local building projects over the years. "What about the Markson character's lover, the young soprano? Her name wouldn't be Taylor, would it?"

"That's her!" His expression registered surprise. "How did you know that?"

"My girlfriend is one of her students."

"Really? Her name wouldn't be Daphne, by any chance?"

"Yes, it is! How on earth did you know that?"

"I met her just this morning, over at Ms. Taylor's home. She's quite an attractive girl. You're a lucky young man."

"Don't I know it."

"She's quite the singer, too," he went on. "I saw her at Saudade over at the Shops. She really does up those old Brazilian numbers. I didn't know anybody was into that stuff anymore."

"The music still has its fans," I told him. "In fact, our shared affection for those classic bossa nova tunes—and the work of Antonio Carlos Jobim, in particular—is one of the things that first brought Daphne and me together. You just can't beat that breezy sound of freedom, you know, the uncanny *lightness* of it! And that simple joy about being in the world, it's a feeling that's hard to come by these days." I put down my drink and stared into it, speechless. "But let me process all of this," I began again after a moment. "It's pretty amazing. From what you're telling me, Olivia Taylor and Robin Markson actually *were* lovers?"

"That's what it looks like. Had you suspected it?"

"From what Daphne told me, all Livy ever said was that they worked together when Markson was here in Miami. But somehow, she got the idea that there was something more going on."

"People never tell you everything, believe me."

"Amazing," I repeated. "Wait until I tell Daphne! That is, if you think it would be all right."

"As long as she keeps it close to her chest. What about you? Are you acquainted with Ms. Taylor yourself?"

"Not much. Mainly through Daphne. I've been to a couple of parties at her house, the occasional recital . . ."

"But given that," Nelson said, "what do you think of her? I mean, what kind of a person do you think she is?"

"I'm not sure what you mean. She's a tremendous voice coach, I know that. Daphne thinks the world of her."

Nelson kept his gaze riveted into my eyes. "What I'm getting at, though, do you think she's on the up and up?"

"The up and up?"

"You know," he said. "I don't mean to impugn anybody's character or anything. I'm just asking whether you think that, by and large, she's an honest individual."

"Honest?" I didn't manage to hide the surprise in my voice. "I'm not sure I would know. I've always assumed she's an upstanding person. Like I said, Daphne regards her very highly, and I generally trust her judgment on people. But why do you ask? Do you have any reason to suspect that Livy's not on the 'up and up,' as you say?"

"For one thing, when I interviewed her this morning, there were certain indications that she wasn't leveling with me. It's nothing definite, but I'm afraid she may be hiding something."

"I don't think I can help you there."

"I know this stuff is pretty personal for the lady. But we have a murder investigation going on, and we need some answers."

"I understand."

"And there's something else I've come across. Something more . . . concrete . . . that's bugging me."

"What's that?"

"This one's a bit of a stretch, but I found a scuff mark in Markson's suite that could have been made by a wheelchair."

"And you think that wheelchair could have been Livy's?"

"It's just a theory. Throw it at the wall, see if it sticks."

"Aren't there ways to confirm your suspicions?" I asked. "Wouldn't there be a residue? Something?"

"The problem is, housekeeping scrubbed off the mark before it could be analyzed."

"It seems to me," I ventured, "that there are plenty of things that could leave a scuff mark on a wall. Anything from those cleaning carts the maids use, to somebody's golf bag . . ."

"You've got a point there," Nelson said, looking across the lobby with a blank expression. "An excellent point." He punctuated his remark with a another bracing belt of his drink. When he turned toward me, he resumed in a more casual tone.

"I watched *La Bohème* last night," he said. "It wasn't half bad. Had my kid Sara in tears."

"It's definitely one of the greats."

"You know, I wouldn't mind seeing more opera," he went on. "But is it all that heavy tragedy kind of stuff?"

"For a glimpse of the lighter side," I offered, "you might want to take a look at *La Sonambula*." At his request, I wrote the title on a cocktail napkin and handed it to him. After thanking me he sat holding the napkin in his hand. He was obviously mulling something over.

"Listen," he finally said, "I hate to ask you to do this, but you've been so helpful . . ."

"Go ahead," I told him.

"I know I'm out in left field on this wheelchair thing. Maybe even in the stadium parking lot! But it would be helpful if you could somehow find out what model Ms. Taylor uses. We have so few leads, you see, and I need to rule some things out. Once something like that gets in my head, I can't stop until I get rid of it. I'd rather not upset the lady by going down there again. I wouldn't want her to think that she's a suspect or anything. I mean, I realize this thing is far-fetched. But if there's some way you could get that information—discreetly, I mean—you'd be doing me a big favor."

I told him that I would see what I could do.

"Thanks for meeting with me."

I said that I was glad to help and invited him to call on me anytime.

"I might be doing that." He slid off his stool and held out his hand. "I just might be doing that."

We shook hands and he stepped briskly away, through the lobby and out the front entrance. Daphne was singing over at Saudade, and I would have liked nothing more than to stop in. But I had an assignment to get off, and the evening wasn't getting any younger. I headed for home.

Chapter 9

THAT TOM OWENS was a nice kid. I didn't learn much from him, but talking to him did me good. It brought me a solid tick closer to the world of Robin Markson. Maybe it was Owens' girlfriend's connection with Olivia Taylor, or Owens' fascination with Markson's art. Then again, maybe it was just the way Owens reminded me of what a young Robin Markson might have been like.

I left the hotel and headed for home. Just for the heck of it, I took out my cell and rang the Ocean Cab Company. I asked for the manager, explained who I was, and inquired about a pickup at Taylor's house on the night of Markson's murder.

He said that he would have to get back to me.

On the way up the Intracoastal I stopped by the Diaz condo. Lily answered the door.

"Lieutenant Nelson, what brings you here?"

I asked if I could speak to Mr. Diaz.

"He's not here, I'm afraid. He's working."

"Oh, of course. I guess I'm not used to the evening hours you musicians keep."

She asked if there was anything she could do for me.

I told her I'd come to return the DVD her husband had loaned me, *La Bohème*. She asked if I had liked it. I told her that I thought it had some nice moments, even if it was a bit of a tearjerker.

"My daughter Sara loved it," I added. "She wants to be a singer."

"Oh," Lily said. "Does she have a teacher?"

"The kind of singing she does," I explained, "I don't think they have teachers for."

"What kind is that?"

"You know, the kind the kids listen to. I don't know the names anymore. I'm more of a Beatles type, if you know what I mean. The occasional Three Dog Night . . ."

She looked like she wasn't quite sure what I was talking about.

"You know," I went on, "they wear a lot of dark clothing and stick metal objects in their facial features. Except with Sara there's no metal. That's where Lori—she's my wife—draws the line."

"I think I see," Lily said, smiling. "Still, voice lessons couldn't hurt. Once your daughter develops her instrument"— that's what she called Sara's voice, her *instrument*, the same way her husband, José, had referred to his own voice when I interviewed the couple—"she can use it for anything she likes."

"I guess you're right. Maybe I'll mention it to her. But I should probably tell you, on a cop's salary . . ."

"If it's the right thing, there's usually a way to work out the finances. That's what I typically find to be the case, at any rate."

I told her that I'd think about it and handed over the DVD. Then I took the napkin out of my pocket, where Owens had written down the title of that other opera, and showed it to her. I told her that the opera had been recommended by someone else I had been speaking with.

She looked over the napkin. "*La Sonambula*," she purred.

"Oh, yes, this one is quite different than *La Bohème*. A comedy of considerable lightness, with a touching sentimental undercurrent. It's an excellent introduction to the Bel Canto period. The early years of Italian opera, that is. And for my money, none of the Bel Canto composers wrote gorgeous melodies like Bellini."

"That sounds good," I said. "I don't like too much tragedy all at once. I see enough of that on the job."

"You know, I'm quite sure we own a copy. Sit tight a moment. I'll be right back."

Before I could protest, Lily Diaz whisked off into the condo and came back with the DVD. "Here," she said. "Give it a look. I'll bet you'll like it."

I told her that I didn't want to impose on their generosity.

"Think nothing of it," she said. "It won't be missed. Enjoy!"

I promised to take good care of the DVD, thanked her and said goodbye. On the drive home, like I usually do, I mulled over the case. Nothing definite was yet taking shape, but I didn't feel completely depressed about our progress. It was still early in the investigation, I told myself, and I was already getting a bead on Markson's life. I was getting to know the people he knew, learning about his work, relating to him as an individual. Now, at that last thought—relating to Markson as an individual—a picture of beefy old Sergeant Delaney, my first mentor in homicide, barged uninvited into my mind. Delaney, God love him, was a big fan of objectivity. He always said that if you get emotionally involved with a case it will cloud your judgment. Besides, he used to say, over the long haul, it will wear you down. I respected Delaney. He was a good teacher. But we're different types. Me, I can't help but get interested in the life of a victim. And it hasn't kept me from solving cases, or moving up in the department. Was it wearing me down? That was a harder one to answer. Maybe Delaney had a point on that one. Slowly, like the steady drip of water on a stone. Little by little, year by year, until there's nothing left of the stone . . .

It was something to think about.

I looked forward to meeting with my team in the morning. Hopefully Sanchez would have more information on Kessel. I didn't really like him and I didn't trust him. As for the necklace, I had given up on finding it on the street. Sanchez hadn't turned up any leads and the trail was growing colder with every passing day. The Olivia Taylor angle wasn't adding up to anything in particular, either, and I couldn't see any clear way forward. My brain was tangled up with all the loose ends. I knew it would make better sense after some good downtime. I needed Lori and my family and pressed a little harder on the gas pedal.

She had dinner ready for me, and Sara and Andrew were watching the tube, as usual. It looked like more vampire stuff. Lori brought my plate to the table and sat down. I remarked that I was concerned about the amount of television the kids were watching—and the nature of some of it.

"I don't know if it's healthy," I said. "All the vampires and blood. It seems a little seedy, doesn't it?"

"Do you want me to censor them?"

"I don't like the word *censor*. I just wish they had more wholesome activities to occupy themselves with."

"They were both in school all day. I suppose that was pretty wholesome." She smiled her gently teasing smile.

"You'd like to think so."

"I wouldn't worry about it, sweetheart." She placed her hand over my arm. "It's their way of winding down. I don't think they take it too seriously."

She sat quietly while I ate for a while. Then she said, "Actually, Andrew was hoping you'd get home before dark, so the two of you could go over to the park and practice his batting."

That, of course, was Lori's way of being the great mom she is. She was taking up for her son, letting his old man know that he didn't sit around watching bloodsuckers because that was his first choice. But I couldn't escape the obvious implication: if I was around more, my son would have something better to do with his free time than watch the boob tube. I lost my appetite and stopped eating.

"Not hungry?" she said.

"Just thinking."

We looked into the yard together in silence. After a moment, she spoke out of the blue.

"He does seem to be staying in more since we took away his skateboard."

She was reading my mind, the way she does sometimes. "Yeah, but what choice did we have?"

The year before, Andrew had started to hang with some neighborhood ne'er-do-wells, and he got himself busted for using his skateboard in prohibited areas. I felt like I had to teach him something about respecting his community's laws and customs.

"We did the right thing," Lori said.

"Then why do I feel lousy about it?"

"Some things—like raising a child, for example—are a work in progress. Rome wasn't built in a day, you know."

"If I had my druthers, I'd be around more for him, for all of you. But the workload never seems to let up."

"You'll figure something out."

I wasn't so sure, but Lori's faith in me has always had a calming effect. I squeezed her hand and kissed her. While I finished my dinner she asked about the case. I told her where we were with it, and she wished me luck.

"I've got some entertainment for tonight," I said as I carried my plate over to the sink. "If anybody else is up for it, that is."

"What's that?"

I went to the other room, returned with the DVD Lily Diaz had loaned me, and showed it to her.

"Another opera?" Her smile seemed a bit forced.

"You don't look too thrilled."

"No, I'm game." She looked over the cover. "This is all just new to me. How do you pronounce this one . . . *So-nam-bu-la*."

"That sounds about right. But look, I don't want to force it on anybody. I realize it's like bringing work home . . ."

"That may be true," she said, "but a new influence or two wouldn't hurt around here."

She looked into the living room. On the TV screen, a pretty teenager was about to plunge her fangs into her girlfriend.

"Sara did seem to like that other one," I said.

"True. I don't know about Andrew, though."

I told her what Lily Diaz had said, about this *Sonambula* being lighter. "It's more of a comedy."

"You never know," she said. "We can give it a try. And if it helps with your case, so much the better."

Lori was accustomed to getting involved with my cases in one way or another. It was the way I worked, digging into the lives of the unfortunate individuals whose tragedies colored my daily life. She'd gone to jai alai matches, tried deep-sea fishing, explored the Everglades, and even taken up gem cutting, all because of the many crazy things my perps or victims had been involved with.

While she cleaned up the kitchen I went in to talk with the kids about the opera. The undead were done biting each other's necks, and I gave it my best shot. With the vampire show's credits still rolling, Sara got off the couch and broke into song.

It was that number from *La Bohème* I had heard her humming the night before.

"Do I have to hear this?" Andrew croaked.

I commented to Sara that her mouth must be feeling better, but she didn't break her stride. She was floating around the room, wielding a feather duster like a fan.

"It's not sounding any better, that's for sure," Andrew chortled.

Sara reached a leg around to kick him, but he rolled onto the couch and broke into laughter. I told my baby that I thought she had a lovely voice, and she hugged me and said that she would be thrilled to see another opera.

"We'll just have to convince the barbarian." She waved the feather duster toward her brother. He put on a caveman face, grunted, and hopped around the room in an ape-like crouch. I pleaded with him on the basis of family solidarity. I also promised to spend Saturday afternoon practicing his batting if he would give the opera a try. I even hinted at clemency on the skateboard rap.

"Nothing like a little bribery to move the savage beast," Sara said.

"I'll take it," Andrew returned. "It's a deal." Then he addressed his sister. "I guess this is what happens when you get your *wisdom* teeth yanked. Ha!"

I didn't catch her retort because I went into the kitchen to fetch Lori. She was putting together a snack tray and getting some cold drinks. After I helped her carry everything to the living room, we all got seated and put on the opera.

This one—*La Sonambula*—featured a winsome lass who lives in this picturesque Italian village a couple hundred years ago. The whole gimmick of the show revolves around how the girl, Amina, is afflicted with a sleepwalking habit, and how it gets her in dutch with her main squeeze, Elvino. The show opens at the couple's festive engagement party on the town square, and it's clear the two youngsters are deeply and truly in love. But that very night, Amina's nocturnal rambling kicks in, and she sleep-walks her way into the bedroom of this wolfish count who happens to be holed up in the town inn. Luckily for Amina, the count, who's normally a real louse, behaves like a gentleman for once. Knowing lack of consent when he sees it, he tucks Amina into bed and goes off to crash someplace else. But the girl's troubles have unfortunately just begun, because in the morning the innkeeper, who's a world-class gossip, finds Amina in the count's bed. I guess small towns are the same everywhere, because by evening everybody and his brother knows where the poor kid has spent the night. From that point forward, the whole show is about how Amina tries to convince her fiancé—and the rest of the village—that she isn't the slut they now say she is.

Aside from the slut-shaming, Sara was indignant that the sleepwalker's fiancé didn't trust her enough to believe her side of the story. Andrew said he thought the whole thing was ridiculous, but he enjoyed pronouncing Italian words in his goofy way and rated the main diva an eight on a scale of ten. Sara called him a disgusting chauvinist, Lori said "all that glitters isn't gold," and I was just happy that everyone wasn't falling asleep on me.

The show had a happy ending, at least, because the wolfish count finally reappears and clears the girl's name. Elvino has to eat crow, which I figured was good practice for being a husband and a father, and the opera ends with the townspeople breaking into musical celebration at his and Amina's wedding.

I let the DVD run while the audience clapped forever for the endless curtain calls. Everyone in my clan was in a decent mood. Sara went down the hallway singing, and Andrew got up and said, "That wasn't half bad, Dad. It was decent hanging with the fam." Lori snuggled into me, and I felt like maybe I could do something right now and then. Before he entered his bedroom, Andrew turned and said—"Saturday afternoon."

I told him I'd be there.

Chapter 10

SANCHEZ AND SIMMONS had been working the Kessel angle. Sanchez was doing some research in our archives, and she had Simmons surveilling him.

"It looks like the feds suspected money laundering in the 1996 case," she said at our morning meeting. "There were some convoluted transactions with real estate deals, and some unexplained cash, but after the prosecutor's key witness went missing the case collapsed. They eventually settled with civil fines. I'm waiting to hear from the chief investigator on the case. I should know more by next week. Meanwhile I've been looking into some of Kessel's more recent deals. Today I plan to talk to a few of his associates, ask around."

"What about his alibi?" I asked. "He told me three people could attest to his whereabouts at the time of the murder. Have you checked that out?"

"Oh yeah," she said. "One was his wife. Naturally she backed him up. Said they spent the evening at home and went to bed a little after ten-thirty. The second was the live-in maid. She confirmed the wife's story."

"I wouldn't take that to the bank," Willis chimed in. "He could have easily bought her off. Or threatened her. What's her green card status, anyway?"

"Not every maid in Miami is undocumented, you know," Sanchez said.

Willis held his hands up in front of himself, palms out. "Hey, I'm not trying to start some international incident. I'm just, like, saying."

"All right," I said. "What about the third one?"

"This is the one that's hard to question," Sanchez said. "There's a private security service that patrols Kessel's neighborhood. Apparently Kessel went down the drive around ten, just before he went to bed, to put a couple of letters in the box. One of the security team's agents was coming by, and he stopped and chatted for a few minutes. The contact is even noted in the man's log."

"Fine," I remarked. "But like I've said, if Kessel was involved, he probably wouldn't have done the dirty work himself. He's too smart for that." I turned to Simmons. "How's the surveillance coming?"

Simmons hadn't seen anything unusual. Kessel had gone to his office in downtown Miami, to lunch with one of his associates, back to the office and then home.

I instructed them both to stick with it and asked Willis if anything had turned up at the Shops.

"Not really," he said. "But you might say I'm developing an informant."

"Who's that?"

He hesitated. "She's one of the waitresses at the café."

"And exactly what do you mean *developing* her?" Sanchez asked.

"We've just been getting friendly, I guess you could say. We went out last night."

"Went out? Do you think that's smart?"

"Sanchez," Willis said, "I love you a lot. And I'm sure you're a great mother. But you're not my mother."

"But Sanchez has a point?' I said. "This gal works at the Shops. She could blow your cover."

"Sure Sanchez has a point, but it's on top of her head. Hey, do you guys think I'm some kind of dope? It's not like I told her I'm police. She thinks I own a roofing company."

"A roofing company?"

"Still," Sanchez said, "I don't know if you should be dating her."

"I couldn't help it."

"She was that irresistible, eh? Just like all your other floozies, I suppose . . ."

"Get real," Willis said. "Look, she'd noticed me hanging around the café for two full days. Naturally she got a little curious. Finally Rosie—that's her name—came out and asked what I was doing, spending so much time at the place. Like I said, I'm not a dope, so I wasn't about to tell her I was a cop casing the Shops for a burglar who might also be a murderer."

"So what did you tell her?" I asked.

"I think I handled it pretty smoothly, considering I had to think on my feet. I told her I was hanging around because of, well, because of her."

"Because of her!" Sanchez erupted. "How could you?"

"It wasn't totally untrue. I had noticed her. And I've got to say, she's pretty hot." A thin smile formed on his lips. In his eyes, that faraway look . . .

"You're a real schmuck," Sanchez said.

"Gee, thanks Mom."

"Wait a minute," I said. "This could be the start of something big. It should be clear to anyone with eyes in his head that our friend Willis here needs somebody to take care of him."

"Or take him out," Sanchez put in.

"Whatever the case," I said to Willis, "you're going to have to make time somewhere else from now on. I need you to work on getting some prints. Start with Markson's associates at the opera, and then tackle the hotel staff. I want to see if we can rule out the latents on that music score and the Venus statuette."

"I'm on it."

"While you're at it, why don't you also get some prints from Olivia Taylor."

"Who's that?"

"Isn't that the ex-diva, the one Kessel was involved with?" Sanchez asked.

"That's right."

"The lady with the wheelchair?" Willis piped up. "You really think she could be mixed up in this?"

"I know it sounds a little crazy. But given how she behaved when I interviewed her, I think she's not telling us everything she knows."

"Whatever."

"And Willis, keep it light. I don't want to upset the lady. Tell her it's routine. I'll get you her address."

The meeting broke up. I went to my office with a cup of coffee and stared out the window. I don't know why, but I often solve problems while staring out of windows. I guess the spaciousness of the outdoors inspires me.

Willis's remark about Taylor echoed back at me. Did I really think our opera teacher was mixed up in Markson's murder? She certainly wasn't my first choice. But the more I thought over our interview, the more certain I was that the lady was holding something back. It probably involved embarrassing details from her personal life, some past business with Markson or Kessel that she didn't feel like discussing. You can't expect people to be thrilled to give up their privacy just because you're investigating a murder. But I never like to proceed with those kinds of wild cards in the shadows.

And, as I think back over the case today, I realize there was something else that drew me to the Taylor angle. It may sound corny, but I'm going to put it out there. Love. You heard me right. The more I look at life, the more it looks like love is at the bottom of just about everything. Listen to the songs on the radio. What are 99.99 percent of them about? That's right. What about movies, or the operas my family had started to watch? Look at Willis. Crazy for girls. What's he really after? You got it. Take Sanchez, and her devotion to her kids. What about me? What would I be if it weren't for Lori and Sara and Andrew?

None of us is anything without love.

Taylor and Markson had once loved one another. And it wasn't just a passing fancy—at least not from Markson's point of view. He died while attempting to show the world how much she had meant to him. He no doubt knew she would come to the opera, knew she would see herself in the show and understand that he had never forgotten her. I remembered the tears in her eyes backstage after the premiere.

The guy at Ocean Cab had gotten back to me. There was no pick-up at Taylor's house the night Markson was offed. That didn't surprise me, but it left me with nothing. I didn't feel like I could interview Taylor again. I didn't have a new angle, and it would just seem like harassment. I had hoped that critic, Owens, might be able to shed some light on the lady, but he hadn't been a lot of help. Maybe I had to talk to his girlfriend, Daphne, the singer at Saudade.

There was only one problem. Could I count on her discretion?

I put in a call to Owens. I got his answering machine and left a message. Then I sat at my desk and made a few calls about some of our other cases. A post-it note reminded me to call Markson's daughter. I told her that we were doing everything we could and that she should let the estate executor know about the deposit on the painting.

I asked if her father had mentioned anything about it.

"No," she said. "But my father could sometimes live in a world of his own, with his artistic enthusiasms, his fascinations. Impulsive decisions."

"I see."

"Do you have any idea what happened yet?" she asked.

"We still don't know, I'm afraid. It was most likely robbery. And that brings up something else I wanted to ask you about. Maybe it was one of those impulsive decisions, but your father bought a very expensive piece of jewelry the day before he died. It wasn't recovered at the crime scene, and we're still looking for it. You wouldn't happen to know anything about it, would you?"

"Can you describe it?"

"It was an emerald necklace, from Cartier's. Can you imagine why he would purchase such a fine piece of jewelry, or who he may have bought it for?"

She was silent for a moment. "I spoke to him by phone the night before . . . the night before I flew down there. He told me he had purchased a necklace, and it sounded like the one you're describing. He asked me if I thought it was the kind of thing a woman might like."

"Did he say who that woman might be?"

"No, he didn't. And when I asked, he said—rather coyly, I thought—that it was a closely guarded secret."

"You have no idea who he purchased it for, then?"

"This is a little embarrassing," she began meekly, "but I thought he might have bought it for me. That may sound presumptious, that he would buy me something so special. But he always called me his best supporter, and I thought that, maybe, with this big premiere, well, that he may have made some gesture. He wasn't romantically involved with anyone. There was someone he had been dating out here in Seattle, but he cut things off with her about a year ago."

"I understand," I said. In her voice there was still the unquelled yearning for her father's loving presence. A picture of Sara popped into my mind and I added, "Maybe he did purchase the necklace for you."

"Frankly, I don't really know. If you find it, though, I would like to have it."

I could hear the tears starting and was almost sorry I had called. I told her that I would get back to her and hung up.

I went over to the window. The case was going nowhere fast. But I've often found truth in the old adage that the darkest hour is just before dawn. When it looks most hopeless, that's often when things start to break.

The phone rang. It was Owens, returning my call.

"I was going to call you, anyway," he said after we greeted one another. "I've got that information you wanted on Livy's wheelchair."

"That was fast. I hope it didn't cause any problems."

"No. I feel a little devious, but I told Daphne that I had a cousin who needed one, and that my family was looking for a good model. I didn't like lying, but she'd be pretty upset if she thought you were checking up on Livy."

He gave me the make and model and I thanked him.

"Is that all you needed?" he asked.

"Actually, I called to see if you could arrange for me to talk with her. With Daphne, that is."

"Why is that?"

"I'm just working my leads."

"Do you want to speak to both of us, or just her?"

I told him it would be good if he was there, too. "It might make her feel more comfortable."

"When?"

"The sooner the better," I told him. "Today would be great, if you could arrange it."

He said he would try, signed off, and then called back in a few minutes. He said that Daphne had agreed to meet us at the Shops before her dinner gig at the Saudade restaurant.

Chapter 11 (Owens)

I WAS HAPPY TO MEET WITH FRANK NELSON again, just one day after our first conversation. It helped me feel that I was doing something positive toward resolving Robin Markson's murder. This time it was Daphne he wanted to speak with, though he said he wanted me there as well. He couldn't get the idea out of his head that Daphne's voice coach, Livy Taylor, might hold some key to unlocking the Markson case.

Daphne was nonplussed at first.

"I can't imagine why he'd want to talk with me. What could I possibly have to do with all of this?"

My sweetheart is easily intimidated by law enforcement officials.

"It has something to do with Livy."

"But he's already spoken with her."

"I have no idea how these guys work," I said. "I'm just relaying a request."

"If you think it might help solve the case . . ."

"Nelson seems to be a pretty a busy man. I don't think he'd waste his time if he didn't think it would be useful."

She reluctantly agreed. I assured her that she was doing the right thing and signed off. We were to meet Nelson on the upstairs level at the Bal Harbour Shops at four-thirty.

When I pulled up at the Shops I called Daphne to see if she had arrived, but she was still making her way down Collins. I waited for her at the parking lot, saw her car pull in, and went over to her. The sky was clear and blue, but there were distant rumblings of thunder, harbingers of the storms forecast for later that afternoon.

We climbed to the second level and found Lieutenant Nelson sitting at one of the tables outside the Guantanamera Café. The café had closed. There were a few others making use of the tables to rest from their shopping.

Nelson stood as we approached.

"I think you know Daphne," I said.

He nodded. "Yes, we met briefly the other day."

Daphne returned his nod and we all sat down.

"I picked up a couple things around the corner at the coffee shop." Nelson gestured to three coffees and a few pastries on the table, and we thanked him.

"I appreciate your coming," he said to Daphne.

"I'm happy to help," she said, but her voice betrayed nervousness. She proceeded to pour four sugar packets, one after the other, into her coffee.

"I caught a bit of your act at Saudade the other day," Nelson said. "I guess you already know this, but you're pretty darned good."

She thanked him, blushed slightly, and stirred her coffee. "I've got a long way to go, believe me."

"Not that I could tell. The way you sang those old Latin numbers made me feel like a young man again."

"You're very kind."

I could see that Nelson knew, perhaps through some instinct he had developed over the years, how to soften up an interview subject.

"That was interesting hearing you and Ms. Taylor do your lesson. I suppose there's more to becoming a singer than the average person realizes."

"It can be pretty complicated," Daphne agreed, "depending on how seriously you take it. If we're talking about opera, in particular, the sounds you're trying to achieve are very precise, and the vocal instrument has many facets. Livy likes to say that using the voice for fine singing is like the workings of an orchestra. The brain is like the conductor, and it must get the tongue, lips, jaws, the larynx and throat, lungs and breath, diaphragm, facial muscles—all of these things—working in perfect synchronization. The problem is, she says, that some of the orchestra members—perhaps even the conductor—haven't practiced, some lack adequate training, others aren't paying attention, and some are just plain tired on any given day."

"Have you been studying with Ms. Taylor for long?" Nelson asked.

"Six years."

"Would you say that you know her well?"

"I guess so," Daphne replied, pausing a moment before continuing, "but there's always a certain barrier between a student and her teacher. The student comes with hat in hand. She's looking for knowledge, but also for encouragement and inspiration. You desperately want the teacher's approval, so you're secretly terrified of disappointing her. Our artistic egos are so delicate. And the relationship is never on a completely equal footing . . ."

"But you and Livy have always seemed close to me," I put in. "Like friends, almost."

"That's true, in a way," Daphne said. "The knowledge may flow in only one direction—from teacher to student—but that's not to say the respect isn't equal. Livy was once a student herself, so she can identify with the role I now must play. We're friends the way a mother and a daughter can be friends. There's a great deal of affection there, on both sides. But though the mother may know the daughter inside out, there are usually things about the mother the daughter will never know, as much as she might like to."

Daphne seemed to catch herself, and then she looked squarely at Nelson. "But Lieutenant," she went on, "Ralph said you wanted to speak with me about your investigation. I can't imagine what you think Livy might have had to do with any of this. I may not know everything about her, but I can tell you without a doubt, she's no criminal. She's one of the finest people—maybe the finest person—you'll ever meet. I mean, if you think Livy was mixed up in Robin Markson's death, you're really on the wrong track."

"I didn't say that," Nelson rejoined. "It's just the way we work. When a homicide is committed, you're only left with so many leads. These are the threads that might connect you with the circumstances of the crime you're trying to solve. There aren't an infinite number of them. What's more, they're not necessarily the ones you wish they were. So you grapple with whatever leads you have, and you work them as far as you can.

"Can I level with you?" He rested one elbow on the table and twisted toward her. "In this case we haven't got much to go on. In fact, I'm nearly at wit's end. But I have this much figured out. Ms. Taylor was a very important person in Mr. Markson's life. At least in his past. Did you happen to see his opera, *Biscayne Bay*?"

"No, but Ralph told me about it."

"Then you know the story."

"Yes. Ralph described it to me."

"Ralph told me you weren't aware that Ms. Taylor and Mr. Markson were on intimate terms when they were younger."

"I hadn't been aware of that before . . . well, before all of this happened," she said. "Livy once mentioned that she used to work with Markson, when he was here in Miami. Then, last fall, when I was working on an aria from one of Markson's operas, she dealt with the music in this extraordinary fashion. So delicate and thoughtful! That made me wonder if they hadn't been closer than she let on. But it wasn't anything definite. Now that I know they were lovers, of course, it all makes perfect sense."

"Would you say that Ms. Taylor is secretive in general?"

"Not particularly, why?"

"What you mentioned a moment ago, about her not telling you everything, I get that same feeling when I speak with her."

"Can you be more specific?"

"For one thing, the afternoon of Mr. Markson's murder, he phoned Ms. Taylor. Now, you would think that after all they'd meant to one another, and how he'd come to town to conduct this opera that's all about her, they would have had quite a lot to talk about."

"And?" Daphne said.

"When I asked Ms. Taylor about their conversation, she said that he had just called to say hello. And that was that!"

"Sometimes," Daphne said, "after two people have been involved together and split up, there's not much left to say."

"I hadn't thought of that." Nelson took a moment to slowly stir his coffee. "I haven't had much experience in that department, knock on wood."

Daphne bent over and took a quick sip from her cup. "It's not like Livy's been sitting on the shelf all these years, you know. She's an attractive woman, and she hasn't lacked for admirers. Nothing has ever stuck, but she's certainly been in a relationship or two."

"Granted," Nelson said. "But I still think there was more there than she let on to. The day I visited, the day I met you at her house, I got that same impression. Maybe there are things she's not comfortable talking to me about. Are you sure she hasn't mentioned anything about her dealings with Mr. Markson? Anything at all?"

"Nothing comes to mind."

"What about this. Has she ever spoken to you about her relationship with Donald Kessel?"

"Kessel? Who is that?"

"Her ex."

"I've never heard of him."

Nelson looked at me with a touch of helplessness in his eyes. All I could offer in return was a non-committal shrug. He leaned in again and addressed Daphne with an air of confidentiality.

"Daphne," he said, "let me ask you something. You're a woman, and you seem to have some understanding of these things. I'd like your angle on this."

"Okay."

"Mr. Markson, the day before his death, purchased an emerald necklace worth fourteen thousand dollars. He bought it from Cartier's, here in the Shops."

"Okay."

"Now the necklace is gone. It was last seen by a maid in Markson's room at the Sheraton the day of his death."

"Do you think it was taken in the robbery?"

"We don't know. We don't even know for sure that there was a robbery. I figure he must have bought the necklace for someone special. A lady, more specifically."

"That makes sense."

"The funny thing is, as far as we can determine, he wasn't

involved with anyone. What do you make of that?"

"I'm not sure what to tell you," she said. "A composer might buy gifts for his lead singers at a premiere. But the quality of the necklace you're talking about—you said an emerald, with diamonds, worth fourteen thousand dollars?—that would be a little extravagant, I would think."

Nelson emitted a weary exhalation. "I know this isn't really your department," he said. "I just thought I'd put it out there. Thanks for listening."

"Of course." Daphne rummaged in her purse, opened her cell to check the time and said breathlessly that she had to get things set up for her gig at Saudade. Nelson thanked her again and asked her to call if she learned anything that might be useful. She stood up, brushed my cheek with a kiss, and walked off.

"Wonderful girl you have there," Nelson said as Daphne disappeared down the stairway to the lower-level shops.

I shook my head in acknowledgment.

He relaxed into his chair, grew thoughtful. "You two seem pretty serious about one another."

I told him that we were.

"Been dating long?"

"A little over four years." I spoke distractedly, still picturing how nice she had looked walking away from us.

"I suppose you two plan on getting married," Nelson said off-handedly.

I gave him my stock response. "I suppose that could happen, one of these days . . ."

Nelson fiddled with his spoon. "One of these days," he repeated thoughtfully. "You know, I was just speaking to one of my younger colleagues the other day. He said something very similar, and I'll tell you what I told him. You want to be careful, I said, because *one of these days* can have a way of dragging on until *one of these days* becomes *none of these days*. Life seems endless when you're young, but you'd be surprised how quickly the years can clock by."

Nelson was invading uncomfortable regions of my personal space, and I didn't respond.

"I don't mean to be intrusive," he remarked, apparently sensing my mood. "Maybe I'm just trying to understand the way things work these days. I have a couple of kids not much younger than you, and I'd like to know what to expect. Me and Lori—that's my wife—we met in the tenth grade. Aside from a brief period, when I sort of lost track of where I belonged, we've been together ever since. To be honest, I wouldn't have it any other way. So when I see a young man like you, and you've got the devotion of a marvelous girl like that, I can't help but wonder what you're waiting for. If you're not right for each other, aren't you just wasting each other's time? And if you are, why not make it official? That way, you both know where you stand."

"It's not always so clear cut," I heard myself explaining, surprised at a creeping urge to confide in this man, who was practically a stranger, like he was my favorite uncle. "The thing is, Daphne's got her music. I've got my own artistic ambitions. We both need our freedom, at least for the time being."

Nelson let my remark hang in the air before responding. His expression was skeptical. "Do you think that's how Daphne feels about it?"

"I believe we're in agreement on that."

Why was I suddenly sounding defensive?

"Hmm." He allowed himself another pause before resuming. "I imagine you two live together, like most young people in your situation . . ."

"Actually, no." Seeing the surprise in Nelson's eyes, I felt

compelled to explain what I have come to regard as some species of personal failure. "I've proposed it," I said, "but Daphne's
a little old-fashioned in that respect. She says that living together would make things too easy. That we'd never have to decide
if we want to make a real commitment to one another. I can't
help thinking she's been influenced by Livy on that one."

His curiosity was piqued. "Really," he said, "why is that?"

"Daphne was raised by her mother," I explained, "but she
was never really there for her. As for the father, he was AWOL
from the get-go. Of course, that's another story. . ."

"But all too common nowadays," Nelson remarked.

"Yes, it is. In any case," I went on, "lacking family support
like she does, Daphne has come to see Livy as more than a
vocal coach. She's more like a life coach, if you know what I
mean. Though Daph has never admitted it, I suspect Livy has
cautioned her against getting in too deep with someone who's
not ready to make a serious commitment."

"Given what we know about Ms. Taylor's life, I can see why
she might feel that way."

I agreed. "But anyway," I said, "the long and short of it is,
we keep our separate apartments. It's like what Katherine Hep-
burn famously said about Spencer Tracy: why get married,
when you can just live next door and be friends?"

Nelson smiled and looked off into the distance for a long
moment. Then he ceased fiddling with his spoon and fixed his
gaze on his empty cup. "Freedom," he said, "there's a lot to be
said for it. But only if it's the kind of freedom that brings you
happiness into the bargain." He lifted his eyes to mine. "After
all, that's what we're all after, isn't it? Happiness? Let me tell
you something I've discovered. Sometimes, if you give up one
kind of freedom, you may get a bigger kind in return. The kind
that brings real contentment, instead of just running around

willy-nilly. But listen, I should apologize. I'm starting to sound like some old know-it-all. Anyway, thanks for coming."

He rose from his chair.

I invited him to call on me at any time, if he felt it might be useful, and stood to shake his hand. He walked away and presently disappeared down the stairs to the Shops' lower level.

As I sat down again I thought over the approaching evening. There was no place I had to be, so I decided to stay at the Shops and watch Daphne's act at Saudade. I felt a sudden urge to get closer to her, to see her in a new and clearer way. Perhaps I had begun to wonder what freedom would mean to her, the kind Nelson had spoken about. A freedom that would bring both of us real, lasting happiness . . .

There was still half an hour before Daphne started her first set. I didn't want to show up early. She likes to center herself before a gig, she says, and she apparently considers my presence a distraction. I decided to take a walk on the beach and come back for dinner.

An effervescent crowd pressed around the hostess station in front of Carpaccio. In the shady foliage of the manicured laurel trees, the big black birds gathered with their raucous twittering. When I got to the avenue I looked over at the Sheraton's towering form. Tall and erect, pristinely whitewashed, its presence was almost otherworldly. The setting sun painted its façade a faint rose; inchoate vegetation massed around its foundations in darkly fertile clumps.

I had meant to cut through the resort to the beach, but the sight of the imposing structure brought to mind in newly trenchant fashion the tragedy for which its precincts, so lovely to behold, had willingly offered a setting just a few nights ago. The pedestrian signal changed to walk, but I could not move.

The solid breeze that rustled down the avenue from the north seemed to push me bodily away. I turned and walked south along Collins Avenue.

I was surprised by my visceral aversion to the hotel. Only three days ago I walked with Daphne through the grounds, out of what I have concluded was a primal need to come close to the scene of Markson's murder. Yesterday I met Nelson at the lobby bar. But today it was suddenly different. The turnings of grief are strange and mysterious. I had come to be repulsed not merely by the violent circumstances of Markson's death, but by anything associated with them.

What is more, as I ambled past the workaday shops and restaurants that line Collins south of the hotel, I detected the beginnings of a seismic shift going on within me. I sensed that Markson's murder—and my involvement with the case through Frank Nelson—was working a vital turning in my life.

As of yet, I had no idea where such a turning might lead.

My conversation with Nelson began to reverberate in the chambers of my mind. He had insinuated, in his subtle, casual way, that Daphne might not be happy with our relationship. Could he be right? At first I struggled to dismiss the thought, for it threatened long-established notions. The moist air of the coming storm bathed my face, cars cruised slowly down the avenue beside me, and the humble signage of that district's World War II era shops composed a shifting mosaic along the way. I tried to lose myself in the bric-a-brac of the evening, but Nelson's words kept pinging back into my brain.

"Do you think that's how *she* feels about it?"

Allowing myself finally to consider the question, I realized that I couldn't say with certainty how Daphne feels about our cozy arrangement. Perhaps I don't want to know. My precarious, salad-days lifestyle, supported by my poorly paid work for the

Gazette, has served my purposes admirably. The job's flexible, and often scant, hours allow me to devote handsome stretches of time to my novel, the grand work upon which I have pinned all my hopes of glory, success and ultimate freedom!

Antes de morirme, quiero echar mis versos de alma!

When Daphne came into my life, it must be said, a new element was added. It is an element of decided sweetness, with a glory all its own. Life would be immeasurably poorer, I had to admit, without our sentimental operations. What is more, she has come to be a lodestar of sorts for me, keeping me pointed toward true north when self-defeating impulses threaten to come to the fore.

I peered through the windows of a kitschy shop, four blocks south of the Sheraton, at outsized lawn statuettes and gaudy chandeliers. A pair of enameled greyhounds stared ever alert across the avenue; behind them, two life-sized centurions stood at sternly bronzed attention. In the presence of these mute witnesses, I considered Nelson's remarks anew. Was the man seriously suggesting that Daphne and I *marry*? He spoke of freedom. But isn't marriage a form of bondage, where you surrender your personal inclinations to the needs and even whims of another? And doesn't it imply other problematic things as well, things like children, a steady job, yard work, and Saturday chores?

Had Nelson considered, or was he even aware of, I wondered, what the life of an aspiring novelist entails (late nights working on notes and revising chapters; a constant exploration of the world and of the self; deep study; and an ongoing investigation into all that makes up the human condition)? Does he realize that all of that must be squeezed in around the brute necessity of making a living, of keeping body and soul together? I could not conceive how I might fit marriage—and God forbid, children—into my life. Perhaps, I thought, after my great, grand novel is finished, I will be more at liberty to consider the question.

For the present, however, I couldn't see it.

The sky was darkening, the northerly breeze gaining force. I continued on a couple of blocks and then turned at an old drugstore where the lunch counter advertised a full breakfast for $2.99.

When I arrived at the Shops the battered sky was black and blue. Sparse but heavy raindrops pelted the sidewalk; the blackbirds fluttered in and out of the laurels in a state of great agitation. I rushed across the parking lot, past Carpaccio, and made my way around to Saudade. The high, complex tones of Daphne's voice—bearing sun and rain, ocean breeze and occasional strikes of lightening!—reached me before I arrived there. When I came upon the restaurant, where wrought iron tables surround a koi pond in one of the lower corridors of the mall, she smiled over her microphone at me. The sound of her voice merged in a sort of tropical splendor with the rain spattering on the mall's glass canopy three stories above us.

I gave the waiter my order and sat back to enjoy the music and, even more, the one making it. Yes, sitting there watching Daphne sing, I realized anew how much I love every single thing about her. She approached the timeless melodies she sculpted in air with sincerity and respect, and I knew how hard she worked to make each note exactly as good as it could be. She was positioned on a stool in front of Stan, her pianist, and rarely looked at their audience except to acknowledge, with a faint nod, the occasional applause.

Her eyes, her hair, her voice—that smile!—everything about her called out my desire; and I wished she were in my arms that very moment. Lieutenant Nelson's words echoed again in my mind: "What are you waiting for?" I wasn't sure I had an answer, except that I have always had a very personal destination, and have convinced myself that I cannot tether my fortunes to anything that might slow me down until I reach it.

My reflections were interrupted when Daph started in on one of Jobim's old and famous tunes. I knew the lyrics by heart, thanks to the liner notes of albums I have worn out the grooves on. But tonight those words struck me with a stark and novel urgency:

> "Sad" is to live in solitude
> far from your tranquil altitude,
> "Sad" is to know that no one ever can live on a dream,
> that never can be, will never be,
> Dreamer awake, wake up and see . . .

I was obviously keyed up, because as I listened to Daphne sing "Triste," Jobim's words began to make me feel decidedly worried. It was just a song, it is true, one that Daphne sings at every gig. Yet tonight there was the feeling that she directed her efforts especially at me, that she sang about *us*. Oblivious to my inner turmoil, she mouthed preposterous things: that her lover was an airplane; that his single-minded craft soared through an atmosphere so remote and rarefied, that her heart broke with the strain of yearning and waiting!

It went on like this for verse after excruciating verse, so that by the time Stan played his last soft chord, topping it off with a delicately ascending bit of filigree, it was a certified fact: Daphne was the sad one of the song, and I the blasted airplane, flying high and out of reach, expecting her to live on a dream that could *never* be. A wave of anguish came over me, for I could hardly bear to think that Daphne, whom I adore with all my soul, might be sad on my account. And though we have agreed that marriage isn't for us, it now seemed clear that it is I who has enforced that view on our situation, as Lieutenant Nelson so adroitly suggested when we spoke earlier. As for Daphne, it would be precisely like her to go along with things, because she's just the kind of woman who wouldn't want to make life any harder for me than it has to be.

She sang out the rest of her set, old chestnuts she does so well, and when she and Stan stopped for a break she came over and sat with me. While we held hands and shared a tiramisu, I told her, in every way I could, how marvelous I think she is. I wanted to dispel any sense of sadness she might feel on account of us—the *triste* of Jobim's song. And as we polished off the last delicious morsels of ladyfingers and mascarpone, I suggested that I sleep at her place after the gig.

"I'm sorry, Ralph," she said, "but I have a lesson tomorrow. I'm not prepared, and I need to get up first thing and get to work."

"I promise I'll get out of there early," I cajoled.

"I really need a good night's sleep," she said decidedly. She massaged the back of my hand with her thumb. "You know, if you come over . . ."

"I miss you," I said.

"I miss you, too. But since we've decided to live our separate lives, we can't always have it just the way we want it, can we? After all, I've got to take care of my career."

It wasn't usually this difficult, and I didn't know what to say. We sat in silence for a long while and sipped our drinks. Then she changed the subject.

"Personally, I don't understand Lieutenant Nelson's fascination with Livy. I think he's grabbing at straws."

"You might be right. But he's not a bad guy, as far as I can tell."

"I just hope he doesn't harass her. Men can be so insensitive."

Stan gestured to Daphne that it was time to get started again, and she walked over and joined him at the piano. I barely heard her first few numbers, absorbed as I was with feelings of rejection. It wasn't the first time she has turned down an offer to spend the night, so why was I taking it so hard? Nor was it the first time she has spoken of having to keep up her career, remarks I have always credited to the camaraderie of two struggling young artists. Why then did I now feel that she was making a point? Namely, that her career is the only solid thing she has in this world, because she's in love with a schmuck who won't commit. Perhaps I've been so hardheaded all along, I thought, that I've failed to observe the obvious.

Men can be so insensitive.

Chapter 12

COLLINS AVENUE WAS BUSY with Friday traffic when I went out to the parking lot. It had been a long week, and I couldn't think of anything more I could do on the case. At our Monday team meeting we would review where things stood and decide how much more effort our current leads justified.

I decided to knock off for the day. Maybe I could catch up with the kids and have dinner with the whole family for a change. Unfortunately, when I called Lori she was over at her friend Brenda's. They were getting things together for a catering job they had on the books for Saturday.

"I told you I'd be here, remember?"

"Yeah," I said, "I guess you did. I have so much going on right now . . ."

"That's all right."

"How long are you going to be?"

"Probably most of the evening. There's still quite a bit to do."

"I see. Maybe me and the kids can go out to dinner."

"I don't think that will work tonight, hon."

"How come?"

"Andrew's over at Jeff's. They're all going to the new Batman movie. And Sara has a date . . ."

"A what?"

"You heard me, a date."

"Wait, when did this happen?"

"What?"

"Dating."

"Sweetheart, she's in the eleventh grade. It shouldn't be that shocking."

"Maybe not, but why didn't somebody tell me?"

"It just came up today. I didn't think you'd mind."

"Who is this guy, anyway?"

"Can't we discuss it later? It's all very safe, believe me."

"All right."

"What are you up to?" she asked.

I told her that I had finished early for a change.

"And no one else is free. Poor baby."

"I'll survive."

"I wish I could be home. We'd have the place to ourselves."

"Maybe you can rush it up over there."

"I'll try."

We signed off and I stood watching the cars on Collins. Everybody seemed to be in a hurry, but I had no particular place to go. I did have the Diazes' DVD in the car, though, so I decided to head up the avenue to Hallandale and return it.

I took the elevator up to the seventh floor and rang the bell. Diaz came to the door. He was in a big rush, just like everybody else. He had on part of a tuxedo, but the cummerbund wasn't fastened and the bow tie hung in a tangle around his neck. He was out of breath.

"Oh, Lieutenant," he said, "good to see you. Come on in while I finish tying this stupid thing. Have a seat."

He gestured to the dining table as he stepped up to a mirror and began to struggle with the tie.

I sat down.

"Sorry," he said, "but I don't have much time. We have a show tonight. I just rushed back after rehearsals to grab a bite with Lily. I'm due back at the opera house in half an hour."

"Are you still doing Mr. Markson's opera?"

"Yes, in fact, we are. They'd only planned two nights, but there's been so much interest, they've extended the run."

"I guess Mr. Markson would be thrilled."

"I'm sure he would be."

He had finished his tie, and now he was wrestling with the cummerbund. "I'd like to think that the interest isn't just because of, you know . . ."

"The crime?"

"Exactly. But we did get some excellent reviews. I'd prefer to think that the enthusiasm is genuine."

He had finished with the cummerbund now and went darting across the room.

"Maybe I should skedaddle and let you finish getting ready."

"It's no bother," he said. "What was it you wanted to see me about?"

"I just came by to return your DVD." I showed him the cover.

"Oh, how'd you like it?"

"It went over pretty well with Lori and the kids."

"By the way, how's the investigation coming?" He was now digging in the drawer of a desk near the balcony doors.

"Nothing new, I'm afraid."

"Are you still figuring it was robbery?"

"That may be what we end up concluding. We may never know, frankly."

He stopped digging for a moment and turned to look at me.

"That would be upsetting," he said.

"We're doing everything we can."

"I know you are."

"There is one thing you could help me with," I said after a moment, "—if you're sure you have a free minute."

"Of course." He started to buzz around the room again, turning over things and collecting papers . . .

"Olivia Taylor."

"Livy? Okay, what about her?"

"Would you say that you know her pretty well?"

"Probably as well as anybody. We used to hang out constantly in the old days, when Robin was here in Miami. And since Lily and I returned to town, we've kept up pretty regularly."

He came to the table and stood before me, keys in hand, his jacket folded over one arm. "What is it you want to know?"

I stood up. "Don't take this the wrong way," I said.

"Go ahead. I know you have a job to do."

"What I'm wondering is, do you think that she can be trusted?"

"Wow," he said, "I didn't expect that! Livy, trusted? I've never had any reason to doubt her. I mean, she's one of our closest friends. As far as both Lily and I are concerned, she's an absolute gem of a human being. Why would you even ask that?"

"That's not easy to explain," I said. "But she was one of the few people Mr. Markson spoke to after he arrived here in Miami, and we need all the information we can get. I just don't think Ms. Taylor has been completely forthcoming with me."

"Women can be very mysterious, Lieutenant."

"I've been married for twenty-five years, Mr. Diaz. You don't need to tell me that."

"Anyway, now I really do need to go. But I wouldn't doubt Livy. You can take that to the bank."

I tapped on the DVD where it lay on the table. "Thanks again for the loan," I said. "I appreciate your kindness."

He picked up the box and looked over the cover. "Your family enjoyed it, you say?"

"They seemed to. At least they didn't hate it."

"Wait a minute." He draped his coat over one of the dining chairs and set his things on the table. Then he stepped over to the shelf where he and Lily kept their music and movies. He returned in a moment with another one of the shiny plastic boxes. "Here, why don't you try this one? It's quite famous. For what it's worth, I've sung the lead a number of times myself."

Rigoletto, the cover said. It showed a hunched old man descending a set of rugged stone steps in some old European town. Before him, a young lady lay flopped across the stage looking about as dead as a door nail.

"I couldn't," I said. "You've been too generous."

"Not at all," he protested. "I'm always thrilled to gain a new opera fan. And who knows, it might, in some way, help you with the case. But I really do need to go now, or the company will be putting out an APB on me."

"We wouldn't want that."

"No, we wouldn't. Just a moment," he added, "I'll go down with you."

After stepping into the hallway to say goodbye to Lily, he returned and grabbed his things. We went out the front door onto the condo's exterior walkway. It looked like the sun would soon be setting, all orange and glowing, over the pinelands and marshes to the west.

"I really appreciate everything you guys are doing," he said as we walked to the elevator. "I want you to know that."

"We're just doing our jobs."

"But it's a job very few people could do, or would want to."

"I could say the same for yours."

He nodded and we boarded the elevator. When we got down to the parking lot he extended his hand and said goodbye. I watched him walk to a black Saab, get in and speed off.

I guess it was that fabulous view from the seventh floor of the Diazes' building, but I suddenly wanted to get in the car and drive out toward the west. It was like I wanted to catch that setting sun. What the heck, I figured, no one was home and I had nothing pressing to do for a change. The traffic was heavy while I made my way to the Tamiami Trail, but the cars thinned out as I drove over the marshes and canals of the Water Conservation Area. The sun plunged toward the earth ahead of me.

Cruising over one of the Conservation Area's low bridges, I was reminded of the time I brought Andrew out there. We had fished off that bridge, and I recalled promising him that we would take the next opportunity to come out again, maybe rent a boat. Unfortunately, that was three years ago, and we had yet to come back. It wasn't that my intentions weren't good. It's just one of those things that got lost in the ongoing shuffle of school, chores and an unending stream of murder cases. Then I remembered that I had promised to work on his batting practice the next day, and I felt good that we were at least going to spend some time together.

Out around Big Cypress Swamp, just as the sun turned into a magnificent, incandescent ember, I pulled into a turn-off with a view of the marshes. With the light breeze against my back, everything was so subdued I hardly noticed the rumble of the rare passing car. Time seemed to stop. Several egrets and a great blue heron hunted out in the wetlands. A convex golden sheen indicated the presence of a turtle half-submerged on a sunken log. I figured the swamp was probably also loaded with gators, and wondered if the turtle would soon end up on their dinner menu. Killers everywhere, I thought.

I was surrounded by them.

That big glowing ember sank into the horizon and doused itself in the marshes. Funny, I thought, you'll never catch that setting sun, no matter how hard you try. You'll never catch your life by running after it, either. Maybe you've got to stay in one place for a while, I said to myself. Let it come to you.

About that time my phone started to go off. It was Sanchez.

"Hey Chief," she said. "I've been trying to reconstruct Kessel's movements, like you asked. This afternoon I went over to the Sheraton to take a closer look at the surveillance tapes. What's left of them, anyway."

"Not a bad idea."

"I thought you'd be interested to know what I found. The system captured our man showing up at the front entrance."

"Whoa! More than interested. When was this?"

"Two days before the murder."

"What else have you got?"

"Not a lot, I'm afraid. He goes into the lobby and stands off to one side for a few minutes. He looks confused, like he's not sure what he's there for. Then he disappears down a side hallway."

"The one toward the villa suites?"

"No, the other direction."

"Any other sign of him?"

"Not that I could detect. Maybe we ought to interview him again."

I thought for a moment. "Let's not do that just yet. I don't want to tip him off. We already have him under surveillance. We'll see what he does. We'll have this in our back pocket if we need it."

"Got it. Have a good weekend."

"Good work. See you Monday."

Kessel at the Sheraton resort, what was that all about? Had he intended to murder Markson, he could have been casing the place. But assuming his alibi was solid, and he was clever enough to hire someone to do the deed, why compromise himself by lurking around the hotel two days prior to the icing?

In any case, it was another complication to throw into the hopper. Was this some kind of game changer? We would hash out the implications at our Monday morning team meeting.

It was getting dark, so I got in the car and headed home. The place was deserted when I arrived and I went in the kitchen and grabbed a beer from the fridge. I'm not a big drinker, but I felt that I could use a little something. I sat at the table with that opera Diaz loaned me, turned the DVD case over and read the write-up on the back.

The opera, it said, was about this lonely old man, the *Rigoletto* from the title. He was a jester at the court of some wealthy duke and, let me tell you, he sounded pretty disgusting. It wasn't that he was old, withered and had a humpback. The real problem was that he had crap for morals. His employer, the Duke, was apparently a real lech, and Rigoletto's primary job function was to procure innocent young girls to feed the Duke's insatiable sexual lusts. If there was anything appealing about old Rigo, it was that he had a sweet and charming daughter himself.

The back cover didn't give away the rest. It just said that Rigoletto would come to feel the pain of a "father's curse." That reminded me that my Sara was out on her first date. Every father with a daughter has a curse, I thought to myself. The problem is that we all know what men are like. A lot of us, anyway. We're out to put as many notches in our holsters as we can, just like this Duke character, while the girl naively thinks she'll be well and truly loved. She doesn't yet realize that most males don't have the vaguest clue what love is until they're at least forty, fifty years old.

If they're lucky.

I set the DVD on the table and stared out the kitchen window at the shadowy back yard. I got to thinking about Diaz down at the crowded opera house, Lori over at Brenda's and my kids out having fun, and I started to feel a little neglected. There was nowhere to go and no one to see. I did have the opera DVD, though I wasn't sure I wanted to delve any further into the "father's curse." Finally, for lack of anything better to do, I went to the living room and popped it in the player.

I won't bore you with the details. You can see the show yourself sometime. It's supposed to be one of the classics. But stop reading if you like surprises, because here's the spoiler: In the end, it's Rigoletto's inexperienced child herself who falls prey to the Duke's come-on line. It gets even worse than that, but I'll stop before I completely ruin the ending for you.

Fortunately Lori came home just as the DVD was finishing. The story didn't make me feel any calmer about Sara and her date, to say the least. I made Lori sit on the couch with me in the dark, holding hands for a while and just being quiet. I told her about the opera.

"That's just the kind of thing that makes me worry about my little girl," I said.

"She isn't so little anymore, in case you hadn't noticed."

"That makes me even more worried."

"Sweetheart, don't you think we've raised her well? I'd like to think that Sara has good sense. The boy she's out with is just a classmate at school. He's no duke with a string of conquests behind him, I can assure you that."

"How old is he?"

"He's a younger man. Tenth grade."

"Really?"

"We've got to let her grow up. That's what you want for her, isn't it?"

I sat and pondered the question in silence.

"Maybe you don't?" she said.

Maybe I didn't, I agreed. "I've missed so much time with her, with all of you. Especially since my promotion to team lead. The pace has been relentless. The killings never stop. It's so hard for me to . . . back off . . . accept defeat."

"I admire your sense of responsibility," she said after a thoughtful moment. "You know that. But as much as we'd like to, we can't stop time. And we definitely can't turn back the clock. All we can do is make the most of what's here today, and of whatever tomorrow may bring."

She was right. "Make the best of today," I repeated. "I guess the devil's in the details."

"Come on," she said. "Let's go to bed."

"With the kids still out?"

"Andrew's spending the night, and Sara promised to be home by midnight. Don't worry, I won't fall asleep until I hear her come in."

"Andrew didn't forget about our batting practice, did he?"

"No, of course not. He made a point of asking Jeff's folks to bring him home first thing so he wouldn't miss it."

She laced her arms around my neck and kissed me more powerfully than I had been kissed in a long time. "We're all alone," she whispered in my ear. "We can make all the noise we want."

I was down the hallway in a minute flat.

I must have passed out, because I don't remember Sara coming in. Come morning, though, everyone was present and accounted for. We all had breakfast together. My girl looked especially radiant.

"I understand you had a date last night," I said.

"He's just . . . a friend."

"Your mother specifically used the term *date*."

"Whatev."

She smiled between bites of English muffin. Her face seemed to glow even brighter.

"All I can say," Andrew wisecracked, "is I sure feel sorry for the dude."

"Shut it," Lori said.

Sara flung a glob of jelly at him. It took my sternest father look to restrain him from retaliating.

"Nice guy?" I asked.

"I think so."

Still that smile, that glow.

"As long as you don't get carried away."

Ignoring the knowing smiles that passed between Lori and Sara, I turned to Andrew and asked if he was ready for some batting practice.

"I've been looking forward to it all week, dude."

After we finished eating Andrew and I rustled up the baseball gear and drove over to the local park. As we strode onto the field I remembered how I'd first taught him to throw, catch, field grounders and bat when he was just a tyke. I had been a decent high school third baseman myself, and I wanted to expose my son to a sport that left me with a lot of fond memories. It was clear that he had some talent for the game, and he really enjoyed it, so I made sure he participated in Little League. Naturally I was thrilled when he made the junior varsity team his freshman year. Now he was starting shortstop, and I anticipated a bright career on the varsity team as an upperclassman.

Standing on the pitcher's mound with a bucket of balls

beside me, Andrew at the plate, his bat cocked, his stance taut and ready, I couldn't help see that tyke I once knew. I could see how much he had grown, of course, but also how much he still had to grow. I hoped, when the time came, that I would be able give him some clue of what it takes to be a man.

We were just getting warmed up, and he was starting to knock them pretty good, when my cellphone went off. I hated to answer it, but I was on standby, like any other weekend, in case the regular shift couldn't handle the workload. Besides, there was always the possibility that Lori or Sara needed me.

As soon as I heard the dispatcher's voice on the line my heart sank. There had been three killings the previous night. They were the ones that we knew about, anyway. The weekend homicide shift was overwhelmed. I was directed to get my team to Hialeah posthaste, where the bullet-ridden body of a young man had been found in an alleyway under a pile of garbage.

I knew Andrew was disappointed, but he put up a good front.

"We'll catch it some other time, dude," he said.

One thing I love about my boy, he's endlessly understanding when it comes to his old man. But I couldn't help thinking, when's the *other time* going to be? How many *other times* do you get before there are no more *other times* left?

I put an arm around his shoulders as we walked to the car and promised we would use my next free day to get back to the batting. Then, on the drive home, I brought up the idea of going fishing again.

"You remember when we did that, out at Great Cypress Swamp?"

"Seems like forever, dude."

"It has been a few years."

"That would be cool with me."

When we got to the house I popped in to change and get my gear. As I went through the door Andrew gave me some kind of sign I think is Hawaiian. "Give 'em hell, dude!" he said.

I started toward Hialeah. On the way I got in touch with Sanchez and Willis and asked them to meet me at the crime scene. As for Simmons, he was still heading up the team surveilling Kessel. I didn't want to pull him away from that.

Another dark alley, another body. Nine separate bullet wounds. People all over the place, but nobody saw or heard anything. A fat lady weeping her eyes out. It must have been those operas I'd been watching, but I had the feeling there should have been music coming down from the sky, maybe pouring out the windows of the buildings. It would say all the things that nobody standing around, messing with or looking at the body, could say. I have no idea what such music would sound like. But then, I'm not a musician.

I'm a cop.

Sanchez pulled up not long after I got there. We hardly needed to talk about this one. We'd seen it all before. When Willis arrived we started on the usual rounds, looking for witnesses, checking into the victim's background, talking to his friends and family. Suffice to say that I was barely home all weekend.

We had our team meeting on Monday morning. The weekend case was heading in the usual direction. The kid had drug connections and a record like a racing form. We were getting stonewalled at every juncture, but we had a bad actor or two who might crack with the right kind of pressure.

After we finished going over the new case we took up the Markson investigation. First I asked Sanchez to tell the team about Kessel's cameo appearance on the Sheraton's surveillance system.

"Jeez," Willis said, "do you suppose he could have been casing the place, figuring his angle of escape after he wasted our victim?"

"The problem with that theory," I said, "is the man's got a watertight alibi for the time of the murder. And even if he paid someone to take Markson out, it wouldn't be very bright to be hanging around the eventual crime scene a couple days before the icing. Maybe the man just had an appointment with one of the other guests at the hotel. After all, they're the kind of high falutin' circles Kessel travels in."

That's when Simmons dropped the bombshell. "Maybe this will be of interest," he said as he laid a photograph on the table.

The day was bright. In the background was a blue glare that could only be Biscayne Bay. One of Ocean Cab's units was parked at a deserted dock, and pulled up near the cab was a well-polished, late model Lincoln Mark IV. Standing beside the cab was a neatly dressed man. He was no longer young but tall and erect of bearing. Though the image was blurred, due to the use of a telephoto lens, I could see that the standing figure was Donald Kessel. He was accepting a package from someone in the cab. All you could see of the cab passenger was an arm thrust out the window, holding a brown paper bag.

It looked like Simmons and his team had been doing their job.

"Tell me more," I said. "For instance, whose arm is that coming out the window of the cab?"

"That's your friend the opera coach."

"Are you sure? Because I've gotten the distinct impression, from all and sundry, that Olivia Taylor hates Kessel's guts."

"We followed the cab to her house and watched her go in."

"What about Kessel?"

"We called for back-up. One of our other units picked

him up."

"And?"

"He went home. Took the package inside with him."

"God, I'd give anything to know what was in that bag."

"Me too," Willis said. "Heck, Slim, why didn't you move in? Grab the goods?"

Simmons looked lost for a moment. His eyes darted around the table. "I don't know," he said. "Frankly, I wasn't sure I had probable cause. I didn't want to do anything that might screw up our case . . ."

"No guts, no glory." Willis settled smugly back into his seat.

"Simmons has a point," Sanchez broke in. "He didn't have a warrant. So the question is whether the hot pursuit exception would apply. Since neither Taylor nor Kessel has been named a suspect, how could he claim they were handling evidence from a crime?"

"Sanchez is right." I turned to Simmons. "Sometimes Willis gets a little gung-ho."

Willis rolled his eyes at the ceiling.

"The question is," Sanchez said, "where do we go from here?"

"Exactly," I agreed. "I've suspected all along that Ms. Taylor hasn't been forthright with me. And now, with this . . ."

"It certainly makes you wonder," Sanchez said.

"It certainly does. And there's one other element," I went on, "—concerning Ms. Taylor, that is. I haven't mentioned it before because, frankly, it just seemed too far-fetched . . ."

"Chief," Willis came in, "I don't think anything's too far-fetched for this squad."

"You're part of the team, aren't you?" Sanchez said with a friendly smile.

"But what's the development?" Simmons asked eagerly.

"Well," I said, "you know me. I just can't leave things be. I decided to revisit the crime scene the other day, and I noticed a scuff mark on the wall of Markson's room. The thing is, it looked like it could have been made by the wheel of a wheelchair. I've done some research since then, and I've calculated that the height of that mark from the floor would perfectly match a mark made by the very same model that Taylor uses."

"Did you get a sample," Willis asked, "check with Forensics?"

"I went back over there the next day, but the mark had been cleaned off."

"There are plenty of things that can make a scuff mark," Sanchez said.

"I know that. That's one reason I've been reluctant to put too much stock in it. But this meeting with Kessel is a game-changer. Taylor claims to have nothing to do with the man, now they're meeting on a deserted dock and exchanging mysterious parcels. On top of that, we also now know that Kessel showed up at the hotel two days before the murder. If we only knew what they were handing off. Maybe we can get a warrant to search Kessel's home. I guess we'd want to do his office, too."

"It sounds like an uphill battle," Sanchez offered.

She had a point. To get a search warrant, I would need to convince some judge that we had a reasonable expectation of finding evidence related to Markson's murder at the searched premises. What's more, I would have to specify what I expected to find. Unfortunately, all we had was a brown paper bag, contents unknown. Still, this drop was as close as we'd yet come to a breakthrough on the case. Though we hadn't named either Kessel or Taylor as suspects, neither one of them had inspired my confidence. Now we had Kessel at the Bal Harbour resort, and he and Taylor exchanging some object on a deserted dock.

And all this after Taylor tells me she hadn't seen the man in decades!

"You're right." I said to Sanchez, "A warrant wouldn't be easy. But if I really stretch it, I might be able to make a case."

"You haven't got a lot to go on."

"I've got motive, at least for Kessel, along with his visit to the hotel. And now this suspicious meeting with Taylor . . ."

"Good luck, Chief."

"Let me work on it." I looked around the table at my team. "Have we got anything else?"

"I got those fingerprints you asked for," Willis said.

"Anything interesting?"

"I turned them in to the lab. They'll have something for us later today."

"Were you able to get Taylor?"

"No problem."

"How'd she take it?"

He rested back and began to examine his fingernails. "The lady was a little surprised, but after I told her it was strictly routine, she took it calm enough. You want to hear something interesting? She said I'd make a good baritone. With a little training, of course. Apparently she appreciated the quality of my voice."

"You're such a lady killer," Sanchez said. "By the way, how's your little honey over at the Guantanamera Café?"

"We hung over the weekend," he said offhandedly. "I went to a picnic with the family. And when I say family, I mean the whole works. There was grandma and grandpa, aunts and uncles, cousins galore, children all over the place. I'd say their clan occupied a good quadrant of one of the city's parks. The food was to die for, that's for sure."

"So it's the *family* now," Sanchez said. "And how did you all get along?"

"Most of them were super nice. But I got to tell you"—and here his expression grew more serious—"there were a few rough-looking types there. They had the tattoos, hoodies, the whole racket. I wouldn't doubt if they were gang members, frankly. Heck, they're probably in our files."

"Wow," Sanchez said. "You really know how to pick em."

"Look," Willis shot back, suddenly defensive, "Rosie has nothing to do with those roughnecks. They hang with her sister, Talia. Apparently one of them—Stevie, I think his name is—has the hots for her. Rosie's not at all happy about it, let me tell you."

"Rosie's not at all happy," Sanchez crowed. "Listen to him! You'd think they'd been bosom buddies for years."

"What have I got to do to make you happy?" he croaked.

"Please," I interrupted. "You two are as bad as my kids. Willis, make sure you keep your nose clean, will you?"

"Naturally."

"By the way, have you got anything more on the surveillance system?"

"I've spoken to everyone on the security team who has anything to do with it. Run background checks. They're all spic and span. Ex-military, most of them. All of their alibis check out for the night of the murder. This isn't the first time it's happened, by the way, this glitch with the system. They've had their security contractor in, and they think they've finally got the problem sorted out."

I gave assignments for the day and broke the meeting. I kept Sanchez and Willis on the weekend shooting and told Simmons to keep watching Kessel. As for myself, I was going upstairs to speak to the Captain. A number of high-powered individuals had weighed in on the case, including the mayor, and the

Captain had asked me to keep him informed of any major developments. I told him that I intended to seek a search warrant on Kessel's home and business. I also requested another officer or two. I wanted to keep an eye on Taylor as well as Kessel, and I was going to need more manpower.

The Captain wasn't buying my case.

"What on earth have you got, Frank? A guy who doesn't like the way he's portrayed in an opera? Oh, and he makes an appearance at a resort frequented by just his sort of people every day? Now, there's the nice little singing teacher you've got a hunch ain't leveling with you. Uh-huh. And the fact that the two of them met somewhere. I'm going to need more than that, my friend. Kessel might not be squeaky clean, but he's got friends in high places, including on the Board of Commissioners."

"I thought you'd say that," I countered. "But you didn't mention the package. That package is what's eating me. She's supposed to hate the man. Why would she be giving him something? Why meet on some isolated dock? Why not visit each other at home, or at some café, like normal people?"

"Frank, it's not our job to know why everybody in South Florida does what they do. What we need is some kind of probable cause that will hold up in a court of law, and I don't see it."

Two no's from the Captain was all you got. There was no point in arguing the matter. I went back to my desk and spent an hour organizing my thoughts on the new case. Then I began to dig into the rest of our unsolved inventory. It was beginning to look like the Markson case would soon join them, moulder away in our files, perhaps forever, while we devoted our efforts to the mayhem *du jour*.

I hadn't been at it long when Ben, one of the fingerprint techs, called from the lab.

"I've got some news for you."

"Really?"

"We've got a match on that music score."

"Yeah?" I said. "Who is it?"

"It's this Olivia Taylor."

"Whoa! What about the statuette?"

"No matches there, I'm afraid. One of the partials could be, but there's not enough to be certain."

I thanked Ben, straightened in my chair, and tried to contain my excitement. The fingerprint match clearly proved that Taylor had handled the music score at some point. It was now therefore an irrefutable fact that she hadn't been honest with me, since she claimed not to have seen Markson before his murder. It didn't prove that she murdered him, or that she knew anything about it. Still, it was a shot in the arm just when I was losing hope on the case. I went back to the Captain's office and asked him to reconsider the search warrant for Kessel. I also wanted an arrest warrant for Taylor. She had been caught in a lie, I told him, and she was a proven master at stonewalling. It would probably take something more potent than another friendly visit to shake the truth out of her.

The Captain wasn't overwhelmed by the new evidence, but I wasn't about to let it go until I got my two no's.

"She claims not to have seen the victim for twenty years, and we find her prints on the music score he handled as he was dying. Come on, Chief, what's it going to take?"

"What about the weapon, that statuette? Anything there?"

"Not really. A possible."

Puzzlement covered his face.

"I know what you're thinking," I said. "Some medically challenged singing teacher isn't about to murder anybody, right? On top of that, how she could pull it off, even if she wanted to?"

"That about sums it up. Besides, you're also asking for a search warrant on Donald Kessel."

"I am, but let's assume you're right. Let's say Taylor couldn't have pulled off the icing. That's where Kessel comes in."

"What are you suggesting, that they're in this together?"

"That's a possibility. Who knows how crazy people can get."

"I can see a possible motive for Kessel—his portrayal in the opera—though it's pretty thin gruel, if you ask me. But what about Taylor? She wasn't portrayed unfavorably in Markson's show. In fact, from what you've told me, she and Markson were a romantic number when they were young."

"But that's just it, they *were* a number when they were young. And he deserted her!" I felt suddenly inspired. "Let's say, for the sake of argument, that she's carried around a buried rage all these years. From what we've learned about Kessel, he's got connections that are less than savory. There's a strong suspicion he had a witness taken out in a tax case ten years ago. Maybe Taylor and Kessel have been friendlier than she's been letting on, lovers even. We don't know what kind of tangled relationships existed between these people. Might exist still, for that matter! Or here's another thought. Maybe Kessel used Taylor to get to Markson."

"I think you've been watching too many operas. But you do have those music score prints . . ."

"And the package," I said. "That package drop is the thing that's really stuck in my craw."

"But what do you think you're going to find at Kessel's place?" he took up again, aimlessly sweeping through some papers on his desk. "In order to get a warrant, you have to be looking for something specific. You know that."

"We're looking for that package."

"Do you even know what it looks like?"

"A brown paper bag."

"Sweet Jesus," he said.

"Just let me run with this one, boss. I've got a strong feeling on it."

The Captain heaved a sigh and shook his head wearily. "I think the brown paper bag is pretty damned vague. But you do have Taylor's prints at the murder scene and, like you say, she's obviously been lying to us. I won't stand in the way of your applying for the warrants. Just don't tell anybody I okayed it."

I thanked him and left his office. I didn't blame him for being skeptical. Maybe I was grabbing at straws. Perhaps I *had* been watching too much opera. Lover's revenge, passion and all that. Or maybe it was just that the usual banality, another icing over money and drugs, had me bored stiff. Still I had to follow my gut, so I got my coat and drove over to the courthouse. It turned out to be my lucky day. The judge was a friendly: that is to say, not one in the same party to which Kessel regularly makes sizable contributions. She was no more convinced than the Captain, but she gave me the warrants anyway.

"Lieutenant Nelson," Judge Solinas said in a near whisper, "I've known you for several years. I know you're a solid detective, so I'm just going to take your word on this one."

My initial reaction was elation. In fact, I almost did a victory dance as I strolled over to the Bayside Marketplace to find lunch. But while I sat in Harry's Grill, watching carefree tourists stroll by, a sinking feeling began to take hold of me. With the sun shining brightly on all those relaxed and smiling people, and Biscayne Bay throwing off slivers of silver light, a nagging voice in the back of my head whispered that, in my ardor to solve the case, I may have gotten ahead of myself. It had been a long weekend, I reflected, working brutal hours on the drug shooting. My mind was on overdrive. I sat back with my beer, watching the tourists, and tried to calm my brain, ratchet things down to some normal kind of thinking . . .

I went through my encounters with Taylor and found it hard to believe, as I had all along, that she could have committed this murder—or even been party to it. The voices of the Diazes, Ralph Owens and Daphne Courtwright, decent people all, rang in my ears, attesting to her character and goodness. Now, of course, we had the lying, the fingerprints and the package drop. But still I couldn't completely wrap my mind around it. I didn't know what to think, to tell the truth. I felt confused, on thin ice. In some crazy universe I didn't understand. I didn't want to make a fool of myself or, what's worse, the Department.

Robin Markson came to mind. He was quite a different type than me, but I felt I would have liked him had I had the opportunity to know him. From what I saw in his opera, and everything I had been told, he seemed a guy that anyone with any class would like. Thoughtful and decent. He wasn't perfect, mind you, but who is?

What would he want me to do? I wondered.

I pondered the question all through lunch. Markson's opera came before me, and the way he had portrayed Olivia Taylor. I recalled their youthful joy and how, in that incredible farewell scene, she sang of her unconditional and undying love for the man. If she was the perp, she would have to pay the price. But there was one thing of which I was certain. Markson wouldn't want me to trouble Taylor unless it was absolutely unavoidable. Finally, after considering everything over coffee, I decided to pocket the warrants. For the moment, anyway. There were still a few days before the time limits ran out, and we could always execute later. It may seem crazy, after all the finagling I had done to secure them, but I didn't want to proceed until I felt more sure of myself. In my initial excitement over the fingerprint match, I had gotten carried away. Solinas gave me the warrants against her better judgment, so it was all on me. I didn't want evidence to get cold, but I wanted more clarity before we went barging into people's homes with lethal force, dragging them into the station, getting their names on the evening news. In a day or two, I figured, my head would be screwed on a little straighter.

I thought of Ralph Owens. He was the closest thing to a Robin Markson I had and, through his gal Daphne, my best connection to Taylor. I called him and asked if he could meet me again, six o'clock, at the Sheraton Bal Harbour bar.

After that I ran down Sanchez. She was knee-deep in the weekend shooting, but I asked her to take a break from the new case and meet me at the resort at eight.

I had an idea.

Chapter 13 (Owens)

"I GUESS YOU'RE GETTING sick of hearing from me."

I recognized Frank Nelson's voice. "Not at all," I said.

"I wonder if you'd mind meeting me again."

"When did you have in mind?"

"Later today. Six o'clock, if possible."

"Where?" I asked.

"The bar at the Sheraton?"

Given my strong reaction to the hotel on Friday, I thought of suggesting another meeting place, but decided that with Nelson's steady presence, I could handle it. "Are there new developments in the Markson case?"

"One or two."

I told him that I would be there and we signed off.

What might the new developments be? I wondered. I had thought about Robin Markson a good deal over the weekend. It was no doubt my experience with Daphne on Friday evening: how, after singing slyly allusive love songs to me, she put me off about spending the night. Our relationship seems to be coming to a place where something has to give, and I could not help but consider our situation in light of Markson's opera. It was his final statement about life, if you will, and for that reason seemed to command a special attention.

Among many and varied other thoughts, I could not escape the crucial conclusion that Markson, looking back from the vantage of his fifty-odd years, could see nothing he so much wanted to write opera about as Livy Taylor, the tender companion of his youth. With all the intervening years, a marriage and a daughter, and a career full of energy and inspiration, his essential touchstone remained that girl whom he had somewhat carelessly left behind as a young man.

I considered Livy Taylor, a woman of tremendous poise and dignity. She is a person of special grace and yes, female allure. If she has grieved over Markson, there seem to be few lingering signs of it. She goes about her life, immersed in her world of song, pouring herself into her students, and—all too rarely—sharing her still luminous orphic gifts in local recitals.

Daphne and I are still young, I reflected, as Markson and Olivia once were. What will become of us in the years ahead? I realized that I have no plan worthy of the name, and found myself willing to accept the possibility, spurred by Frank Nelson's pointed probings of our relationship, that Daphne wants something more solid than I have yet managed to offer. How much longer can we drift along as we have been doing? There is one thing of which I am certain: I don't want to end up like Markson, longing for a past that can no longer be retrieved.

When I arrived at the hotel I came across Nelson pacing inside the entrance. He peered up a broad set of steps, with a handicap ramp beside it, that led from the lobby to the garden villa wing.

"Looking for someone?' I asked.

Nelson turned. "Oh," he said, seeing me. "No, nothing like that. I'm just trying to sort through something on the case."

I didn't feel it would be right to ask what he was talking

about. He shook his head a couple of times, as if solidifying some conclusion he had drawn, and then approached me.

"Thanks for coming again," he said. "If this keeps up, we might need to get you a badge."

I told him that I would be more than willing to provide any help possible on the case, for as long as it might take.

"It really bucks me up to know there are still conscientious young people out there," he said. "We could use whole platoons just like you."

I assured the Lieutenant that there were many in my generation who could be relied upon to do the right thing.

"I'm sure that's true," he said. "It's probably the kind of youths I normally hang with. Mostly gang members. Why don't we get a drink?"

We walked over to the lobby bar and took a couple of stools. There were several other patrons, deeply tanned and flush with sun and ocean. A tennis tournament played on the television screen that hung from the ceiling. Nelson ordered drinks. Iced tea for him, beer for me.

"You said there were some new developments."

"You could say that."

I waited for more, but Nelson didn't elaborate. We drank together in silence until he spoke again.

"I imagine you've spent a good deal of time around artists and musicians."

"I suppose so," I said. "Through my work for the paper, I've met and talked to a considerable number of them. And, of course, there's Daphne."

"Right."

"Why do you ask?"

"I've been wondering," he said, "and maybe you could tell me, what kind of people they are. Because you see, I've never had that much to do with artistic types. On balance, would you say they're as reliable as the average person, not as reliable, or perhaps just about the same?"

Inwardly wondering whether Nelson's question was even a valid one to pose, I told him that it was certainly a difficult one to answer. "I guess you could say," I began, "that artists, as a group, are different in some ways than other people. I wouldn't draw too hard a line, however. Most people have something of the artist in them, even if it manifests itself only in their penmanship, or the way they drive a car or trim their hedgerow. As for those who devote their lives to works of the imagination, for whom art is a *calling*, there is probably some degree of qualitative difference. In such people there is greater need to express what is felt, and a greater desire—an irresistible one, actually—to make manifest the connections we all feel on an unconscious level, but which most of us are content to leave unspoken and unrealized."

Nelson squinted his eyes at me. I wondered whether he followed my exegesis, but his gaze widened and he said, "Right, go on . . ."

"As to whether artists are more or less reliable than the average person," I said, "that's probably impossible to answer. An uninformed person may think that artists are lazy, or that they lack both self-discipline and a proper respect for the customs and sensibilities of their fellow human beings. Others may opine that artists are show-offs, exhibitionists, or simply overly emotional. Impulsive, and thereby untrustworthy. There's some truth in all of those accusations, but each could also be said of many people who are not artists. The fact is, many artists work harder than most other people. They may be more emotional than others, and for that reason, it is true, they can be unpredictable. But that's part and parcel of their calling. For what is the purpose of art, if not to make manifest the emotional chaos the rest of us are required to keep under wraps, but without which we would all surely perish? Every man and woman, when you look at it, has to manage his or her emotions. Artists are also capable of doing so. Morally, some are certainly better than others. But like the general run of humanity, few are either saints or demons."

"It sounds like you've given the issue a good deal of thought," Nelson remarked.

"I guess I have," I said, "though I wasn't aware of it until you put the matter to me. But I'm curious," I added, "what brings you to ask such a question?"

"It's this thing with Olivia Taylor," he said. "It just keeps getting stranger and stranger."

"These are the new developments you referred to?"

"Yes, they are. But listen," he said, "I've asked you this before, but now I need to ask you again. Can I count on your absolute discretion?'"

I told him that he could.

"Well then," he went on, "we've done some fingerprinting. And get this. Olivia Taylor's prints are on the music score we found next to Markson's corpse the morning after the murder. Right alongside the bloody prints of Markson himself!"

"Really?"

"And this after she says she hasn't seen the man for twenty-some years. Then, over the weekend, one of our men witnessed her handing off something to her ex, who she also claims she has nothing to do with, on a deserted dock."

I was so flabbergasted by Nelson's report that I didn't know how to respond. We sat in silence.

"It's all pretty mysterious, don't you think?" he said.

"It's more than mysterious. Crazy, even. But I don't see what it all means. What's this about her ex? Kessel's his name? What was she handing off to him?"

"We'd love to know. We have a warrant to search his home, but there's no guarantee we'll find anything. Here's another complication. We've placed Kessel at the hotel two days before the crime."

"What do you make of that?" I asked.

"I don't know, frankly. The man has a good alibi, so we're certain he didn't murder Markson directly. We're considering the possibility of a hit, but Kessel seems too seasoned a player to make a cameo appearance on the hotel's security cameras two days before his paid assassin takes out his victim."

"You've got me at a loss." I stared into my drink.

"It could be that Kessel was merely at the hotel to meet a business acquaintance," Nelson took up again. "Either way, this meeting with Taylor over the weekend looks awfully suspicious. There's one thing we do know for certain. Taylor's fingerprints are on that music score, the one Markson handled with blood-ied hands as he lay dying on the floor of his suite."

"But what are you saying?" I still felt perplexed. "Has Livy become your prime suspect?"

"I don't know what to think." He stared across the hotel lob-by. I imagined he was searching through his mind for some-thing helpful, some precedent from his years as a detective. "She doesn't strike me as the kind of lady who would bonk someone over the head with a statuette," he finally said, but after a pause added, "but people can really surprise you."

"Lieutenant, I think I know enough about homicide cases to know that you need a motive. What kind of motive could Livy possibly have had for murdering Robin Markson?"

"Leaving aside the far-fetched," he replied, "like, say, rob-bery, I'd go with something more personal. Looked at from a certain angle, Ms. Taylor may hold Markson responsible for messing up her life. I mean, her illness was nobody's fault. But Markson deserted her when she needed him most. How would that make you feel? Anybody? Who knows how much rage she's lived with all these years. She may have gone over there with no intention of hurting him. It had been decades since she'd seen him. Now here he is, enjoying this great success, and she, who gave him the best years of her youth, is nowhere. It's possible they had an argument. She flies off the handle. All that pent-up rage comes out in one, superhuman effort. These artist types can be pretty emotional, impulsive. You said so yourself. I'm not saying she meant to kill him. Things happen. Who knows?"

I couldn't believe what I was hearing. Livy Taylor, murderess! Struggling to process it all, I sat shaking my head in disbelief.

"I know it sounds wild," Nelson went on. "That's the reason I wanted to talk with you. Along with a search warrant for Donald Kessel's place, I'm holding an arrest warrant for Ms. Taylor. Naturally, I'm reluctant to move forward if I'm out to lunch. I got to thinking about Mr. Markson, and I'm sure he wouldn't want me to cause any trouble for Ms. Taylor if I was off on some wild goose chase."

"But what are you asking me?" I got out after a moment, "—whether I think Livy could have murdered Markson?"

"Something like that," he conceded. But as I tried to find a way to respond he interrupted me. "Wait a minute," he said. "That's asking way too much. At this stage, not a man jack of us knows what happened. Anything else is nothing but idle speculation. I guess I just wanted to bounce my ideas off somebody, see how kooky they sounded."

"You've certainly got me wondering. You think you know

people, but . . ."

We sat and sipped our drinks, both lost in our own thoughts.

"If I could talk with Daphne about this," I offered after a minute, "I might be of more help. She knows Livy a good deal better than I do."

"I thought about talking to her myself," Nelson said. "But she seems awfully devoted to Ms. Taylor. Wouldn't she just go on the defensive?"

"Maybe. But her input could be invaluable."

"The thing is," he said then, his jaw tightening, "I can't risk a leak. If Taylor knew that she was now the focus of our investigation, she could secret evidence. Even abscond. If you were to speak to your gal, could you guarantee her keeping mum on it?"

"I think I could."

"*Think* isn't good enough," he rejoined soberly. Our drinks were getting low and he asked if I'd have another. I accepted, and we sat in silence while the bartender took care of our order.

"I know you and Ms. Courtwright have been dating for a few years now," Nelson said after the bartender set another iced tea in front of him, "so please don't take this the wrong way. But what I'm wondering is, how well do you really know her?"

I had trouble responding. Nelson, perceiving my difficulties, went on.

"I know it seems an odd question," he said. "But I've seen people shocked at the behavior of a person they've shared the same bed with for ten, twenty—even thirty years."

His remarks set me back on my heels. Here I was, sitting at a bar with a man I'd known only a week, and he was probing the most vitally important areas of my existence. More than that, he was asking the most important question anyone could have asked at this moment in my life: *how well do you really know her?*

I took a long, hard sip of beer and felt suddenly confessional. Nelson has a way of making you feel like exposing yourself unreservedly. Maybe that's what has made him a successful detective . . .

"I like to think I know Daphne pretty well," I began haltingly, thinking outloud, still mulling the matter. But then our experience at Saudade on Friday evening came to mind and I added, "There are moments, however . . ."

I hesitated.

"What is it?" Nelson broke in. "You seem reluctant to say what's on your mind."

"It's probably just one of those Mars-Venus things."

"As in, men are from Mars . . ."

"Yes, that. There are times Daphne and I feel so close, we get each other's way of thinking almost automatically. But then, at other times, her thought processes are like some unfathomable mystery."

"Welcome to the club, my friend." Nelson swirled the ice cubes in his tea. "But you know," he continued, watching the cubes circulate one last time before resting his elbow on the bar and turning to face me, "maybe they're supposed to be mysterious. In fact, sometimes I think it's only after you give up every attempt to rationally understand them that you really begin to appreciate the magical creatures they are. After all, isn't that why you wanted her to begin with? To bring some mystery into what would otherwise be a pretty dull existence?"

I couldn't argue with Nelson's reasoning. "Maybe I'm too fixed in my own way of thinking," I said, sorting through my own confused thoughts. "Or perhaps Daphne's goals and mine aren't as closely aligned as I'd like them to be."

"Really?" Nelson sounded incredulous.

"You probably haven't got the time . . ."

"No." He looked at his watch. "I've got a few minutes."

"Okay, then," I said, "if you're sure I'm not holding you up. Remember when we met the other night. You, Daphne and I?"

"Of course."

"Well, some of the things you said got me to wondering. You know, about different kinds of freedom, time running out . . ."

He took a slug of his drink and laughed. "I hope you won't pay too much attention to the ramblings of some old cop."

"But some of it made a good deal of sense. In any event, later that evening I went over to Saudade to see Daphne's act."

"She's a great singer."

"Yes, she is. But we had a talk, and, well, this is a little personal, but when I asked if I could spend the night, she put me off. What's more, I got this weird vibe from her—maybe it was just me—but that she was trying to tell me something."

"What was that?" he asked, though I sensed that he already knew the answer.

"The implication," I told him, "was that she would like more from me than what our non-committal dating relationship has so far been able to deliver."

Nelson rested his elbows on the bar and he smiled lightly. "She wouldn't be the first gal in the world who longed for a more serious commitment from her boyfriend."

"I know," I replied. "But I thought things could be different with me and Daphne. Her being a musician, I thought she could understand my situation . . . as a struggling writer . . ."

"She may be a musician, but she's still a woman."

"It may be hard for you to understand," I barged on apace, not willing to alter my line of reasoning, "but I feel like marriage, for all the good things you can say about it, would throw my life for a serious loop." I rested my head in my hands and massaged my temples with my fingers.

"How is that?" he asked. "I know you mentioned it before, but I'm not sure I completely get it."

I described to Nelson my long-standing dream to create a grand, great American novel, all the time and effort required, the need for solitude and peace. "What with making a living, and taking care of myself," I told him, "I haven't got half the time I need for writing as it is. If Daphne and I were to get married—and what's more, have kids—I can't imagine how I could fit in my literary work. On top of helping with household chores, and childcare, I'd probably need a more steady job. And that woud mean more fixed—and longer—hours."

Nelson thought in silence for a long moment, seriously considering, or so it seemed, what I had shared. "You'd be surprised what a person can do when he's motivated," he said finally, with an authority that was hard to question. "Who knows, you may be able to work out some alternative arrangements. You might even have a good deal more to write about, with a lovely wife, raising a family. After all, isn't that where life really happens, in those connections to others who mean something to us? Where people absolutely depend on each other? Isn't that where we find out what we're truly made of?"

His remarks sounded irrefutably true, grounded in some hard, real-world experience I could only guess at. But they ran against my own settled views. I have come, that is to say, to look upon all the working stiffs and Harry Homeowners with a sort of pity, convinced that they ignobly abandoned glorious dreams when they gave up the kind of freedom I still enjoy, a freedom from any commitments that cannot be broken at will . . .

Nelson seemed to read my mind.

"I know it sounds contradictory," he said, "but it's been my experience that it's only after you obligate yourself unconditionally to another person, or other people, that you begin to feel truly free. Because, you see, in tying ourselves unconditionally to others, we gain the freedom to be what we're built to be. That is, creatures who look after one another. I'm not talking about just for the moment, but for all of time. Of course you have to pick them intelligently. Make sure it's somebody worth devoting yourself to, to always be there for . . ."

He caught himself short, took a sip of his drink before he continued in a friendly, casual tone. "Look," he said, "I don't want to sound like I'm trying to tell you how to live your life. I'm sure there are plenty of right ways to go about it. But you might want to think about it. That Daphne seems like an awfully nice girl, and I get the idea you're pretty fond of her."

"More than fond. The truth is, I can only imagine how empty life would be without her."

Nelson shook his head thoughtfully. "Thanks for your time," he said, "but I've got to get going. Go ahead and talk to your gal about our new developments. That is, if you're sure you can count on her keeping it quiet. I'll let you decide."

He got up, slugged me gently on the shoulder with the side of his fisted hand, and walked off toward the front desk.

Chapter 14

I LEFT OWENS mulling over his life while he finished his beer. I really feel for these younger people, trying to wend their way through the world, hoping to make that special connection. I know it isn't easy, and I feel grateful that Lori and I got that one figured out. We have our occasional dust-up, like any couple, but we never question whether we're headed in the same direction. In a lot of ways, I guess you'd say, we are each other's direction . . .

I went to the front desk and asked for the manager on duty. A Marge Cantrell came out of the office. I told her who I was and asked if the hotel had a wheelchair that I could borrow for a while.

"Is someone injured?" she asked.

"No, nothing like that."

"Well, we do have one, but it isn't electric or anything, just the old-fashioned kind you have to push."

"That would be perfect," I said. Then I asked if the suite where Markson was murdered was occupied.

"No," she replied. "We haven't felt right about putting anyone in there just yet."

I told her I had some work to do in the suite, and she had the desk clerk program a key for me. Then she made a call about the wheelchair. I thanked her and took a seat on one of the upholstered chairs among the potted plants in the reception area. About that time Sanchez showed up.

"How's it going, Chief? You said you had an idea."

One of the housemen was coming into the reception area pushing the wheelchair. I excused myself to Sanchez and went to greet him.

"I think I see what you're getting at," she said when I pushed the wheelchair over to her.

"That's right. We're going to conduct a little experiment, and you're going to be the guinea pig."

"I'm game," she said. "But I'm wondering, besides Taylor's unexplained meeting with Kessel, what have we got on the lady?"

I told her about the fingerprints on the music score.

"Really? And she claims she never saw Markson?"

"That's right."

"Either Ben has made a rare mistake, or the lady's been caught in a whopper, hasn't she?"

"Looks that way."

"What about our love goddess?"

"Our love . . . ?"

"Venus. The statuette, the weapon. Any matches?"

"No luck there, I'm afraid."

"Lástima," she sighed. "Well, let's get to work. What do you want me to do?"

I pushed the chair over to the hotel's front entrance and Sanchez got in. I asked her to wheel up the ramp to the hallway that led to the villas.

"How did that feel?" I asked.

"Not too easy. If that lady wheeled this thing up this ramp, she's got more muscle than you would think."

We rode the elevator to the second floor corridor for the garden villas. I had her wheel into the room, checking for anything that might have created an obstruction getting through the suite. The front hallway was tight, but there was enough space for her to get to the living room. Next I had her work her way around the coffee table to where Markson's body had been found. We didn't have Venus de Milo on hand, but Sanchez used her fold-up umbrella to try and whack me over the head as I stood over the wheelchair. She couldn't reach me unless I bent over.

"Who knows," she said, "maybe he did bend over for some reason. Maybe she lured him close with the promise of a kiss. You know, some kind of female wiles . . ."

I told her that Taylor didn't seem the type.

"You'd be surprised," she said. "But it didn't have to happen like that. What if they were struggling? She could have been standing up, for that matter. Like you told me the other day, she doesn't necessary use the chair all the time." Sanchez stood up and took my arm, put it around her waist. "There," she said, "like that. Maybe it was him that wanted to kiss her. Then, while he held her, she could have reached over . . ." She reached behind her, toward the credenza where the Venus de Milo had sat. She raised the umbrella over her head and brought it down on me slowly . . .

"All right," I said, "I guess there are a number of ways she could have whacked him." I was starting to wonder what Lori would say if she saw me and Sanchez like that. Not that I thought Sanchez was trying anything funny. That's the last thing I would think. I released my hold and she got herself situated back into the chair.

After that I laid on the floor, right where Markson's body

had been found.

"So here I am—Markson, that is—dead now, or dying. I'm lying on the floor. What do you do?"

"Easy, I'm out of here."

"Can you get around me?"

"It's tricky, but with a little maneuvering"—she was grunting a little—"there it is. I'm out of here."

I stood up and considered Sanchez's trajectory away from the body. I remembered the crime scene investigation, the pool of blood that had seeped from Markson's head wound.

"I wonder if she could have gotten out of here without getting blood on the wheels?"

"That would probably depend on how fast he bled."

"It's something to check into. There could still be traces on the wheels of her chair."

Sanchez took a little notebook she always carries out the pocket of her suit jacket and made a note.

"Okay," I said, "where to now?"

She brought a hand to her chin and thought for a moment. "Putting myself in Taylor's shoes—or her seat—I don't think I'd leave through the front of the hotel. I just murdered somebody. In a fit of passion. I got carried away, and now I'm scared. I feel guilty. I'm not a cold-blooded killer, no career criminal. I've got to get out of here, but I feel like all eyes are fastened on nothing but me. I'm certain that everyone I meet will see murder written all over my face."

"Sounds reasonable." I moved over to the sliding glass doors, looked through. "We can rule out her leaving through the steps off the balcony. She'd never get that chair down. She'd have to leave the suite through the door to the corridor."

Sanchez agreed. "So if I recall right, that leaves two basic options. There's an elevator right around the corner, and one at the end of the hallway toward the beach. This one's closer, but she would have to make her way through the pool area."

"Let's try the close one," I said. "I think the lady would want to get out of this hallway as quickly as possible."

Sanchez briskly wheeled herself over to the door of the suite. When she maneuvered backward to open the door, one of the wheels of the chair ran up against the wall and scuffed it. "Ha—look at that," she said.

"Interesting."

We left the suite and waited at the elevator. When it reached our floor we took it down to the pool level and came out near the koi pond. It was around nine o'clock, about the time Markson canceled his dinner reservation at Carpaccio. The pool area was deserted. Sanchez struggled over the stone pathway that curved on a rise past the waterfall area and then descended around the cabanas. She used the friction of her hands to keep the chair from getting away from her. I could see the color rising in her face, the way she bore down on the wheels . . .

"How's it feel?"

"Not easy," she said, "but doable."

She kept to the margins as much as possible, avoiding the brighter lighting closest to the pool, and eventually worked her way between the tennis courts and the poolside bar, which had shut down at dinnertime. When she reached the terrace between the bar and the iron fence that encloses the resort grounds, she pulled up.

"Now what?"

"She obviously couldn't have gotten over that fence," I said. "She'd have to go through the beach gate."

"Fine." She remained still for another minute, catching her breath. After she recovered, she made her way through the gate and onto the paved pedestrian path that runs along the shore there. I knew the options from this point. Her closest route of escape would be up the path to the inlet, and then over to Collins Avenue on the sidewalk that runs along the inlet's seawall.

"The only tricky part," I said, "is there's a stretch of sand from the end of the path to where the sidewalk along the inlet begins. It wouldn't be easy to get through that in a wheelchair."

"How long is it?"

"About a hundred feet."

Sanchez grasped the chair's wheels and, hunkering down, said, "Let's get her done."

She wheeled over the level footpath's four blocks to the inlet and then, for the last stretch, plunged into the sand. She only bought about five feet, though, and she fought hard for every inch of beach.

"It's too damned hard." She panted with exertion. "My arms are burning."

"What if you had more time?" I asked. "Maybe she did it in increments. For all we know, she spent all night out here. Then again, depending on how she feels on any given day, the lady can get around as well as anybody. Maybe she pulled the chair the rest of the way, or just abandoned it here."

"Maybe, but this sand isn't so easy to walk through, either. And if she abandoned the wheelchair, she would have had to purchase another one. I don't know . . ."

Sanchez was probably right. If Taylor offed Markson, she most likely exited the hotel in some other direction.

We pulled the chair over to the sidewalk that runs along the inlet. Just to be thorough, I had Sanchez wheel out to Collins Avenue. Taylor could have caught a cab from there if she had somehow managed to make it through the sand. I would check back with Ocean Cab. If I struck out there, we'd canvas the other companies, see if anyone picked up a lady with a wheelchair on the side of the road. I figured we should also check with the other outfits on a possible pick-up at Taylor's house. Finally, just for grins, I would poll the nearby hotels and condos, see if a loose wheelchair had turned up.

We pushed the chair back down Collins to the hotel and conducted the same experiment using the elevator on the beach end of the villa corridor. That put us out near the tennis courts. Sanchez was easily able to wheel around to the service drive on the south side of the hotel and out to the avenue. The only problem was, that drive ran directly past the security office at the hotel's service entrance.

"She would have been pretty conspicuous," she said.

I agreed, let Sanchez go for the night, and returned the key-card and wheelchair to the front desk. It was an interesting experiment, but not as conclusive as I would have liked.

When I got to the house it was almost ten o'clock. The place was quiet other than a faint sound of music coming from Sara's room. The only light came from the kitchen. I found Lori sitting at the table with a cup of tea.

"It's awful quiet around here," I said.

"It's been one of those days."

"Is something wrong?"

"You could say that."

I sat catty-cornered from her. "Are you going to tell me about it?"

"It's Andrew, I'm afraid. And you're not going to like it."

"Like what? What's wrong?"

"I made him go to his room until you got home. I figured you'd want to deal with it."

"Deal with what?"

She messed with her tea, lifted the bag up and down a couple of times. "Skateboarding where's he's not supposed to . . ."

"What? Again?"

"A couple of uniforms delivered him to the house about two hours ago."

"Where was he?"

"That's the crazy part," she said. "It was the exact same place as last time, that nice town center with the brickwork around the fountains. It seems it's precisely the places you forbid them to use that are most attractive, and with a perfectly good skateboard park within walking distance!"

"Who was he with?"

"The same kids as last time. Tommy, whose parents are chronically AWOL, and whose breath reeks of dope. And Darryl, who's two grades behind in school now."

"I thought we had an understanding." I felt bewildered.

We sat in silence for a long moment. Then she said, "You know, hon, maybe Andrew thought you had one, too."

"Had one what?"

"An understanding."

"Huh?" I didn't get what she was driving at.

"Think about it. You promised to give his board back when he agreed to watch that opera, right?"

"All right, and I did . . ."

"And in the same breath you also mentioned practicing batting with him."

"So?"

"Well, look what happened. You got through all of fifteen minutes of baseball practice before you were called back to work. Maybe, from Andrew's perspective, you let him down on your end, so he doesn't have to hold up his end of the bargain."

"That's so screwy," I said after thinking on it a moment, "it might be exactly how that wacky adolescent brain is operating. I mean, he seemed cool with it Saturday when I dropped him at the house. After all, he knows what my job involves."

"Of course he does. He's a good kid, and he believes in you. And I'm sure he wants murderers to be captured and brought to justice. But he also needs his father—now more than ever, when he's trying to figure out how to grow into manhood. He's not mature enough to sort it all out in any logical way, so he does something like this as a way of getting our attention."

"This is that acting out thing you've mentioned before?"

"Mm-hm."

"They never cease to amaze me. But I guess he didn't ask to be brought into this world, did he?"

She smiled. "That was our doing, if I recall . . ."

"I recall, too, and with great fondness."

I kissed her. "Hello," I said.

"Hi."

"I better go down the hallway and talk with him."

"I guess you better."

I knocked at Andrew's door. Nothing. Nor did he bother to greet me when I opened it. I crossed the room to where he sat gunning down mutants on his gaming station.

"I hope you're not spending too much time on that stuff. It's awful violent."

He tossed his head in a gesture he sometimes makes to clear his bangs from his eyes. "No more violent than being a cop," he said flatly. He didn't move his eyes from the gaming station.

I didn't bother to point out that I hadn't discharged my service weapon in eight years. "Do you mind turning that off for a minute, so we can talk?"

"Sure." He took a couple last potshots before pausing the game. Then he just stared into the screen.

"Your mother told me what happened."

"I figured she would."

"My first impulse was to just get angry and punish you."

"I figured that, too."

"I think it would be more useful, though, to try and get to the bottom of how you could screw up so blatantly."

"It was just some skateboarding."

"We've been through this before," I said. "I know it's fun, and sure, it's not like you're out holding up liquor stores or shooting up. I'm proud that you're such a darn good kid. But that's why this is so puzzling. It's not that skateboarding is in itself wrong, of course. It isn't. But you know how much effort—and money—the city put into creating that nice space over there. It's a place everybody in this community enjoys. The last time this happened, if you recall, we went over there so I could point out all the craftsmanship that went into the brick and terrazzo, all the money the city spent on the place. As I remember, you clearly saw how your boarding was marring all that beautiful artistry. I can't believe you went back over there again."

I waited for a response, but he sat in silence, glumly looking at his frozen mutants. I don't know what irritated me more, the mutants or his silence. I did know that after my long day, I wanted nothing more than to sit down and relax, and my own kid wasn't helping me get there. I made my best effort to keep calm, but it wasn't enough.

"You realize how this makes me look at the department?" I could hear my voice tightening. "With all the bad actors we've got to keep track of, a couple of fine officers had to waste valuable time keeping some punky kids who ought to know better from wrecking up the community."

"So, you're calling me a punk?"

"I didn't say that." I sensed that I was getting off my parenting mojo. I was too tired for this, but I tried to explain. "You know how tough my job is," I said. "I've got a stack of unsolved murder cases yay high on my desk, and more going on every week."

"What are you saying? You haven't got time to raise your own kid?"

That stung, and the smirk on his face told me that he knew he'd hit pay dirt. Something ignited inside me.

I marched across the room and snatched up his skateboard. "Okay," I said, "if you can't be more cooperative, no more skateboard." Then I came back and pulled the plug on the gaming station. Kneeling beside the console, I confiscated the power supply. "This is gone, too. How's that for your wise-ass comments? Are you happy now?"

"I guess you are."

"I'm not!" I barked and slammed the door behind me. Sara had come into the hallway to see what all the racket was about. I forcefully calmed my breathing as I approached her.

"It's all right, sweetheart," I said, "just a little necessary disciplining . . ."

She raised her eyebrows. That didn't make me feel any better.

Lori was still sitting at the kitchen table when I returned.

"It didn't sound like that went too well."

"It didn't."

"Tomorrow's another day," she said. "You'll work it out. Sometimes it takes a few tries, but you always manage to find the right thing to do."

"I'm not so sure."

"I am. Come on, let's go to bed."

When we reached Andrew's room she sent me on ahead. I heard her crack his door. "Time for bed," she said. "And try not to irritate your father unnecessarily."

Something I couldn't hear came mumbled from inside the

room.

"I know," she replied. "But try and forget about it. Think more about what *you're* doing. Everybody has a bad day sometimes."

Chapter 15

ANDREW WAS IN THE SHOWER when I left in the morning. I called through the bathroom door that I would talk with him when I got home. Then, on my way through the living room, I got this feeling like something was caught in my throat. I went back down the hall, opened the bathroom door a crack and, with my face bathed in hot steam, said, "I didn't mean to insinuate that I thought you, personally, were a punk." I went back to Lori's and my bedroom, retrieved the power supply for his X-Box, and laid it on his bed.

The team was at headquarters for our eight o'clock. Seeing their expectant faces around the table, I realized they were waiting for some direction on the Markson case. We had Taylor's fingerprints on the music score, and there was the hand-off to Kessel. I knew how they felt, because I'd been in their shoes plenty of times. They were hoping I would say that we could move in for the kill. The satisfaction of catching a perp is fought hard for, and it doesn't come half so often as you would like.

I told them that I'd gotten the warrants.

"What are we waiting for, Chief?" Willis said. "Why don't we execute? Bust 'em?"

"I don't know," I said. "I've got a funny feeling on this thing."

"With all due respect," Sanchez said—and God love her, she said it with a smile—"don't you get a funny feeling on just about every case?"

Willis and Simmons got a kick out of her remark, and I didn't mind them having a laugh at my expense. With the mess at home, I felt like maybe I was due for a humility adjustment.

"Maybe I do," I said. "But I never want us to get too sure of ourselves. There's too much at stake. The safety of our community, for one thing. And when it comes to accusing our fellow citizens of grave crimes, there's peoples' reputations, the most precious thing they'll ever own."

That settled them down some, but they didn't seem thrilled. "The big chief and Judge Solinas weren't crazy about our case, either," I went on, "if you care to know the truth. I'd like to bust whoever killed Markson as much as anybody. But I don't want us going off half-cocked."

"But Taylor's fingerprints . . ." Simmons said.

"That's right," I agreed, "they're hard to explain. But I don't want to act prematurely. I'm not sure the fingerprints and the drop alone could win us a conviction."

"What about the officers watching the lady?" Sanchez said. "Did they have anything to report?"

"Nothing unusual. She stayed home all day Monday, gave a couple of singing lessons. In the early evening she watered her garden."

She turned to Simmons. "What about Kessel?"

"He spent most of the day at his office," Simmons said. "He only went out once, around one o'clock."

"Where to?" Willis piped up.

"I'm not completely sure," Simmons said. "After leaving his building, he ducked into this alleyway that runs along the side, and I lost him for a while. When I caught up to him a few blocks away, he was on his way to the bank. It's possible he stopped somewhere else in between."

Sanchez sat back in her chair, thinking. "I don't know about this," she said after a moment.

"About what?" Willis asked.

"Aside from his erratic route, don't you find it odd that Kessel goes to the bank himself, when he has scads of underlings who can run those kinds of errands?"

"I'm not sure what you're getting at," I said.

"I'm not sure, either. It just seems strange that a big-shot developer, with an office full of employees, runs his own bank errands. Call it a *feeling*, if you want."

She gave the others a knowing look.

"Maybe it was a personal matter," Simmons said.

"Yeah," Willis chimed in. "Maybe it was *real* personal, like something he didn't want anyone else to know about."

"Like something he got from Taylor in a brown paper bag, perhaps?" I suggested.

"What if he got wind that Slim here was tailing him," Willis said, "and went through that alleyway to shake him?"

Simmons' glance toward Willis didn't reveal a hint of emotion. He turned to me. "Can we search the bank?"

For that, I told him, I'd have to go to the chief again and back to Solinas. Sanchez had either pointed us toward a brilliant piece of police work or we were groping at the wind. It's often that mundane detail, the kind of thing you're tempted to pass by, that becomes the key to solving a case.

"First I think I'll slip over to the bank," I said, "ask a few questions . . ."

"What about the warrant on the lady? Taylor?" Willis asked.

"Let's sit on that for now. We can always execute tomorrow,

or the next day."

He looked frustrated.

"Think about it," Simmons said, turning to Willis. "It wouldn't be smart to bust Taylor before we find out what Kessel's up to. That would just tip them off. That is, if they're in this thing together."

"Chief's right," Sanchez said. "We ought to wait."

I was thankful to Simmons and Sanchez for coming to my rescue. The fact is, I simply had no real stomach for arresting Taylor. Maybe I felt sorry for her, after everything she'd been through with her medical problems, Markson and Kessel. Maybe I liked her. Then again, maybe my gut just told me that she couldn't be a killer.

"I'll make you a promise," I said. "If we don't get a breakthrough by Thursday, we'll execute the warrants. I'm not strong on the possibility of finding that brown paper bag, or anything connected with it. Kessel's way too smart for that. Just the same, I'll visit his bank. How about last weekend's case? Any leads?"

"No," Sanchez said. "We're getting the usual stonewalling. No one wants to talk. We're applying as much heat as we can."

"Keep at it."

"Will do."

"Anything else before we break up?"

"There is one other thing," Willis said in his off-the-cuff way, "—though it probably isn't especially relevant."

"What's that?"

"You remember Rosie?"

"Rosie?" Sanchez said. "You mean your little sweetie at the Guantanamera Café? You're really smitten, aren't you?"

"What are you talking about?"

"I can hear it in the way you say her name, that look in your eyes. Look, you guys. Look at him!"

"Who are you, for chrissake," Willis said, "Ann Landers or somebody?"

Sanchez laughed. "I think it's delightful, actually."

"All right you two," I said. "We've got work to do. Let's get on with it."

"That's what I'm trying to do." Willis laid a sidelong glance toward Sanchez. "Like I was saying, it's about Rosie. Or, to be more precise, it's about her kid sister, Talia."

"Isn't she the one who hangs with thugs?" Simmons asked.

Willis shot a withering glance in our newbie's direction.

"What about the sister?" I asked. "Talia's her name, you say?"

"Yeah, Talia. Anyway, I found out last night that she works at the Sheraton."

"Last night?" Sanchez said. Her eyes took in Simmons and me. "Things must be getting serious, two dates! Or is that—dare I say it—three? We may be going for a new record."

"Cool it, Sanchez," I said. "Didn't you hear what Willis just said? The sister works at the Sheraton."

"Yeah, along with a hundred other nice Cuban girls. What's that got to do with the price of cigars in Havana?"

"I'm not saying it has anything to do with anything," Willis said. "But if there's any scuttlebutt going around the resort staff—something, say, they don't feel comfortable talking to a cop about—I could work it through her."

"And how would you do that," Sanchez asked, "without blowing your cover?"

"My usual forte," he said with his smug smile, "creative police work."

"It certainly won't hurt to keep your eyes and ears open," I said. "We can use all the help we can get."

After instructing the team to stick with their assignments, I broke up the meeting. Then I went out to the lot, got in my car, and headed downtown to Kessel's bank. The manager was able to put me with the bank officer who had handled Kessel the day before. I asked her what his business had been.

"He just wanted to get into his safe deposit box," she said. "Nothing out of the ordinary."

"Do you happen to know why?"

"No, I don't. Is he under investigation?"

"Not exactly. We're just checking out some leads."

"I think it was about one o'clock," she said. "I walked him back to the safe deposit room and let him in. Then I left him alone, as usual. We always allow our customers privacy when they're at their boxes."

"So you have no idea what he needed the box for?"

"Not really."

I decided to take a flyer. "He didn't happen to have a brown paper bag with him, by any chance?"

She abruptly looked up from her desk. "Funny you should ask that."

"Why is that?"

"On his way out, he balled up a paper bag and tossed it into the trash receptacle. It caught my eye, because the first time he missed, and he had to bend down and pick it up."

"Which receptacle?"

"That one, over by the door. But your bag won't be there. The trash cans are emptied at the end of each day."

I went through the trash anyway, just in case. The girl was right. There was nothing but botched deposit tickets and old check stubs.

I thanked the bank people and rushed back to the station. It was time to go to Judge Solinas for another warrant, this time for Kessel's safe deposit box.

The Captain wasn't thrilled to see my shining face.

"My problem," he said, "is probable cause."

"So what's new?"

"Listen, I agree, there's a lot here that looks fishy. But that doesn't mean a judge will permit a fishing *expedition* through some financial institution. If you had some idea what you thought you might find, it would be different. You could say you're looking for the paper sack, but that's history now. Can't you come up with something a little more concrete? Something with the vaguest chance of tying your suspect to the crime?"

I groped for a response, until a spark of inspiration struck. "It seems ridiculous," I said, "but the one thing I can think of is that emerald necklace, the one that went missing from Markson's suite."

"You're saying the singing teacher wasted Markson so she could make off with a necklace?"

"I said it's ridiculous," I conceded. "I could see a crime of passion. But there's no way Taylor strikes me as a thief."

"Then why bring in the necklace?"

"You wanted something concrete. That's concrete, isn't it? It's worth fourteen thousand dollars."

"I don't think fourteen grand means diddly to a guy like Kessel."

"I don't either."

The Captain swiveled around in his chair. He stared out the window into the parking lot, the way he does when you throw him some curve ball he doesn't feel like dealing with.

"I've got a strong feeling about this one," I said.

"And the warrants you got on Kessel the other day," he said without turning around, "what's happened with them?"

"I decided to pocket them for a day or two."

"You had a strong feeling about them, too, didn't you?"

"I believe you're right, Sir. But then I got another strong feeling about them, and I decided to hold off for the time being."

He didn't say anything. Standing in front of his desk, I noticed his thinning hair, the shiny bald spot at the back of his head, and how bright the sun looked striking the date palms that surround the station's parking lot.

He swiveled around again.

"Nelson," he said, "you're a pain in my neck. But you do solve cases. I've got too much going on right now to sort through this mess any further, so I'm going to have to rely on your judgment. If you can get it past Solinas, it's okay with me."

Don't ask me how, but at the courthouse I was able to convince Judge Solinas that we had a reasonable expectation of finding evidence relating to Markson's murder at Kessel's bank. By the time I finished there, the bank was closed, so I decided to go in the next morning. I would take Sanchez with me. The bank didn't keep copies of their customers' safe deposit keys. We'd have to crack the lock, and that lady is a wizard with a drill.

I returned to the station and spent some time with paperwork at my desk. On my way to the canteen for coffee I passed the station bulletin board. It was covered with the usual notices: departmental directives, photos, and a slew of personal items (officers selling cars, somebody looking for a housemate). I slowed down only enough to take a casual look, but for some reason a flyer announcing a job opening jumped out at me. It said they were looking for an officer with at least ten years on the force for a community liaison position. Regular hours, it said. That's what caught my eye. *Regular hours.* I stopped long enough to read over the announcement three times.

While I relaxed with my coffee, the family was on my mind. I didn't feel good about the way I had handled Andrew. I could perfect my lectures on being responsible to a tee, I realized, but if I didn't invest more time in my son, it wouldn't amount to a hill of beans. What is that saying, *they have to know you care, before they care what you know?*

Lori was right, like she usually is about these things. I had let Andrew down, broken promises. Not followed through. Now here I was, demanding one hundred percent compliance with our precious adult rules and regulations. I wasn't thinking about things from my son's point of view. Kids have their rules, too, I reminded myself. There are things they can't help, like the need for their parents' time and attention. I thought about my drive out to the cypress swamp the week before. Whatever happened to the fishing trip I had promised him three years ago?

Lost in the shuffle, like so much else.

Then Lori came to mind. I pictured all the evenings she had spent on her own, keeping herself busy somehow. A beautiful and charming woman, who could no doubt have any man she wants. And what about Sara? Here she was dating. Before I batted an eyelash, she'd be married. In the wink of another eye, her kids would be in college. Where would I be?

Chasing down thugs, twenty-four-seven.

On the way back to my desk I stopped at the bulletin board and stood staring at that job notice. I wasn't actively seeking a career change. But with images of a less stressful life flashing across my mind—topped off by quiet evenings at home with the fam—it struck me, quietly but decisively, that that liaison position might just be the cure for what ailed me. The funny thing is, my self-image was so wrapped up in being a detective, the idea of a different kind of life also seemed to scare me in some way. I felt shaken inside, deep in my core, at the idea of making a change. After a minute or two I started to get embarrassed, standing there in front of the bulletin board, lost in confusion. I shot glances in both directions to make sure that no one was watching. Then I pulled the job notice off, folded it and put it in my breast pocket. I needed some time to sort out my feelings. In the meantime, I didn't want anyone else to go after the job.

Before settling back into my paperwork I resolved to have a good talk with Andrew when I got home. We could go out in the yard and toss the baseball around . . .

Midway through the afternoon I got a call from Ralph Owens. He wanted to meet with me, and he wanted to bring his girlfriend, Daphne, along.

"I don't think I've ever seen her this upset about anything," he said. "This whole idea of Livy being busted seems to crush her. She begged me to set up a meeting with you."

"We can't alter the course of a criminal investigation," I told him, "no matter how much it might upset people. With all due respect for Daphne's feelings . . ."

"I understand. But she's absolutely convinced that she can change your mind. If you'd just consent to meet us, I'd really owe you one."

I owed the kid one or two myself, I figured. Besides, maybe his gal had some kind of game-changer to share with us, something that would get Taylor off the hook. Nothing could have made me happier, to tell the truth. In spite of my resolution to get home early enough to spend time with Andrew, I found myself saying, "How about our usual spot, six o'clock?"

He hesitated for a moment, then he said that he and Daphne would be there.

I wrapped things up at my desk and left the station early. I wanted to go by the Diazes' to return their DVD. I also wanted to get their reactions to our latest developments.

They had just finished eating when I arrived. I stood in their doorway holding the screen door while Lily walked from the dining table and past the kitchen, which was just inside the condo's front door.

"We're having an early dinner," she said. "With José's hours at the opera, it's the only time we have for a leisurely meal."

"We'll have a break after this run, darling," Diaz, who now approached the door, said. "What can I do for you, Lieutenant?"

I told him I had come to return their DVD.

"Oh, thank you. I hope you and your family enjoyed it."

"They didn't join me for this one," I said. "I guess you could say that I enjoyed it on my own."

"I see."

"Also, I thought I might update you on the case, if you have a moment."

"We'd be interested in any information you might have," he said. "I have a few minutes before I have to skedaddle."

They invited me in, and once we were all seated on the balcony, I told them that our investigation had begun to focus on Olivia Taylor.

It was a good thing Lily was sitting down. Her face went white, and she gasped for breath.

"Livy!" she said. "That's incredible!"

"It's unbelievable!" Diaz piped in. "I can't conceive . . ."

I told them about the fingerprints on the music score, the meeting with Kessel over the weekend . . .

"There must be some explanation," Lily said.

"I'm sure she would never harm Robin," Diaz added.

"She doesn't strike me as a killer, either," I said. "But you'd be surprised. Things happen. People lose their tempers. They don't mean to kill . . . and then it's too late."

"I'm dumbfounded," Diaz said. He bent forward and held his head in his hands. "We just saw Livy over the weekend, at her recital. It's impossible to believe . . ."

"It is crazy," I agreed. "But the clincher is," I went on, "why has she been lying to me, if she's got nothing to hide?"

Lily had begun to regain her composure. "Can't we talk to her? I'm sure she could clear this up with a simple conversation."

"I've got to ask you not to do that. We're in the middle of this investigation, and if you were to interfere, you could make it impossible to find out what happened to Mr. Markson. You wouldn't want that, would you?"

Diaz took Lily by the hand. "Of course we wouldn't. We very much want you to solve the case. We just hope Livy can be spared any unnecessary discomfort or embarrassment."

"We haven't done anything yet," I said. "And we may not need to. If she's innocent, she'll be cleared in due time. Meanwhile I've got to ask you to maintain complete silence about what I've just told you."

Still looking bewildered, they agreed.

"I'm certain you'll find a perfectly reasonable explanation for everything," Lily fretted as she and Diaz walked me to the door. "Do please treat her carefully. She's been through so much, and she's such a sweetheart."

I told them that I'd proceed with all possible sensitivity and said goodbye.

From the Diazes' place I headed to the Sheraton. I wasn't looking forward to meeting with Owens and his girlfriend. I figured I was in for a repeat of Lily Diaz's upset about our investigation. I got there early and ordered a drink.

The usual suspects were at the bar, perfectly tanned, well-manicured types. There were a few men and a couple of women, all carefree and relaxed. One of them chatted with the bartender. The same tennis tournament as the day before was on the TV that hung over the bar area. A soft afternoon light poured in through the windows that gave out onto the beachside grounds.

As I sipped my scotch, I looked toward the hotel entrance and remembered them wheeling Markson out on the gurney. I wondered whether he had used the bar during his brief stay at the hotel. Perhaps he occupied the same seat I was in while he had a drink with Diaz, watched tennis while the two friends chatted about their own game or old times. Here was a guy who had lived a very different life than mine, involved in art and music, delicate and beautiful things. Not thugs and perps, narc addicts and serious jail time. But from what I'd learned, his life was not without its struggles or difficulties. It seems that few of us escape them. That's one of the crazy things about hanging out at places like the Sheraton Bal Harbour Beach Resort, where everyone seems so happy and contented, full of ease and comfort. If you don't think too hard about it, you can believe that their lives are free of trouble or care. But if you do think about it, you know it can't be so.

It's an interesting illusion, though, while it lasts.

I thought about Markson's opera, and especially about that man at the back of the stage, no longer young in years, who gazed over the Pacific Ocean and reflected back on his youth. He was thinking about Olivia Taylor, how they'd tried to be there for one another way back when. I can't say the man had regrets about his life, but he was recognizing the beauty of something for what it was. A real connection with another human being. I realized that I had that three times over—Lori, Sara, and Andrew—and felt damned lucky. I dug in my breast pocket to check for that job announcement I had pulled off the station's bulletin board. Just touching it gave me a sort of lift.

I didn't want to miss my chance to enjoy what even as sharp a guy as Robin Markson came too late to realize is what makes the world go round.

Lost in my thoughts, I didn't notice Owens and his gal until they were standing beside me.

"Thanks for agreeing to meet with us," Owens said.

"It's the least I can do." I stood to greet them. "You've been real helpful to me." I offered them seats and got them set up with a couple of drinks.

After they were situated I addressed Daphne. "I understand how upsetting this is for you."

"That's an understatement." She was already breathing harder than she should have been.

"I don't want you to think I feel any personal ill will toward Ms. Taylor. She seems like a real nice lady."

"You can't possibly know how nice she is."

"There are just too many things that aren't adding up."

"The other day," she said, "you mentioned her not saying much when you asked about her conversation with Mr. Markson. But you can't expect her to want to share her private conversations with everyone."

"That may be. But I imagine Ralph told you about the fingerprints. And the clandestine meeting with Mr. Kessel. Ms. Taylor told me she hadn't had any contact with Mr. Markson other than a brief phone conversation. So how could her fingerprints have wound up on Markson's music score?"

She shook her head. "I don't know. I'm no crime expert. But Mr. Markson certainly had his score at the rehearsals. Maybe he loaned it to someone. One of the singers, for example. They may have shown it to Livy. She often coaches members of the opera company."

"That's a little far-fetched, don't you think?"

"Maybe, yes. But not as far-fetched as Livy being a criminal. She's the sweetest, kindest person in the world. Not a murderer. When you tell it, you make her sound so sinister. You make her sound like someone I know she isn't!"

"Horrible things can happen to perfectly decent people," I said. "How do you know she didn't lose her temper? Maybe she threw that statuette. People do such things, you know. Push somebody. Hit them. They don't intend serious harm. And then, there they are, murderers."

She dismissed my comments with a resolute shake of her head. Her loose, dark hair rocked back and forth. "If you arrest her, won't she be on the news, in the papers? It would be so insulting for your officers to manhandle her, push her around. Lock her up. She's a great artist. She can't be treated like some common criminal."

"Wait a minute," I said. "We haven't gotten that far yet. We still have some time. A couple of days, anyway."

She looked me squarely in the eyes. "Lieutenant," she pleaded, "isn't there anything I can do to convince you that you're on the wrong track?"

"I'm open to suggestions."

"Could I talk to Livy about all of this? I'm sure there's a perfectly understandable explanation for everything."

"That's one thing I won't be able to permit," I said. "The integrity of our investigation relies on our suspects not knowing they're being surveilled. Ralph told me that we could rely on your confidence, and I'm banking on that."

She looked at Ralph. He nodded his agreement.

"Poor Livy!" Daphne shifted awkwardly and precipitously off her stool, pulled her purse from the seatback, and stormed off sobbing toward the front entrance.

Ralph got up to follow. "I'm sorry, Lieutenant," he said.

"She's just a little frustrated."

"Women," I sighed. "Not that I'd want them any other way."

Owens started to go. I restrained him with a hand on his shoulder, and he turned to face me.

"Yeah, Lieutenant?"

"Remember, I'm counting on your—and her—discretion."

"Don't worry. She's emotional right now, but she promised she would keep this under wraps. She'd never go back on her word. You can count on that."

I watched him stride out of the hotel and disappear into the early evening twilight, following his gal. I still couldn't understand why he wouldn't want to make it legal.

As I headed for home, it struck me that I had just divulged ongoing details of our investigation to not merely one, but to four separate parties. What's more, there wasn't a single one of them that I could say, with absolute certainty, wouldn't talk out of class. But I had known from the start that this case would be different, that the usual rules wouldn't apply. I felt it that first day at the crime scene, when I sensed that this Robin Markson character would change my life in ways I couldn't yet fathom.

I had a lot on my mind, and now I had to go home and face Andrew. I shouldn't have called my son a punk. Or even insinuated it. That was out of line. It wasn't true, for one thing. For another, how is something like that going to make a kid feel, when his own dad doesn't believe in him?

Just for some extra-legal skateboarding.

I'm no psychiatrist, but I'd been parenting long enough to know that a good portion of what went down with Andrew could be chalked up to venting my own frustrations on my kid. He was wrong to ride his skateboard in the town square. But I could have handled it differently, with a little more understanding for the struggles he was facing. I remembered how lonely and helpless I felt as an adolescent—until I met Lori, anyway. It didn't help one bit for me to blow up at him. The only positive side to the whole mess was that it made me confront the doubts that were slowly working their way into my own life, doubts about the pieces that didn't quite fit together anymore . . .

It was time to do some backtracking. I'd go home and have a mano a mano with the boy. Spend some quality time with him. The evening was young.

But when I got home, with dusk falling across the front lawn, the place was dark and empty inside. There was a note from Lori on the kitchen table. I'm at my catering job, it said. Andrew at Jeff's. Sara out with Joe. Dinner in the fridge.

Sara out with Joe. That was the boy from last week.

I took my dinner out of the fridge (a delicious roast beef sandwich with all the trimmings) and ate at the kitchen table. The place seemed quieter than I could ever remember. After I ate I put my plate in the sink and wandered into the living room. I didn't feel like watching the tube, listening to music or surfing the web. Once again I had scored some precious free time, I reflected, and once again, all I wanted was to be with my family. And they weren't there. They couldn't be expected to sit around waiting for me, I said to myself, in case I might eventually show up.

After a minute I went down the hallway and opened Andrew's door. I wasn't looking for anything in particular. I just wanted to see my son's space. His ball mitt hung on its peg on the wall. I remembered buying that mitt for his last birthday, securing that peg to the wall.

I told myself that somehow, some way, we'd be all right.

It got to feeling too lonesome inside, so I went out and sat at the picnic table at the back of the yard. While I sat there, sipping a brewskie, I reviewed the Markson file in my mind. We were going to execute the warrant on Kessel's safe deposit box in the morning. That seemed to promise a break in the case, but it wouldn't be smart to start counting chickens. It was perfectly possible that Kessel's bank visit had nothing to do with his meeting with Olivia Taylor. He had a brown paper bag with him, but for all we knew it was from a sandwich he bought for lunch.

Beyond that, there was my continuing difficulty with the idea that Taylor, a soft-spoken lady of culture and refinement, with upstanding friends and glowing references, had bonked Robin Markson to death with Venus de Milo—even if, by the crazy logic of our investigation, manifold indications seemed to be pointing in her direction.

But what if, I suddenly thought, my prejudices were clouding my judgment? Olivia Taylor was both female and differently abled. Each of those factors, to my mind, was practically a disqualifier for murder. Together, they seemed to rule it out entirely. But wasn't I being unfair, I asked myself, both to women and to the differently abled? That is, to assume that a partly wheelchair dependent woman couldn't commit a murder if she wanted to? I felt I owed Taylor some kind of apology, either for suspecting her unjustifiably of a heinous felony, or for assuming she was incapable of pulling off an icing because of her gender and health difficulties.

It was all too damned confusing, to tell the truth, and I pushed the case out of my mind. I thought of Lori and wondered if she would be home soon. It's great, I thought, to have one person who's always in your corner, even when you're making a complete fool of yourself. *You always find the right thing to do*. That's what she had said when we discussed my dust-up with Andrew. I was glad she believed in me like that, although

I questioned whether I deserved it. And her remark begged an important question. What's everybody supposed to do, including me, while I'm figuring out what the heck the right thing to do is?

Chapter 16

I WAS LOST IN MY THOUGHTS when the cell phone started to chirp. It was a struggle to wrap my mind around what I heard on the other end of the line.

It was Willis. His voice was muffled.

"I need back-up."

"What?" I asked. "Where are you?"

He gave me his location. It was a service road that runs behind a shopping center in Hialeah.

"What on earth are you doing down there?"

"No time to explain. Just back me up. Got to go."

He hung up. I rushed into the house, grabbed my keys and Glock and went out to the car. I put the siren on the dash and sped toward Willis's location. On the way I called Dispatch and asked for some uniforms.

When I reached the location Willis had described a couple of our units already blocked the service road. Their whirling blue lights fractured the still night. I parked and walked past them.

Willis lay in the alley. One of our uniforms knelt beside him and cradled his head. I showed the officer my badge.

"What happened?"

"Says he was jumped. Our units took pursuit but we lost them. We've got an ambulance on the way."

"How's he doing?"

"He'll live. Just beat up."

I crouched down. Willis had a couple of ugly contusions on his face and blood dribbled out of his nose and mouth. He peered at me through swollen eyes.

"I'm okay," he said bravely, "don't worry about me."

"Sure, you look great. Never seen you better. Why don't you tell me what happened."

"They . . . ambushed me." He spoke in a hoarse whisper. "I barely saw it coming."

"Who ambushed you? What were you doing down here, anyway?"

"Following them . . ." He tried to shift around to face me, but after grunting in pain, he gave up the effort and collapsed onto his back again.

"Don't hurt yourself. The ambulance will be here any minute." I let him catch his breath, and then I asked, "Who was it you were following?"

"Rosie . . ."

"You were following Rosie?"

"No . . . her sister . . ."

He rocked his head back and forth, groaned and went out on me. It was probably a concussion, I figured. At least I hoped it was that simple. An ambulance siren came crashing through the darkness. After they got him in I followed to the hospital.

It could have been worse. He was concussed and contused and two ribs were busted. They had also managed to break one of his ankles, but there was nothing that wouldn't heal in time.

I sat by his bed until he came around.

"I came as fast as I could," I said when he opened his eyes.

"I know you did, Chief. I appreciate it."

"No thanks needed. You'd do the same for me."

I gave him some water. He took a long draught through a straw.

"I could leave you alone," I took up again after a minute. "But if you feel up to it, why don't you give me the story while it's fresh."

"It was that gang Rosie's sister hangs with."

"Did you recognize any of them?"

"Sure. They knew me too, believe you me. Ouch!"

He had moved the wrong way.

"Hurts, huh?"

"The anesthetic must be wearing off."

I went out to the nurses station and asked them to send someone to the room. Then I returned to Willis's bedside.

"Okay," I said, "we were talking about this gang Rosie's sister hangs with. Why on earth were you tailing them?"

He turned away. "I realize this probably doesn't pass departmental muster, Chief. But it was . . . Rosie."

"Rosie? Was she with them or something?"

"No, Chief. It's like I said the other day. She's been worried about her sister, Talia, hanging with these roughnecks. So I decided to do a little case job on Stevie and his crew. See what they're up to. If I didn't find anything, I could reassure Rosie they're not bad actors. If I did, well, we could bust 'em."

"Let me get this straight," I said. "You went down to Hialeah to conduct an unauthorized surveillance, by yourself, without proper back-up . . ."

"Aren't I entitled, like any other citizen, to go where I want? There's no law against following somebody around, is there?"

"Willis, you've got to remember that you're a cop. First, last, and always. Anything you do takes on the color of authority.

We've got to draw a very careful line between our private lives and our public duty."

"I know, Chief." He grimaced. "I didn't think it would come to this. I was just trying to do Rosie a favor."

"What exactly happened down there?"

"There's not much to tell. Like I said, I decided to surveil these guys a little. Find out what their racket is."

"Yeah?"

"Rosie didn't know anything about it. She still thinks I'm a roofer."

"Fine."

"Anyway, after I finished my shift with Sanchez, working the new case, I went over to this crummy bungalow where some of these dudes live."

"Uh-huh."

"I did the usual. Waited around awhile. A little after dark six or seven of them came out and piled into one of their cars. I followed them down to that shopping center in Hialeah. They parked the car off to one side of the service road where it was covered by some brush. That by itself looked pretty suspicious. Then they sauntered off past the dumpsters behind the shopping center."

"All right, I get it."

"I parked my car, got out and followed." Willis's eyes took on a special kind of focus, like he was still peering down that dark service road. "I hadn't gotten more than twenty paces when I sensed that someone was watching me. That's when I called you." Again he tried to turn to face me, but grasped his rib cage, winced and turned away. He looked straight ahead, back into that dark night, his face clouded over with confusion and bewilderment . . .

"The next thing I knew, they were on me. I didn't have a

chance."

"Did you have your service weapon with you?"

"No."

"Badge?"

"No, I left them in the car. That way, if I got into some kind of fracas, I wouldn't blow my cover."

"At least you were sharp enough to think of that."

"You want to hear something funny? They said they knew I was following them all the way from the bungalow. They must have had a good laugh on me. Ouch!"

I went to the door and called down to the nurses station again. "Hey," I barked, "can't you get somebody in here? My colleague's in pain." I went back to Willis, gave him another sip of water.

"Did they say anything else?"

"Stevie did most of the talking. 'Listen, you piece of shit,' he said. 'I don't know what your game is, but you better cut the crap.' Then—get this—he asked me if I was some kind of informant."

"I'm not surprised."

"I'm just a simple working man, I told him. That's when they started with the kicking. They really ought to make ribs harder than shoes . . ."

He started to laugh but caught himself short with another wince.

"Anything else?"

"Yeah," he said. "After the kicking, Stevie grabbed me by the collar and got up in my face. Real close and personal. He said if I didn't tell him why I was casing them, they were going to waste me."

"I guess that got your attention."

"Not really. I told him the truth. That Rosie was sick of her sister hanging out with a bunch of bums."

"That must have gone over real swell."

"That's when they started with the face."

"I'm glad they didn't do worse. But those punks didn't know they were messing with one of Miami-Dade's finest. I'll see their wagons get fixed good and proper. You can count on that."

"Chief," he got out.

"What?"

"Do me a favor, will you?"

"What's that?"

"Don't go after them just yet."

"What? Don't you want to see them busted?"

"Of course I do, just not right away. I've got a hunch I might be onto something here. Something bigger than an assault charge, that is."

"Sure, they're probably involved in some criminal enterprise. Drugs, most likely. But remember, Willis, we're homicide detectives. We've got eleven unsolved murders on our hands this very moment. We can't afford to go following every whiff of criminality all over the Sunshine State."

"I'm just asking you to do this one favor for me. You're always saying that hunches are important. Well, I've got one on this thing."

I figured what Willis had was two broken ribs and a seriously injured pride. In brief, the whole thing was way too personal for any good to come of it. Still, lying there with his torso bandaged, his foot in a cast, and his face looking like Frankenstein's monster on a bad day, he was hard to say no to.

He reached over and took me by the arm. "Chief," he said, "this girl . . ."

"Rosie?"

"Yeah, Rosie. I know we practically just met, but I've never felt this way about a woman before. There's like this strange need to take care of her. Protect her. It's as if I'm responsible for her or something. I don't know what it is, but . . ."

I would have told him exactly what it was, but I didn't want to alarm him while he was injured. "All right," I told him. "we'll do this one your way. You're going to need some time to heal. I won't pursue this thing until you're back on your feet. Then we can talk it over. Good enough?"

"Good enough."

The nurse finally came in with the pain meds, and I left the hospital. They were supposed to keep Willis overnight. I'd check back with him in the morning.

When I got home it was the wee hours and I slipped into bed beside Lori. She turned over just enough to kiss me, grunted and rolled over again. I was worn out but couldn't sleep. There was too much going on. In the morning we were going to Kessel's bank. Whether or not that turned up anything, I had promised the team we would execute the other warrants on Friday, two days away. We would arrest Taylor and search Kessel's home and offices. I wasn't particularly jazzed by any of it. I used to get as much a thrill out of these operations as the next guy, busts that promised that longed-for closure on our cases. But it was increasingly coming to feel like been-there-done-that. Maybe I was growing out of what by rights was a younger man's—and woman's—game.

I wondered how Andrew was doing. I didn't want him to become one of those sullen teens who hates his old man. At least I didn't want to give him any good reason to hate me. And what about Sara and this Joe character? Could young Joe be the me that I had been to her mother? Could it be that serious? Lori and I were no older than them when we first started dating. It was way too early to tell, but still . . .

I should have been sleeping, but the middle of the night is when I get most of my discretionary thinking done.

I eventually dropped into a deep snooze, but before I knew it the six-thirty alarm hit me like a slap in the face. Sanchez and Simmons were waiting at the station. I could see that they were anticipating big things from the search of Kessel's deposit box. Though I didn't share their enthusiasm, I understood it. Since Simmons didn't have anything pressing on his agenda, I invited him to ride along. After all, he had been the one who made the connections on the brown paper bag. On the drive over I reminded both of them to exercise the utmost courtesy toward the bank's officers and staff.

After I went through a couple layers of red tape, the lady I had spoken to the day before let Sanchez and Simmons into the safe deposit room and showed them the box. I stood outside the door and chatted with the bank manager while they drilled the lock.

Sanchez's face lit up like a Christmas tree the moment they opened the lid. Simmons held the box while she lifted out a mass of that fluffy white paper they wrap gifts in. She dug into it and there it was, a fourteen thousand dollar emerald necklace.

She brought the bling out to where I stood with the bank manager, and when she dangled it toward the windows it caught the morning light in a thousand different ways. You almost wanted to shield your eyes. She held its ends up to either side of her neck like she was wearing it.

"Not bad, eh?" she said.

I asked to see it and she handed it over. I wanted to sense the weight of it, see what it felt like to hold in my hand. It had real substance, a definite and inescapable mass. I thought about Markson, what he must have felt like when he purchased it.

Whoever he bought it for must have been as radiant to him as the gems that studded its chain, hanging in sizable teardrop shapes.

Sanchez and Simmons were jazzed. This seemed to nail our case, even if it was over-the-top bizarre. That necklace was the last thing I had expected to find, in spite of the stipulations in my warrant request. We discussed it on the way to the station.

"I just can't believe the motive could be robbery," I said. "A crime of passion I could understand. But Taylor doesn't strike me as the type who would knock someone off for a necklace, no matter how posh it is."

"Whatever the motive," Sanchez said, "she had the goods. On top of that, she lied to you about it—among other things— and handed it off to Kessel in a highly suspicious manner."

"What if," Simmons began, reasoning out loud, "she went to see Markson. She was still angry, after all these years, about the way he'd abandoned her. She sees this necklace, which, let's say, he had bought for some young honey he was interested in. That would be the normal thing, wouldn't it?"

"Fine, go on."

"The rest is obvious, isn't it? She flies into a jealous rage, knocks him over the head with the statue. Maybe she throws it at him, gets a lucky shot. Then she figures, what the heck, here's the necklace, I may as well take it. She may have felt like it was her due, that, somehow, it should have been hers."

"I don't know," I said, "but I like the way you're working. Keep it up."

"What about the Kessel angle?" Sanchez said. "Why would she hand it over to him? And why was he lurking around the hotel, two days before the murder?"

"Got me," Simmons said.

"Maybe we'll have to ask them."

"So, we're going to bring them in?" Simmons asked.

I hesitated to respond. Despite the now crushing mountain of evidence pointing to Taylor, I was still having a hard time with the idea of arresting the lady.

"Chief," Sanchez said, "Simmons asked if we're going to book them."

"Of course we are." What else could I say, with the two of them looking at me like that? By any logic you could conceive of, both Taylor and Kessel were mixed up in Markson's death.

We already had an arrest warrant for Taylor, and to be on the safe side, I told them, I would also get one for Kessel. I would put everything in place for the arrests that afternoon, and we'd conduct them first thing in the morning.

I dropped Sanchez and Simmons at the station and drove to the hospital. When I got there Willis was being prepped for discharge. The swelling in the eyes had gone down and the doctor said there had been no injury to vital organs. They had set him up with a pair of crutches and he had a patch over one eye. He walked slowly out of the hospital, groaning with each step.

I drove him to his place, got him situated and asked if he needed anything.

"I'm fine, Chief. Don't worry about me. I'm just sorry I can't be in on those busts tomorrow."

I promised that I'd give him a full report. "Just get yourself well," I said. "And don't hesitate to let me know if there's anything I can do for you."

We said goodbye and I drove to the station. My first stop was the Captain's office.

"I can't conceive how," he said, "but it looks like you may have actually stumbled onto something."

"I prefer to think of it as the seasoned intuition of a veteran investigator."

He laughed. "Yeah, and I prefer to think that you're full of crap."

"We do have the perps."

He looked up at me from under his brow. "Pride goeth before a fall . . ."

He had me there. "You're right, Chief," I said. "Who knows where this thing might go from here."

"We'll see."

That's what I loved about the Captain. He was always so damned unmovable about everything.

I went to my desk and put together a plan for the busts. Then I went to the courthouse to get the second arrest warrant from Judge Solinas. She was as surprised as the chief that my hunches about Taylor and Kessel had yielded pay dirt.

"Lieutenant Nelson," she said in that world-weary way of hers, "you never cease to amaze me."

Chapter 17 (Owens)

I RECENTLY READ A BOOK by an anthropologist who studies the evolution of man and woman, and how these disparate creatures have struggled together through eons of existence on this planet. Men and women are built so differently, this scholar argued, in terms of their hormonal drives and reproductive imperatives, that we would profit by seeing them as two separate species, utterly distinct, who have negotiated a nearly unbridgeable gap in order to ensure the continuation of *homo sapiens*. I don't know that I would go so far, but there are times when I would almost subscribe to the concept . . .

I have just seen Daphne, and I am still reeling from our conversation. First let me state the bald fact: she has divulged every detail of Lieutenant Nelson's investigation to Livy Taylor.

I was flabbergasted.

"You gave me your word that you would keep all this to yourself," I said, not without a hint of pique in my voice.

"I don't remember giving my word, per se."

"Now, honey, don't start with the *per se*. You either gave your word or you didn't. When I told you that I had news of the investigation, but I couldn't share it unless I could count on your confidence, didn't you agree?"

"I don't remember agreeing."

"If I remember correctly, you moved your head in the up and down motion that normally means yes, isn't that right?"

"Maybe I was simply indicating that I understood, not that I had agreed to anything!"

I threw up my hands in exasperation. "Didn't Lieutenant Nelson make it plain that the integrity of his investigation rested on our continuing discretion?"

"He may have," she said off-handedly. "I can't be expected to remember everything anyone ever said." This was followed by one of those prolonged silences, where I sometimes feel like some early Egyptologist staring at a bunch of indecipherable hieroglyphics, trying to figure out what she's thinking.

"Doesn't Nelson's investigation mean anything to you?" I finally ventured.

"No," she said flatly. "Livy has never hurt anyone, and I know she never could. So if the integrity of Nelson's investigation means that he's going to hassle Livy, his investigation has no integrity, as far as I'm concerned."

How could I argue with logic like that? The worst part was, I couldn't help realize that there was some kind of logic going on there. It was simply different than my kind of logic. Maybe it was the logic of a completely different species, who could say?

"But I gave Nelson my word," I protested. "What am I going to tell him now?"

"Is that all that matters," she returned sharply," what you're going to say to Lieutenant Nelson? Where do we women fit in with this good old boys' network, if I might ask? But I don't guess that matters, as long as you have your honor and your secret handshakes, the integrity of your investigation and all that nonsense . . ."

Why was my Daphne suddenly channeling Gloria Steinem?

"Honestly," I said, "I don't know what you're talking about."

"You don't know what I'm talking about, really? Look at Robin Markson. He abandoned Livy just when she needed him most. Now he's the lauded artist, and where is she? The subject of a criminal investigation, about to have her life turned upside down. Humiliated and abused. What has she ever done, except to extend her caring to everyone around her?"

She was tearing up.

"How can any of us know what really happened between Markson and Livy?" I put in.

"You wouldn't know, that's for sure."

I was thrown for a loop by that one, for I vaguely knew where this was heading, and I didn't welcome it. "Wait," I nonetheless said, "what do you mean by that?"

"If you don't know, maybe it's not worth explaining."

She clearly had me on the defensive, and she was pressing her advantage. I felt it. We were coming to that point where I would be brought to my knees before the Goddess. I knew it would be painful, but possibly my only means of salvation . . .

"But I think you *should* explain it," I said.

"Okay then, I will. What I mean," and now she spoke with careful deliberation, "is this. Do you know what it means to be devoted to someone, to make a once and forever decision to be there for them, no matter what?"

I was speechless.

"That's what I thought," and now she began to openly cry. "Well, Livy knows," she murmured through her tears, "and I know. Most women know. And we're left standing around waiting for some man to finally grow up and understand that the world doesn't revolve around his plans and ideas, his enthusiasms of the moment. You all want love, but you don't have the vaguest idea how to give it!"

"Honey," I said, "what you're saying hurts."

"I've kept it inside for too long. Now I see it all clearly, and I can't keep quiet any more." At that she gave herself over to a sort of fractured weeping.

I tried to put my arms around her but she shrugged me away. How I felt it, the pain of the Goddess wisdom! The wisdom I both craved and fled!

"Life isn't only about you men, you know." She had recovered herself a little. "You can have all the laws you want, all your promises and discretion, but it's not right to break peoples' hearts. I don't care what you say. Livy's has been broken enough. And I'm not going to sit by and watch somebody else hurt her. I just can't."

I was through trying to win this one.

"I'd better call Lieutenant Nelson."

"If you love me, you won't."

"Daphne," I said, "you're being unreasonable."

"I don't think I am."

"I hope you aren't letting what you feel about our relationship color your thinking on this."

"How can it not?"

I was thoroughly defeated now, and I knew it. For I could not deny that I too wanted our relationship to color her thinking—every bit of it, if possible. I left her apartment, hearing her sobs behind me as I strode down the walk.

Chapter 18

AFTER I LEFT the courthouse I went back to the station and met with what was left of my team, Sanchez and Simmons. I assigned Sanchez to the Kessel warrant. I wanted to go to Olivia Taylor's place myself. After my discussions with the Diazes and Daphne Courtwright, I felt personally responsible for making sure the lady was treated with all due care. Sanchez would take Simmons along, and we would put a team of uniforms at her disposal.

I was afraid Kessel could be trouble.

It was late afternoon when we finished. I went to my desk and called Willis. No answer. I decided to go by his place and see how he was doing. His car wasn't in the drive when I got there, and he didn't answer the door. I figured he must have gone to the drugstore or needed groceries.

After waiting for an hour I started to get worried. Where would the guy be in the shape he was in? What if, I got to thinking, the punks that jumped him the day before came back to finish the job? It would probably fit their MO to take his car while they were at it.

Chastising myself for letting him talk me out of busting them, I got out of the car and went around back. I peered in through the kitchen window but couldn't make out much inside. The place was dark and looked deserted. I knocked on the door and rang the bell. Nothing. I waited another half hour.

No Willis.

I retrieved a crowbar that I carry in the trunk of the car and pried open one of the windows at the back of the house. I wanted to make sure Willis wasn't inside, dead or dying in a pool of blood. I was relieved to discover that he wasn't there.

I called the Captain and asked him to put out an APB on Willis's car.

"Don't you think you're overdoing it?"

"Who knows?" I said. "Maybe I am a little spooked, after what happened yesterday. But the guy wasn't in any condition to be going out."

"If I know Willis," the Captain said, "he's at one of the local watering holes, salving his troubles with a few stiff drinks and a pretty smile."

"You're probably right," I conceded. "It's just you get to thinking about these guys like they're your kids or something. It's terrible what they put you through."

"Been there."

"Yeah, I know." I signed off.

The mention of kids made me think about the ones I made with Lori and I decided to head home. With everything set for the warrants, the Markson case seemed to be cracking. I still didn't know how all the pieces would fit together. But I was confident the answers would come after we got Taylor and Kessel in the station and one or the other of them started talking. Our latest case was next in the queue, but the idea of taking it up again left me flat. It looked like another senseless shoot-up over a few measly dollars, bragging rights or some thug's over-extended ego getting bruised.

While I was driving I got to dwelling on that liaison position from the bulletin board. I was still carrying the notice around with me. Sure, somebody had to take responsibility for getting these bad actors off the streets. But I was beginning to seriously consider the idea that that somebody didn't have to be me.

When I got home everybody was sitting down to dinner. They were surprised to see me come through the kitchen door.

"Why is everybody looking at me like that?"

"We just didn't expect you home so early," Lori said as she came around the table.

"It looks like we've wrapped up a case, so I thought I might knock off at a decent hour for a change."

"I'm delighted." She kissed me and went to the stove to put together a plate for me. Sara said hello, but Andrew just stared sulkily at his food. I took my seat at one end of the table.

"What's up?" I said.

"We were talking about Sara's preparations for her Spring Fling date."

"I see. Would this be the same fellow you went to the movies with last week?"

"Yeah, that's him." She blushed a little.

"Now he's invited you to the school dance?"

"Not exactly."

"What do you mean, not exactly?"

"Things aren't quite the same as when we were young, hon," Lori said.

"I invited him, Dad," Sara volunteered cheerfully, spreading butter on a piece of bread.

"I certainly hope he's worth it."

"It's just a dance," she said matter-of-factly. "It's not like we're getting married or anything."

"I'm glad to hear that, anyway. What about you, sullen-face? How's your day going?"

As soon as the words left my mouth I knew I was on the

wrong tack. I just hated to see my son acting like that. He put his napkin down and left the room. Lori called after him, but I asked her to let him be.

"It's all right," I said. "I'll take care of it after dinner."

Lori and Sara and I chatted about the dance and one of Lori's upcoming catering jobs. After we all finished eating, I went down the hallway and knocked on Andrew's door. He didn't answer.

I opened it a crack.

"I come seeking peace."

"Then don't be calling me sullen-face."

"Fair enough." I felt like I was more on my parenting game than I had been for our last conversation. I sat on the edge of his bed, he at his X-Box.

"I didn't mean to suggest that you personally were a punk the other day." I searched my brain for the right words. "I just meant that busting up community property is . . . a punky kind of thing to do."

He shook his head in agreement. It seems he had thought about things in a more mature light, and he was now back on his son game. His bangs hung down over his lowered face.

"The fact is, I think you're a pretty great kid."

The color returned to his face, the vaguest hint of a smile.

"It was still wrong to ride your board in prohibited areas, of course."

"I know."

We sat watching mutants dash across the screen, ducking behind buildings in burnt-out landscapes, while I struggled to find something meaningful to say to my son: something to make him realize that I loved him, that I wasn't the enemy. I wanted to honor the connection we shared, and to let him know that I cared about that connection as much as anything in this world.

"I haven't been around as much as I'd like to be," I said. "There's always so much work to do on these cases, and it seems like they never stop coming at me."

"I know. Mom says you don't like to let anybody down."

"That may be true. But most of all, I don't want to let you and the rest our family down."

"You're not."

Like I told you, he's a good kid. A great kid.

"I don't know about that," I said. "But I want to tell you this. Things are going to be different around here. I'm looking into another job, one that won't require such long hours."

"I didn't know that." He turned to face me with an expression of eagerness. The truth is, I didn't know that I was applying for the job myself. I had been mulling it over, sure, but it wasn't until I looked into the eyes of a son who needed me that I realized that there was only one right decision to make.

"It's a new development," I said. "The fact is, your mom hasn't even heard. I suppose you're the first to know."

"Does that mean you won't be a detective anymore?" He looked a little disappointed. I think he had grown accustomed to the idea of his old man collaring bad actors.

"I won't be solving cases directly. But public liaison work—that's what this job is—is an important part of the law enforcement picture. If we don't have the cooperation of the community, doing our jobs can be practically impossible."

"I can see that." He bobbed his head up and down the way he does.

"Look at me," I said. "I'm talking like I already have the job, and I haven't even put in the application."

"I bet you'll get it."

We sat in silence a moment.

"Are you sure you won't mind your old man not being a detective anymore?"

"Heck no, Dad," he said. "The fact is"—he looked back toward the X-Box screen—"you'll always be some kind of hero to me, whatever you do."

It takes an awful lot to make a hardened homicide cop shed tears, but the kid just about did it with that one.

"Come on, let's go out back and toss the hardball around a little . . ."

Later that evening I got a call from Willis.

"Thanks for coming around to check on me," he said. "Sorry I stood you up."

"Where the hell were you? I didn't figure you'd even be out of bed."

"I had some things to do."

"Not messing with those pals of Rosie's sister, I hope."

He didn't say anything.

"Willis, I'm talking to you."

"Chief, don't worry about me. I'm a big boy. I can take care of myself."

"Sure you can. How are those ribs?"

"They're just ribs. Nothing to write home about."

"Willis?"

"Yeah, Chief?"

"Don't do anything stupid."

"Me, stupid?"

In the morning I met the team at the station. We went over our instructions with the uniforms and headed out. It was nine o'clock when I pulled up to Taylor's residence. Her maid Alice answered. I showed her my badge and told her who I was.

"I remember you," she said. "We've been expecting you."

Expecting me! What on earth was she talking about? "You must be mistaken," I said. "I didn't make an appointment."

"Just the same, we were expecting you."

I didn't get it, but it didn't look like an explanation would be forthcoming. "Can I speak to Ms. Taylor?"

"I'm afraid she isn't here."

"Do you know where she is?"

"She didn't say where she was going. She just had to get out. She knew you'd be coming, and she wanted to go someplace where she could think a little."

"How long ago did she leave?"

"About half an hour."

"How'd she go?"

"Called a cab."

"Ocean?"

"Yup, same as always."

I went to my car and got on the phone. After I waited in a queue for ten minutes Ocean Cab was able to contact their driver. They gave me Taylor's destination. The cabbie had dropped her at the Sheraton Bal Harbour. I headed for the beach. On the way I dialed up Sanchez.

"How's it going over there?"

"Smooth as glass," she said. "Kessel didn't have a clue and didn't give us any trouble. He barked a little, but I have to admit, he's been a regular gentleman about the whole thing. We're on our way back to the station with him."

"Do you think Simmons can carry on without you?"

"I don't see why not. Why do you ask?"

The fact is, I didn't relish encountering Taylor on my own. I was prepared for a simple meeting at her home and a quick ride to the station, but I wasn't comfortable with the idea of running her down. It wasn't just that she was a woman, though that had something to do with it. It was a sort of delicacy I had seen in her, something I was afraid I might break.

"I could use some help."

Sanchez agreed to meet me in the parking lot of the Shops at Bal Harbour. Then we'd find our suspect.

The day had dawned sunny and clear, but when I arrived at the Shops roiling black clouds poured inland from the Atlantic. The premature twilight must have confused the boat-tailed grackles, because they were roosting in the manicured laurels the way they usually do at day's end. The air was filled with their twittering and squawking.

I sat and waited for Sanchez.

When she arrived I went to her car. She got out, pulled a raincoat from the back seat and put it on. We walked across Collins Avenue.

The hotel lobby was like it always was. Guests lolled or lounged or rushed around, depending on their mood and what they had on their agendas for the day. Some sat near the windows that looked out toward the shore, watching the drama unfolding in the heavens.

Not one of them knew that we were about to collar a murder suspect.

Sanchez and I split up. I asked her to check the hallway where the villas had their indoor entrances, and from there go out through the lobby bar, over the jungle bridge and around the hot tubs and cabanas. I told her that I would meet her at the pool bar, near the beach. I then went downstairs to where there was a café and a few fancy shops and out to the beachside grounds on the lower level. I passed the koi pond and climbed up around the kiddie pool. There was no sign of Taylor anywhere.

When I got to the poolside bar the lifeguards had cleared

the water. The more eager of the bathers milled around in their wet suits hoping the weather threat would blow over. The kids laughed and horsed around the way they do. Some of the guests were collecting their things, getting ready to make a dash for cover. Others were already hurrying indoors. Soon Sanchez joined me. She hadn't run into Taylor, either.

We went through the beach gate. Parked just on the other side of it was an empty wheelchair.

We noticed our suspect immediately. She was down near the water, directly in front of us, sitting on the sand with her arms wrapped around her knees. The surf was picking up, a wild green thrashing in toward the beach. Taylor's unbound hair danced in the wind. A bleach-haired, well-bronzed lifeguard approached her, bent down and asked her something. I figured he was suggesting that she get off the beach. She turned and spoke with him a minute, and he walked away.

"There she is," I said to Sanchez. "Our killer. We may as well get this over with."

"May as well."

"Let's be gentle with the lady."

"I think I can handle it."

A stray raindrop struck my forehead once or twice. I hung back when we got to Taylor and let Sanchez do the talking.

"Ms. Taylor?" she said.

Taylor looked up at her.

"Who are you?"

"I'm Detective Maria Elena Sanchez, Miami-Dade police." She showed Taylor her badge.

"I guess I expected the other one. Lieutenant Nelson, I think it is."

"I'm here." I stepped around to where she could see me.

"Oh, yes."

"Ms. Taylor," Sanchez said, "perhaps we should go inside. It looks like the sky could open up any minute now."

"I guess you're right. That would be fine with me."

I had to admire the way Sanchez was handling things. She spoke to Taylor like she was a beloved aunt or something. I offered Taylor my arm and we walked toward the Sheraton's beach gate. When we got there, I offered to wheel her up to the hotel.

"That's kind of you," she said. "I am feeling a little shaky."

A steady rain was now falling and bathers were deserting the pool area in droves. Only the drinkers stayed put under the cover of the poolside bar's wide, green awning. I rushed Taylor around the serpentine walkways toward the entrance to the café.

When we got inside I stopped short. It occurred to me that we hadn't told Taylor we were arresting her. Hadn't mirandized her. I knew we should take care of those details before our interrogation, but it all seemed too abrupt. With a lady like Taylor, almost uncivilized. I looked at Sanchez and she seemed to read my mind.

"Why don't we just sit in the café awhile," she said to Taylor, "—if that would be okay with you."

"That would be fine."

I wheeled her to a corner of the café, away from the other guests, and eased her chair up to a table.

"Can I get you something?" Sanchez asked. "Tea, coffee?"

"No, thank you. I'm fine."

We all sat in silence for a moment. Then Taylor spoke.

"I know why you're here."

"How is that?" I was miffed about our cover getting blown, and you could hear it in my tone. Sanchez gave me a shut-up-stupid look and spoke before Taylor could answer.

"Never mind that for now," she said soothingly. "It's not important."

Taylor fidgeted with the silk scarf she wore around her neck. "I must look a mess."

"You look fine," Sanchez said.

"I'd feel better if I could get to a mirror for a moment."

I guess those performers never stop worrying about their appearance.

"There's a ladies room around the corner," Sanchez said. "We can wait for you here."

Taylor looked at me as if asking permission. I nodded, and she went off toward the ladies room.

"Now Sanchez," I said, "I know I said gentle. But let's remember, we are here to arrest the lady."

"I know, but I think I get this woman. What say you let me take the lead on this one?"

"Don't you think we ought to mirandize her?"

"We'll get to that if we need to."

I didn't like the sound of that, but something told me I should let Sanchez handle it her way.

"You don't think she'll go anywhere, do you?"

"I can see the bathroom door from here. Why don't you make yourself useful and get us some coffees."

When I got back to the table Taylor had returned and she and Sanchez were talking. Taylor accepted the coffee I offered. She took her own sweet time putting creams and sugars in it.

"Like I was saying to Detective Sanchez," she said when she finished fixing her coffee. "I wasn't trying to run away from you, or cause you any trouble . . ."

"Of course not," Sanchez said.

"I just wanted to be here one more time." Taylor looked through the café windows toward the beach. There were tears in her eyes. "I didn't know what might happen. For all I know, you'll end up convincing some jury that I killed Robin. That's what you plan to do, isn't it?"

"That's a little premature," I put in. "We haven't gotten that far. But there have been some awful strange things going on."

"You mean the necklace, I suppose? And the fingerprints on Robin's score?"

How did she know about these details of our investigation? "They're the main ones," I said with a distinct sense of annoyance.

Taylor looked into her coffee and began to quietly weep. Sanchez glared at me as she passed Taylor a couple of tissues. A few café patrons stole worried glances in our direction.

"It's all right," Sanchez said softly. "We're here to help."

Here to help? I hiked my head at Sanchez as if to say, "Let's get on with it, can we?"

Taylor spoke through her sniffling. "It was out on that beach that Robin proposed to me. The first time, that is. We were so happy then. How could you think I would harm him? He was the great love of my life."

"But the fingerprints, Ms. Taylor. And the necklace?" In spite of my best efforts, my tone betrayed my impatience.

"Give her time, Chief," Sanchez said. "Give her time."

"As for the necklace," Taylor said after collecting herself a moment, "can't you see? That was all I had, the one, concrete thing. They, whoever they are, took the rest away from me. And so suddenly! If I had just had one more day . . ."

She'd completely lost me, but I didn't say anything. I didn't want any more of Sanchez's scolding looks. Taylor meanwhile had broken into another crying jag. Sanchez softly squeezed her hand until she calmed down.

"I'm sorry. This has been so difficult for me."

"Don't worry about it," Sanchez said. She gave Taylor a reassuring look and patted her arm.

"In regards to Robin's score," Taylor took up again, addressing me now, "of course my fingerprints were on it. He showed it to me, that evening. It wasn't easy for him, either." She sniffed a couple of times. "We hadn't spoken to one another for so long . . ."

She fell silent and fiddled with her coffee stirrer for a moment. Sanchez and I waited.

"I could see how beautiful his new music, for *Biscayne Bay*, would sound," she went on abstractedly, almost as if Sanchez and I weren't there. "I could hear it, every wonderful note of it, in my head. I felt so honored that he had composed such a fine opera for me. That's what he told me. He said that he had come to realize that every bit of his work had been an effort, in some way, to make his way back to me."

She brought a tissue to her eyes and burst into another jag of quiet weeping. I grew impatient again to move things along; maybe I was just uncomfortable with all that emoting. I gave Sanchez another frustrated look. She looked back in a way that said, "cool it, I've got things under control," but I couldn't contain myself. "Let's get back, if we can, Ms. Taylor, to that necklace. I'm still not sure I get it."

Taylor looked out the windows. Big, plump raindrops plunged steadily into the koi pond. She blew her nose daintily into her kleenex and stared down at the table. "To you," she said quietly, "that necklace may be nothing more than pretty stones on a chain. But for me, it's all I had left. I suppose you'll take that now. That's why I didn't mention it. He gave it to me, at the hotel. He said that it was a token of everything he wanted to do from now on. For us. He said that he had made a terrible mistake when we were young, and that it had taken him years to figure out where he truly belonged. That's what he said. He was afraid that I would be mad at him. Resent him. But I wasn't, and I didn't. I was just glad that he was finally here again. I've made my share of mistakes, too. I knew it wasn't easy for him to make his way back. For me, it was like a miracle . . ."

It may have been a miracle for her, but it still wasn't adding up for yours truly.

"Ms. Taylor," I said, "the evening Mr. Markson was murdered, he made a reservation for dinner at Carpaccio, across the street at the Shops. Then he canceled . . ."

"Yes, I know!" she blurted out and started to gush again. Sanchez glared. I decided to keep my mouth shut for a while.

"It's all right." Sanchez patted Taylor's hand. "Take your time . . ."

"This is so hard to bear!" Taylor struggled to fight back tears. "That reservation was for us, for Robin and me! I came to the hotel at seven, and we spent some time at his suite. He showed me the *Biscayne Bay* score. But it was all too much, seeing him after so many years. I needed time. I'm not saying that I shut him out. How could I? There are places in my heart where no one has ever been but him, or ever will be. I just needed to be alone, so that I could let it sink in. I've become accustomed, over the years, to dealing with things on my own. It seemed so unreal, after all the time we'd spent apart, struggling through life without one another. You become inured to your loneliness. You can see that, can't you?"

Sanchez nodded sympathetically.

"I told Robin that I would need to think things over. I had slept poorly the night before, in anticipation of our meeting, and I didn't feel up to a night out. I called my ride and went home."

She looked out, through the café's windows, on the rain. It flooded down in opaque sheets and blotted out the sky.

"That's what's so hard to bear," she took up again, pitiably, looking down into the tissues she held in her hands. "If I had only stayed and gone to dinner with him, he would still be alive!"

She went right into another jag. After a minute, she quieted some, stifling her sobs in her kleenex. I looked over at Sanchez. Her eyes were wet, too. I couldn't believe what I was hearing. Is this what our case came down to? But there was still something the detective in me couldn't let go of. Taylor had collected herself again, and I spoke as gently as I could.

"There's just one other thing, if you don't mind."

"What's that?" she sniffed.

"Kessel."

"You mean," she said, "giving him the necklace?"

"That's right."

"I thought I made that clear."

"Not to me. Maybe I missed something."

"Come on, Frank," Sanchez said. "You're not paying attention. Didn't you hear what the lady said? She was afraid that we would take it."

"Yes, I heard. But does that justify holding up a murder investigation? Secreting evidence?"

"I'm so sorry, Lieutenant," Taylor said. "I didn't mean to interfere with your investigation. After all, I knew I didn't murder Robin, so what difference could it make? I was still reeling from his death, and that on the heels of our sudden reunion. I probably wasn't thinking straight. It's like I froze up, emotionally. I only knew that those shining jewels were the one pure memory I had of our brief evening together, and I couldn't risk losing it. I didn't want it tainted by police, and investigations, and murderers." She cast her eyes into her lap. "I guess it's too late for that, though."

"I'm afraid it is. One last thing, though, and then I'll leave it alone. Why give the thing to Kessel? I thought you despised the man."

"He's not my favorite person, that's for sure." She balled her tissue up and daubed her eyes with it. "But I knew he'd do me a favor, and without asking any questions. He owes me a few. When it comes right down to it, he's the only person I could think of who knows how to take care of certain things. Sneaky things, you might say. I just wanted to keep it in a safe place for a while."

"We'll see that you get it back," Sanchez said.

We sat quietly for a moment, while not only Taylor but also Sanchez dried her eyes. Then Taylor spoke, more calmly now.

"There is one favor I'd like to ask of you, Lieutenant."

"Yes?"

"My student, Daphne Courtwright . . ."

"Ahh . . . I suppose she was the one who tipped you off about our evidence. And about the arrest warrant . . ."

"She won't be in any trouble, will she? She's such a fine young person. After all, no harm was done, was it?" Her eyes shone on me with some kind of female juice I don't even have a name for.

I assured Taylor that Daphne would not be charged with a crime for alerting her about our investigation and asked if she would come to the station and make a statement. She agreed, and Sanchez and I saw her across Collins to Sanchez's car.

The storm had passed, and bands of clear steel-blue now streaked the sky behind ragged clouds. I put Taylor's wheelchair in the trunk and told Sanchez I'd meet them at the station.

The Shops' asphalt lot was glistening wet and dotted with wide puddles. It seemed those crazy grackles had gotten wise to the trick the weather had played on them, for they wheeled over the laurels now, shaking rainwater off their wings as they stroked steadily off and away from Bal Harbour.

Who could say to where?

I took stock of our situation. We were back to ground zero on the case. I could have doubted Taylor's story, but why? Hadn't I told myself—and anybody who would listen—that I found it hard to believe that she had whacked Robin Markson, or had anything to do with it? What was more curious was how things had come as far as they had. All of her suspicious behavior led in what seemed an inevitable chain toward her arrest: her evasiveness, the fingerprints, the drop to Kessel, the necklace. In a way, I felt like I had been set up. But by whom? By life itself? For all my vaunted faith in the glories of intuition, this time I had let pure dumb logic take over, and I came up empty-handed.

I had liked Taylor from the moment I met her and didn't want her to be the perp. The only problem was, now we didn't have a thing to go on. I felt dispirited as I walked toward my car, dodging the puddles.

As I put the key in the door I happened to notice, over the roof of my Impala, a black Mustang the same vintage as Willis's in a shaded corner at the back of the lot. Black Mustangs are about as rare in South Florida as sunburn, but something told me that I should check into it. I walked over to the car, went up to the driver's window and, sure enough, there was Willis, slumped down in the low bucket seat. I knocked on the window while I loudly spoke his name.

He turned abruptly as the window zipped down.

"Could you keep it down?" he said in a strained whisper. "I'm in the middle of a bust."

"A what?"

He motioned me to the passenger side, and I went around

and got in. His face wasn't as swollen as the day before. The bruising was deepening to a nice eggplant purple, with hints of half-ripe mango.

"A bust?" I repeated. "What are you talking about?"

"Long story." He peered intently across Collins.

"I've got nothing too pressing on my schedule at the moment."

"It's Stevie and his gang." He glanced briefly in my direction.

I couldn't disguise the disappointment in my voice. "Willis," I said, "couldn't you leave that alone?"

"You wouldn't want me to leave this alone, Chief." He pointed across the avenue. "See those two Caprices pulling in over there?"

"Yeah, they look like a couple of ours."

"That's right. Captain detailed a few plainclothesmen from other units."

"The Captain? You got him involved?"

"You were on your arrest warrant, and we had to move! We've got some more guys in the alley that runs alongside the building."

"It sounds like quite a production just to bust Stevie."

"You won't say just-to-bust-Stevie when you hear the rest."

"I'm waiting."

"After you brought me home from the hospital," he started after staring through the windshield a moment, "I couldn't sit still. They told me to rest, but it was a total no-go. I didn't want to take any more of those pain meds they gave me at the hospital, either. They were making my head fuzzy. Not good. You guys, my team, were making a murder bust, and I'm supposed to lie around zonked out in bed? I decided to just put up with the headache."

"That was probably your concussion talking."

"Maybe. But you know what? I can't say I mind it. The headache, that is. It gives you this kind of edge, know what I mean?" A painful wince punctuated his laughter, and then he went on.

"I do have to admit," he said earnestly, "I was pretty burned up about how Stevie and his boys handled me in that alleyway." He shifted awkwardly in his seat, trying to get comfortable.

"I figured you would be."

"But there was more to it than that. The more I thought about the way they roughed me up, the more certain I was that they were involved in some serious criminal activity. Why else would they get so psyched up about me tailing them?"

"That sounds reasonable. Maybe."

"So what I did, I called over to my drinking buddy, Gregorio Mano, in Intelligence. I had picked up on some of the names of Stevie's peeps, you know, and I asked Gregorio to do a little backgrounding on them."

He took a long look across Collins, toward the Sheraton, before turning back to me and continuing. "One of Stevie's crew, one of his main lieutenants, in fact, is this guy named Raúl. Raúl Gomez. So Gregorio gets back to me, and he informs me that this Raúl character works for a security company as some kind of technician. And you know what? The company he works for happens to handle the Sheraton's security system."

"Sweet Jesus!"

"Exactly. That explained the cameras being on the fritz the night Markson was offed. As closely as I checked out the resort security team, it never occurred to me to check on their outside contractor."

"The more technology we get, the more ways the bad actors are going to find to use it against us."

"That's for sure, Chief. But anyway, after speaking with

Gregorio, I called Rosie and told her that I needed to speak with Talia."

"That's the sister, right?"

"That's right. At first, though, I got to tell you, Rosie was a little peeved. You see, I totally forgot that I'd promised to take her dancing last night. But after I told her about my medical emergency—you know, my little accident down in Hialeah—she told me to come right over. She and Talia were in the living room when I got to the family bungalow in Little Havana. Rosie, bless her heart, she went white as a sheet when she saw me with the patch, the cast. The bandages. She led me over to the couch and made over me for, oh, a good ten minutes. Then I figured I better get on with the show. I got her and Talia to sit back, and I told them about my friendly little encounter with Stevie and his gang.

"When I finished the whole story, like I guess you'd expect, Talia tried to take up for her crummy pals. She said I shouldn't have been tailing them. You should have seen Rosie, then, Chief. She turned on that poor Talia like some crazed alley cat. I mean, she went totally ballistic! 'Look what your no good friends did to Kevin,' she screamed in Talia's face. 'I told you they're a bunch of filthy animals!' I tell you, Chief, that's one feisty little woman."

Willis's face took on a sort of glow, and he gazed off through the windshield at nothing in particular. Then, with a pained grunt, he turned toward me again.

"Now get this, Chief. Rosie grips Talia by the sleeve, and she gets way up in her face. She says she knew all along that Stevie was a no-good crook. What's more, she claimed he was bonking at least a dozen sluts all over Miami. I don't think Talia knew how to respond. She stood there like she was paralyzed or something. I've got to tell you, Chief, I don't think

I've seen a finer shakedown in all my years on the force."

And I'd never seen so much pure admiration in Willis's eyes. He just sat contemplating it all for a moment. Then, after another painful shifting in his seat, and another glance across Collins, he looked over at me and continued.

"I finally got Rosie to calm down," he said, "and we all got seated again. Then I started to press Talia for more information about Stevie's gang. Especially this Raúl character. But she wouldn't talk. She just sat there eyeing Rosie, like she was afraid she was going to her to launch into her again!"

"I can imagine."

"Then, Chief, get this. This was really great. Rosie goes marching off down the hallway and comes back with *Mamacita*. Now, Rosie had told me about Mamacita. She was sweet as pie at the picnic, but Rosie and her siblings live in holy terror of the lady."

"Okay, so . . ."

"So Mamacita and Rosie come clipping down the hallway, jabbering in Spanish about a thousand miles an hour. And before you know it, Mamacita's standing over Talia, glaring at her with these dagger eyes. She pulls her up from the couch and takes her by the shoulders. 'What kind of foolish business you been up to?' she screams. 'You going to talk, young lady! You going to talk!' Talia tried to sass her at first, but the old lady was too much for her. Finally she just turned her face away, collapsed back onto the couch, and started to bawl her eyes out."

Willis took another long look across the avenue. All was quiet over there, just the Caprices sitting peaceful in the clear morning light. He wiped his mouth with the back of his hand.

"At that point," he went on, a broad smile forming on his face, "the funniest thing happened. Mamacita and Rosie, they go over to the couch and sit down, one on either side of Talia.

Naturally, I thought they were going to launch into her again. But instead, get this, they put their arms around her and start to comfort her! Kissing her hair and cheeks. Telling her everything was going be all right! I got to tell you, Chief, that's one crazy family. But for some reason, I really get a kick out of them. Maybe I'm a little crazy myself . . ."

"No comment."

"Funny, Chief. Anyway, after Talia finally collected herself, she asked me, straightforward as you please, to tell her what I wanted to know. All this time, mind you, Rosie and Mamacita are patting her nicely on the knee for encouragement, smoothing her hair . . ."

"Okay, already. But what did you come up with?"

"Chief, it was exactly like I suspected when I found out about this Raúl's job with the security company. Stevie and his gang have been running a theft ring out of the Sheraton."

"I see, and . . ."

"For several months running, Stevie's been pressing Talia for information about valuables in the guests' rooms!"

"So Rosie's sister, this Talia, she's an accomplice?"

"I hope we can go easy on that angle, Chief. You've got to understand, Talia didn't know about Stevie's racket for the longest time. She thought he was just interested in how the other half lives, if you know what I mean. That's how he played it. Cool like. That's what Talia says, anyway. And Chief, I believe her. That family may be crazy, but they're, you know, good people. You can tell about that sort of thing. Know what I mean?"

"I suppose I do."

"The fact is, Talia didn't suspect anything goofy was going on until after Markson got iced."

"Markson?"

"That's what I said. It turns out Talia told Stevie about that emerald necklace the day before Markson was killed. She heard about it from the girl who cleaned Markson's room."

"The one I spoke with? Lucía?"

"Exactly."

"My God. So this Raúl character . . ."

"Precisely. The guy rigged up some kind of remote app, so he could shut down the hotel's recording system anytime he wants. He can even take out selected hallways, or specific security zones, at will. I checked with Records, had them look at all the hotels Raúl's company handles security for. And guess what?"

"I don't think I need to."

"Bingo. There have been multiple security system failures, just before robberies are pulled off." Willis abruptly broke off and pointed across the avenue. "Take a look."

Our plainclothesmen had emerged from the Caprices and were pacing around their cars, speaking into walkie-talkies.

"I think I get the picture," I said. "But why didn't you call me, fill me in? I'm forever telling you guys to keep me in the loop, for chrissake! You could have kept me from making a major fool of myself with Taylor and Kessel."

"Sorry, Chief. It seemed like you were sick of hearing about Rosie. Besides, I knew you were busy on the other busts and, let's face it, I was just operating on a theory here. It was a pretty strong one, granted. But it was still just a theory. I mean, we also had some pretty solid evidence on Kessel and the opera singer."

"We thought we did. I'll tell you about that fiasco after we wrap up these festivities. For now, why don't you just clue me in on what's going on across the street."

"Easy. In short, Talia agreed to cooperate with this little scheme I dreamed up. First, of course, I had to have a serious come-to-Jesus with Rosie. We went out back, on this covered patio, and I told her about my cover. You know, how I'm really a cop, not a roofing contractor."

"How'd she take that? Was she steamed at you for misleading her?"

Throwing his head back, Willis let out a gleeful laugh. "That's the beauty part, Chief! She wasn't upset at all. In fact, it turns out she's rather fond of law enforcement. It took her a minute, naturally, to get what I was saying. But after she understood it all, she put her arms around me and gave me this long, wet kiss. She even said that the idea of me being a cop actually turns her on . . ."

"Okay," I said, "too much information. I get the picture. So you told Rosie about your cover . . ."

"Right, and after our little talk, we went back to the living room and filled in Mamacita and Talia on my situation. As you can imagine, when Talia heard I'm a cop, she acted like she was going to clam up on me again. But with one stern look, good old Mamacita put the fear of God into her. Naturally, I told Talia she wouldn't be in any trouble. As long as she cooperated, that is . . ."

"Okay," I said, "if I'm getting this straight, after your unauthorized surveilling, you took it upon yourself to grant our aiding and abetting suspect immunity from prosecution. Nice."

"But, Chief, listen. This is the golden part. I got Talia to tell Stevie about some high-end bling she saw in one of the other rooms. She did it right there, over the phone, while I listened. I told her to let drop that the guests would be checking out this morning, so we knew Stevie would have to move fast. The hotel relocated the guests to a different suite, of course."

"Okay, not bad."

"Next I called over to the resort's security office. I asked them to keep an eye on the recording system, and to let me know the moment they experienced a failure."

"Good, and . . ."

"Well, about half an hour ago my phone rings. And sure enough, it was the hotel security guy. The recording system had gone on the fritz again, just like I thought it would. I asked him to report it to the security company like always. You know, keep it strictly routine, not give anything away . . ."

"Naturally. So who have we got over there?"

He told me the officers' names. Most of them were old hands I'd known for years.

"Do you mind if I go over?" I said. "I'd like to be in on this." I felt in my gut that this might be the last bust I'd ever witness. I wanted to experience it one last time, make sure I would remember the beautiful feeling of collaring some heartless predator for good and proper.

"Not at all," Willis said. "I'm staying out of the way, so I don't get recognized and blow the operation."

I walked across Collins. When I got to the Sheraton I talked with one of the plainclothesmen by the cars near the avenue. He radioed one of the men in the alley to let him know that I was coming. I arrived just in time for Stevie's arrest. The shock on his face was worth several paychecks.

Willis crutched himself across the avenue so he could have the satisfaction of looking Stevie in the eye while a couple of officers shoved him toward one of the Caprices. We walked back over to the Shops together and Willis went up to the Guantanamera Café to tell Rosie that everything was finished.

I called Sanchez with the news and suggested she release Taylor with my apologies. I asked her to stick around and help Willis interrogate Stevie.

Lori was happy to see me home for dinner. She was even

happier to hear about my interview for the community rela-
tions job. After we booked Stevie, I had gone down the hallway
to personnel and poked my head in the door. Charlie, the human resources guy, didn't have anything going on, so he invited
me to sit down.

When I told Lori what Charlie said (that I'd be a shoe-in for
the job) she didn't say a word. She just came over and gave me
one of those quiet hugs I've come to learn signals deep satisfaction. And relief. She had never complained about my crazy
hours, or about the stress of being married to a man who makes
a habit of pursuing vicious thugs who sport loaded firearms.
But as we held each other there in the kitchen, I felt decades of
tension draining from my wife. Suddenly my decision on the
job felt like one of the smartest, cleanest things I had ever done.

There was a big memorial service for Markson the next day.
We were still finishing up the case (interviewing Stevie's associates, who had been arrested at various locales about the same
time Stevie was busted) but I finagled some time off to attend.

Markson's body had been cremated the day before at a private ceremony attended by only family and close friends.

The memorial service was a different kind of affair. There
must have been nearly two hundred people there, and the
front of the church was decked out with a huge array of gorgeous flowers. Some kind of non-standard preacher spoke a
few words, and then one after another of Markson's musical
associates got up and performed a special number. Usually they
started by talking about what a good friend Markson had been,
what a great guy they thought he was, and how much he had
meant to them. Each one of them heaped praise on his musical
talent as well, and it was all pretty damned touching. Listening
to them speak, I knew I would never regret the time I had spent
in homicide. Any human life is a beautiful thing, and nobody

has the right to cut somebody else's short.

Both of the Diazes sang tunes from Markson's earlier operas, with an accompanist on piano. After that, Livy Taylor came up to the front of the church and sang one of the arias from *Biscayne Bay*, that stunning number from the farewell scene. Aside from the piece being pretty darn gorgeous, and the whole thing being about as poignant as you could get, that lady sang with the voice of an angel. How could somebody capable of making such heavenly sounds ever murder anybody? I found myself imagining what kind of career she might have had, had it not been for her health difficulties.

After the service Ralph Owens approached me. A few minutes earlier I had noticed his gal Daphne congregating at the front of the church with the other mourners.

"I hope you're not ticked at me," he said. "I guess Daphne, too."

"What on earth for?"

"For leaking your plans on the case."

"It came out okay in the end, didn't it?"

"I suppose it did."

"Let me tell you something I've picked up over the years."

"What's that?"

"Sometimes the most illogical-seeming maneuver of a woman ends up being the most brilliantly inspired. And, often as not, saves your bacon."

"That Mars-Venus thing?"

"Something like that," I said. "Take this case. Daphne knew Livy Taylor never would, nor could, kill anyone. I just realized that myself, listening to her sing. Meanwhile, all the logic of the case pointed to Taylor as a suspect. Sometimes, it seems, when a woman has a deep intuition of something inside, she's got the woman-wisdom to ignore what feels like logic, no matter how strong it might appear to be. I think us gents could take a page out of their book on that one."

"Perhaps you have a point."

"What's more," I said, "those females have considerably more courage then we sometimes give them credit for. Take your Daphne. She risked getting busted for obstruction—a pretty serious charge—because she wasn't going to stand by and see an injustice perpetrated on her friend. You've got quite a gal there. But I guess you realize that."

"Oh, I do." He gazed over to where Daphne stood beside Livy Taylor. "In fact," he added, "I have some news to share with you."

"Could it be?"

"Yep, we're going to tie that famous old knot."

I congratulated him. "What brought you around? I mean, everything you told me about needing your freedom, not wanting to get tied down . . ."

"It may sound strange," he said, "but Robin Markson was probably more responsible than anyone for my change of heart."

"Really?"

"He's always been one of my artistic heroes, as you know. And it struck me, as I thought about *Biscayne Bay*, that at the end of his life, the one thing he seemed to truly care about, more than his talent, his achievements, more than anything else, was the time he had spent with Livy. That made an impression on me. I feel like with Daphne, I've got a chance to live the kind of life Markson would have wanted to have with Olivia, had things been different."

"You're a couple of smart cookies, and I wish you both all the luck in the world."

"And Frank," he said.

"Yeah?"

"I want to thank you, too."

"What for?"

"For your advice. You know, about Daphne. You also helped me to see things more clearly. And I've got to tell you, now that I've made this decision, I feel like life's going to be a lot easier."

Daphne was coming over. When she reached us I congratulated her on the news.

"I hope you're not upset with me," she said sheepishly.

"Forget it. I was just telling Ralph that you did the right thing."

She took Ralph by the hand, held it tightly and thanked me for solving the case. "I know it's brought a lot of peace to Livy."

"To a lot of us," Ralph added.

I told them that it was a team effort.

"I hope you and your wife can come to our wedding," Daphne said.

I told her we'd be honored, and I said that I would bring Lori and Sara around to the restaurant sometime to hear her sing. "They'd really enjoy it," I added, and I meant it. I was already relishing the new and more relaxed life I would soon be leading.

Morgan Markson approached me with her friend from the opera and I greeted them both.

"You remember my friend, Donna Sullivan," Morgan said. Her eyes were moist, but there was a look of peace about her.

"Of course."

"I just wanted to thank you again for your efforts on the case."

"Yes," Ms. Sullivan put in, "it's mighty comforting to know we have people like you tracking down these terrible criminals."

"It wasn't just me," I protested. "It takes the whole

department to get these crimes solved, as well as the assistance of the public."

"By the way," Morgan Markson began again, "thank you for taking the trouble to follow through about the painting. I went to look at it the other day, and I just fell in love with it. It was obvious why my father would want it."

"It'll look terrific at the opera house," Ms. Sullivan said.

"The opera house?"

"I'll receive a small inheritance from my father's estate," Morgan explained, "and I've decided to devote a portion of it to buying the painting. The management at the Arsht Center has agreed to hang it in the lobby, with a placard about the premiere of my father's opera."

"I'll have to go down and take a look," I said, and I meant that, too.

I left those two and headed for the exit. Before I got there José Diaz caught up to me. He too thanked me for bringing Markson's murderer to justice.

"Nothing can ever replace my friend," he said. "But at least we can now feel that the value of his life has been upheld."

I said that I understood.

We chatted for a minute, and just as we were saying goodbye Lily came over. I took the opportunity to thank them both for their help with the case. "And for the opera DVDs," I added. "I really learned something."

As I walked off Lily called out to me.

"Yes?"

"That daughter of yours, the one who sings . . ."

"Sara?"

"Why don't you bring her around sometime? I have a few scholarships for worthy students."

"That's a very kind offer," I said. "I'll think about it."

Chapter 19

AS I LEFT the church I noticed Donald Kessel standing at the porch rail looking off in the distance. I couldn't help wonder what was on his mind. Years gone by, I supposed, and things that went down with him and Markson, maybe him and Olivia Taylor, too. He looked so lonesome standing there by himself that, for the first time since I made his acquaintance, I felt something for the man. Maybe people really can change, like he told me at his house.

I walked over.

"Mr. Kessel."

He turned around. "Oh, Lieutenant."

"Beautiful service, wasn't it?"

"Yes, it was."

"I owe you an apology."

"Nonsense. You were simply doing your job."

"Yeah, but in this case, I wasn't doing it too smart. I wish I hadn't inconvenienced you or Ms. Taylor. The evidence was just so confusing."

"With my track record," he said, "I can't very well blame you."

"There was one thing that really threw me off," I went on

again after a moment. "We never mentioned this, but we identified you visiting the Sheraton two days before Mr. Markson's
murder. That really got us to wondering."

"You knew about that, did you?" He looked off down the
street, like he wasn't sure he wanted to go on. But then he
turned to me again and spoke confidentially.

"The fact is," he said, "I went there to see Robin."

"No kidding?"

He cast his gaze downward. "When I was a younger man," he
went on after a moment, "all I could think about was getting to
where I wanted to be, getting a big enough piece of the pie that
people would think I was worth something. Maybe I thought
that would convince *me* that I was worth something. The fact
is, I was hideously insecure. Once you get to my age, you look
back on your life, and you wonder what the hell you were thinking. In my case, I wasn't thinking much at all. The sexual revo-
lution had gone down, and you felt like you were supposed to
be getting all this action. In my stupidity, I thought that money
could get me anything and everything. Even self-respect. It all
seemed like a game, where winning was all that mattered, and
the old-fashioned rules were just for chumps. I was wrong. A lot
of it seems unreal to me now. Frankly, I can't believe some of
the things I did. In short, I went over to the Sheraton because I
felt I owed Robin an apology."

"I see. So did you see him?"

His face grew taut and he looked away again. He spoke soberly. "No, I regret to say I didn't. The truth is, when I got into
the lobby, I lost my nerve. Who knows what he would have
said? I can't expect people to forget the thoughtless things I've
done. I can live with that. I just hope there's someplace where,
one day, we can all forget about it—those of us who are still
here, anyway—and be clean with one another again."

"I'm sure there is, Mr. Kessel," I said. "I'm sure there is."

I left him there on the steps and went to my car. Charlie had been true to his word about me being a shoe-in for the public liaison job. When I returned to the station after the service he told me that he had fast-tracked my application. I was supposed to start in a month. He said they would move some worthy applicant onto our team from another office and, based on my recommendation, make Sanchez the new team lead, with a promotion to sergeant.

I was touched that the Captain said he'd miss me, even if he went about it in his own, special way.

"What's this I hear about some public liaison job?" he said after he called me into his office. "After all the effort I've put into you, you're going to go and flake out on me?"

"As much of a pain in the neck I've been, I thought you'd be thrilled to get rid of me."

"I know I bitch and moan a lot," he said. "But the fact is, you're about as straight an arrow as this force has ever known. I'm sure we'll be seeing plenty of each other in your new capacity."

If you can believe it, after that he came around his desk, shook my hand, wrapped his other arm around me and gave me a sort of stiff hug.

Closing out the Markson case was a relative snap. The unmatched prints on old Venus de Milo turned out to be none other than our friend Stevie's. Starting from the evidence Willis dug up, we were able to tie his gang to a number of other robberies in South Florida hotels. The conviction was a breeze, and the punk will be spending the rest of his life behind bars. Nor will his associates be troubling the fine and decent people of South Florida for the foreseeable future.

I asked Sanchez why she was so soft on Taylor when we

picked her up at the hotel.

"To be honest," she said, "I never had much faith in that angle. It just didn't feel right."

The fact is, the case ended up being exactly what Sanchez had speculated at the crime scene: a botched robbery, the assailant after the emerald necklace. I knew the team would be in good hands with such a cool head in charge.

Willis recovered fully from the injuries he suffered at the hands of Stevie's people, and I'm sure he didn't mind Rosie's tender ministrations. What's more, he became something of a hero with Rosie's mother—Mamacita—for the role he played in extricating Talia from the bad influences she was hanging with. Talia's now engaged to Pedro Hernandez, a fellow officer she met through Willis.

Willis and Rosie got married in a big Catholic ceremony with lots of tropical flowers down in Little Havana. The roasted pork was delicious, and the mojitos weren't half bad, either. Those dance lessons I took with Lori came in handy when the band struck up their salsas and rumbas, and Willis looked real sharp in his guayabera. Those two didn't waste any time starting their family, either. They already have a three-year-old daughter, cute as a button, a one-year-old boy, and another little empanada in the oven.

The wedding of Ralph Owens and Daphne Courtwright was a more restrained, but no less beautiful affair. It was really touching to see Olivia Taylor give away the bride, walking down the aisle with just a little help from—you guessed it—yours truly. The reception was at a swanky Miami club with a broad wooden deck hanging out over Biscayne Bay.

I got to talking to Daphne while Lori was engaged in a deep discussion with Lily Diaz.

"Looking back on it all," I remember saying, "I really have

to admire your faith in Ms. Taylor. If we had shown you a color photo of her murdering Mr. Markson, you still wouldn't have believed it. You'd have said that it was doctored or something."

"I'm sure I would have," she said with a laugh, looking as flushed and happy as you'd expect any young bride just married to the man of her dreams to look. "When you know someone as I know Livy, and know how strong and good they are inside, you know that they could never harm anyone like that."

We looked over the sunset-streaked surface of the Bay for a moment. Then she began to speak again, but haltingly, as if she were testing the waters . . .

"But even had it not been for that—that absolute faith in Livy—," she stammered, "—there was something else that assured me of her innocence. Something more . . . concrete, I guess you could say." Turning back toward the Bay, she seemed to be considering, again, whether she should go on. Seagulls wheeled and squawked over the water, the sun's slanting rays painted their wings with gold. A pelican came tooling by. Still Daphne Courtwright was silent. The suspense began to get to me.

"Well, what is it?" I said. "Aren't you going to tell me?"

"I think I'm afraid to." She scrunched up her face in a funny way.

"I'd wager I can handle it, whatever it is."

"If you promise you won't be upset," she said, "I guess you should know the truth." She twisted toward me and leaned an elbow on the deck rail. "That evening, that awful evening . . ."

"When Mr. Markson was murdered?" I wondered where this could be going . . .

"Yes, that evening," she said. "Anyway, to put it bluntly, I was the one who drove Livy over to the hotel."

"You!" I wasn't able to hide the shock in my voice. I wheeled around and looked out over the Bay. "That would certainly explain why I couldn't find a taxi record."

Daphne spoke freely now, anxious to explain. "Livy was feeling so insecure about meeting Robin after so many years. So at sea. She didn't feel good about just showing up in a cab. Too *alone*. She asked if I would drive her to the hotel. I waited over at the Shops while she met with him."

"I'll be damned."

The gulls squawked.

"A little after nine," Daphne went on, "Livy called and asked me to pick her up. She sounded very happy, but clearly overwhelmed. I went around to the side entrance at the hotel and waited while Mr. Markson accompanied her out to the car. I met him briefly and helped him to put her wheelchair in the trunk. He kissed her so tenderly when they said goodbye. I took her home, and we sat up and talked until the wee hours of the morning. So you see, even if I didn't know Livy so well, I knew she couldn't have been the one who murdered Robin Markson."

I was so flabbergasted I just about dropped my drink. Why hadn't she said something when I met with her and Ralph Owens, not once, but two separate times! How cagey she had been! But how could I be angry with a lovely bride on her wedding day? That same thought, in fact, was probably what had given her the courage to spill the beans in the first place. I turned a bit on myself and gave out a little laugh.

"I'll be," I said. "This sure is a surprise to hear."

She sounded more than a little embarrassed when she responded. "I thought it would be."

"I'm just going to ask you one thing, and then we'll never mention it again. It's that detective mind in me. It can't feel comfortable until all the T's are crossed and all the I's dotted."

"Okay, shoot." She squared herself to me with a sincere and open expression.

"Why didn't you simply tell me about this when I met with you and Ralph? Wouldn't it have saved everyone, including Ms. Taylor, a lot of trouble?"

"I thought of that, naturally. I even suggested it to Livy. But she had sworn me to secrecy. This whole thing with Robin had taken on such significance in her mind. He was the only man she had ever completely loved, and felt completely loved by, in spite of what happened between them. And then, after the . . ."

"The crime?"

"Yes, after that, she was left with their one brief evening together. And the beautiful gift of that necklace. She didn't want any of that tarnished by the rest of the world, with its robberies, its investigations. Its lawyers and courtrooms. It may seem silly to you. It even does to Livy, now. But I had promised that I wouldn't breathe a word to a soul, and I couldn't go back on my word. Especially not with Livy, to whom I owe so much. That's why I kept it to myself."

I didn't mention withholding evidence, obstruction of justice or any other fifty-cent words of that ilk. What did it matter now, on this luscious evening, the Bay afire with the setting sun, and a couple of marvelous young people about to embark on the most glorious adventure two souls can share in this world?

"You make a lovely bride," was all I said. "Please come over and meet *my* soul mate."

We walked over to where Lori was talking with Lily Diaz. When we reached them, Ms. Diaz turned to me.

"Okay, Lieutenant," she said, "it's all settled. Your Sara starts her lessons next week."

"Sara?" Daphne inquired.

I introduced Daphne to Lori, and then Daphne gave Lily

a big hug. It appeared that they were already well acquainted. Lori told Daphne about our singing daughter.

"How fabulous," Daphne said. "She'll be starting with such a tremendous teacher."

Lily squeezed Daphne's hand, and I looked hard at Lori. We had been married long enough for her to know exactly what that look meant.

How are we going to afford this one?

"Lily has some scholarships available," Lori said casually, as though she were just filling me in, "through the opera company. It won't pay everything, but we can easily manage the rest. I'll just take on an extra catering job or two."

I was about to protest, my default reaction to any attempt to slice a cop's salary into more pieces, but what was the point? I was clearly outnumbered, stewing in some kind of female conspiracy I knew it would be futile to resist. It seemed I ought to butt out and let the ladies take care of my daughter. At least on this one. I'd grown to like the Diazes. Maybe this was exactly the new influence my Sara needed in her budding life.

Our conversation presently broke up. The band had taken a break, and one of the musicians in the crowd (the place was loaded with them) was walking toward the bandstand carrying a handsome guitar of polished blond wood. He stopped when he reached Olivia Taylor and they spoke a moment. She rose and they walked to where two stools sat in front of the stage. After they got situated, the guitarist started in on one of those old bossa nova songs. Olivia Taylor spoke briefly over his bright chords, dedicating the song to Ralph and Daphne, and then she began to sing. Everyone's attention, including our little group's, was riveted to the bandstand, so beautifully haunting was the sound of Taylor's voice drifting across the deck and out to the Bay, where it mingled with the soft breeze that played over the water . . .

It's been four years since that evening, but I remember it like it was yesterday. As I had suspected, Sara's lessons with Lily Diaz proved just the thing to help her finish growing up. Later, when Lily said she had taught Sara everything she could, she sent her to study with Olivia Taylor.

It's been a pleasure to continue to see that whole crowd from time to time. They've convinced us that our daughter has some talent, and I gave her my blessing to study music in college if she agreed to minor in computers. Lori said that if we honored what was most important to her, she'd more likely take our advice on other things, and she was right. Sara gave in with barely a grumble. You've probably figured out by now that Lori's the smart one in the family when it comes to parenting. Sara's away at college now, but she still catches up to her old voice coaches when she's home for holidays and summer vacation. That is, when she's not hanging with Joe, who, wouldn't you know it, has become her steady boyfriend.

Shortly after the wedding of Ralph and Daphne an envelope arrived in the mail from the opera company. It contained season tickets for two, with a nice note from José Diaz. It was awfully considerate of him, but I had to return the tickets. Us cops aren't allowed to take gifts from the public. He planted an idea in my mind, though, and a week later I went down to the Arsht Center and sprung for the tickets on my own. I guess I'd caught the opera bug. Since then Lori and I have become quite the fans, what with all the shows at the opera house, Sara's student performances, and the occasional recital by the Diazes or Olivia Taylor.

Andrew will be going away to college himself next year. He made varsity baseball as a junior, just as I'd predicted, and this year he's team captain. I don't guess I need to tell you how proud his old man is. He keeps up his grades to boot, and was awarded a nice scholarship to Florida U. And get this. When he sees younger boys skateboarding down at the town square, he goes over and gives them a little mano a mano about taking care of the community's public structures. I really get a kick out of that one. We've been on fishing trips to the Water Conservation Area at least a dozen times now, and I never miss one of his games.

Lori and I couldn't be happier. We miss Sara, and we're already feeling lonesome about Andrew leaving. But I'm grateful, at least, that the new job has allowed me to finally spend some quality time with both of them. It's good to know that Lori and I will be there for each other, just like always. I'm getting quite accomplished at the rumba, if I don't mind saying, and we've even begun to venture into the wickedly crazy moves of the tango . . .

The End